To evangelists
—and others who tote the mail.

*But you shall receive power
when the Holy Spirit has come
upon you; and you shall be
witnesses to Me. . . .*

**Acts 1:8**

# Preface

IN the house of God there is a golden mail slot. The fact that it is gold should surprise no one, given that heaven is paved with the element. Neither should a brow be raised at the mention of a mail slot in such a high place. After all, spirits communicate with one another just as humans do, and they can't always do so face to face. The account in the book of Job describes the Prince of Darkness talking to God. But even Satan must write a letter or two now and then.

Throughout the universe, parcels fly clicking fast overhead. Small wonder human space travel isn't hampered by all the cosmic commerce: myriad messengers from hell skirt between galaxies, and angels speed words of love from one end of paradise to the other. It is a considerably large miracle for NASA that there have been no serious mishaps.

And it was by this same miracle (whether one chooses to believe it or not) that a simple letter of loneliness—penned by a sinner in hell, smuggled out of the devil's mailroom, winged through the violent furnaces of the underworld, carried over oceans, continents, stratospheres, and gravitational pulls, despite wind, weather, and warring factions of the air, and all the while traveling in the scarcely fastened satchel of a grubby, little demon—should ever come to rest safely in God's golden mail slot. But that is where the story begins.

WWC

# ~ 1 ~

*Down to Gehenna or up to the Throne,
He travels the fastest who travels alone.*

—Rudyard Kipling, *The Winners*

I
N the town of Ellenbach there is a leather mailbag.
It has been there for generations. Passed from veteran to novice nearly a dozen times in the hundred years since the infancy of Ellenbach, the bag has been a vehicle of good news for some and bad for others as long as there were legs to carry it and a willing soul to deliver its contents.

In former years, some carriers have sped with similar bags over the deserts of Asia, all the while facing fierce beasts and fiercer bandits. Others have walked the roads of Rome on their way to the world's farthest corners. Once a whole continent was saved for Christendom when a simple mail carrier took an appeal for help to Paris. Pony Express riders were beset by terrible storms, hunger, and dangers as they rode across the western United States.

But in Ellenbach, the hazards of postal work were of a different nature.

One morning in May, Walter Conniston, U.S. Postal Carrier 1009, took the bag from its shelf above the dryer and ducked his head through the wide strap. Because the bag had not been filled yet, it flapped lightly against the plastic guard that Walter wore to protect his clothing from the oil of the leather.

Walter clumped across the utility room floor then out into the morning. He closed the door quietly, not wanting to wake his wife of thirty years. For even though his feelings for Donna had nearly disappeared, he still respected her. He fooled himself into thinking he couldn't love her anymore, or anyone, for that matter.

But he really *did* love Donna. Yet he saw her slipping from him, growing quiet, retreating into a novel she'd been working on. In Walter's mind, there was only one way to interpret his wife's new hobby of writing. Donna had died and buried herself under a mound of manuscript. But in reality, Donna Conniston, unlike her husband, had found an acceptable way to deal with the pain of losing a daughter to cancer and a son to a military firing squad.

"*Hearts on Fire,* hmmph," said Walter, as he walked along the sidewalk. "Who does she think she is anyway, Elizabeth Barrett Brown?" Of course, he meant *Browning,* but Walter Conniston was not particularly educated.

He had once been happy—and loving, handsome, and patient as rain with his children when they were young. But he was no longer any of those things. Instead he was sad and lonely. And as weather marks a stone, so sadness marked his appearance.

"Hmmph," he said again. "Pecking at that thing until all hours of the night while I'm trying to sleep. Who does she think she is?"

In truth, and Walter Conniston was not interested in truth at the time, he had begun spiraling into despair long before Donna had thought of returning to college to finish her English degree. A doctor in the next county over had told him once that it was nerves and wrote him a prescription for an antidepressant. But Walter didn't put stock in medicine. Straightaway he pitched the pill bottle in a culvert and went back to being sad and lonely.

Nerves wasn't Walter's problem. Neither were the forty-seven other diagnoses hung on Walter Conniston in the last twelve years by shrinks, quacks, and charlatans of the Hippocratic persuasion. At least those were the names Walter slung at them. Most were honest physicians who wished no harm to the ailing mail carrier.

The problem wasn't nerves, and it wasn't strong drink (as some in town supposed), nor was it midlife, codependency, sinus headaches, allergies, iron-poor blood, bipolar disorder, the moon, the stars, or even the hex of a witch who lived on the edge of town and had supposedly practiced her craft on past postal workers when they were late with her welfare check.

No. In truth, the problem that beset Walter Conniston was as plain as the two white tombstones that stood at the easternmost corner of Ellenbach Cemetery. There he'd buried Muriel, and there he'd buried Bent. His only daughter and older son were gone. Gone like the ocean retreating from its shore and leaving in its place broken coral and empty shells dotting the sand. Walter would have given anything to have back the dog tags he'd placed in the casket next to his son's still form. Anything to remember Bent when he was warm and willful.

Their deaths were the root of Walter's sadness. The untimeliness and pain of their absence rankled in his soul and frayed the edges of his conversations and bubbled forth in vitriolic blasts whenever Donna kept him up at night with her typing.

Walter feared loss. *It could happen,* he thought, as he walked his route through the elm-canopied neighborhoods of Ellenbach. *It's like Murphy's Law. Just when a fellow gets happy, something always goes wrong.*

Before Bent and Muriel's deaths, Walter had been immeasurably happy. His wife was a glistening harbor to him then. His children were clothed, fed, and esteemed by their peers. He had a relatively low-interest mortgage, a car that was paid for, a bird dog, a chance to hunt from time to time, and a Briggs & Stratton lawn mower in the garage. And he was well liked by his fellow Ellenbachians. They looked at him and said, "Yes, sir, he's a fine man, that Walter. Nobody alive can tote the mail like Mr. Conniston and be a deacon, too. Yes, sir, he's a fine man."

Then, melanoma took Muriel. And as Walter watched scoops of earth shoveled onto her casket, he no longer had to fear losing his joy. It was gone. And when Bent was executed, Walter didn't try to grasp all the more tightly to Dallas, his remaining son who was nine at the time. Instead, he pretended Dallas didn't exist. And at the age of fifty-six, Walter began an affair with the U.S. Postal Service, much preferring to give his love to something that couldn't die and leave another hole in him. But why he emotionally barred his faithful spouse from his love became a mystery to the people of Ellenbach, for the Conniston romance had always been exemplary. Nevertheless, Walter did it sweepingly.

Long before Donna rose from bed each day, Walter was at the post office going through the predelivery routine of his job. First he sorted magazines and letters into the large, rectangular cases. Then, starting with the last customer on his route and moving backward, he trayed them out according to address in a vertical-horizontal-vertical-horizontal succession. Belvedere's mail on Hampton Way was always turned vertical, Matt Ladd's horizontal, Delbert Ray's vertical, Elias Ledbetter's horizontal, and so forth. After that, Walter went through the packages, taking note of all accountable mail, all holdings, and any sleepers that might have gotten stuck behind the metal dividers during the sorting process. Walter would then sign off for a coil of stamps to carry with him in case the Widow Spradling wanted her usual thirty-two dollars' worth. And when all was done, he would swing his bag over his shoulder and head to the Paradise Donut Shop for breakfast.

He ordered the same thing always: Danish, coffee (black, to jump-start his life), and toothpick. He walked his route until noon, ate lunch in the mailroom, completed his route in the afternoon hours, and arrived home at six in time for the news. Supper he always ate alone in front of the television. Occasionally, he'd toss the ball with Dallas in the front yard until the rooftops burned red and the mosquitoes came nosing about. But only occasionally.

Finally, when Dallas was in his room, the dog fed, the trash emptied, the box scores gleaned for the possibility of a Kansas City Royals victory, Walter would settle down to the thing that had obsessed him since the deaths of his children: the flawless delivery of the mail.

*A man of excellence does one thing well,* he would tell himself at the beginning of each night's routine. He'd spread his things about the living room—his mailbag, his uniform, his service chukkas, his can of mace for the mongrel on Troost—and he would stare at them for a good, long time, like they were icons of sorts. *These are the secure things of my life,* he thought. They could not be torn from him as Muriel was torn. They could not be cast aside by the hand of a general court-martial like Bent.

These things alone were lasting, these solid trappings of a civil servant.

After a while, Walter would clean the bag with a damp cotton cloth and rub it with mink oil. Then he'd clean his shoes with saddle soap. How tenderly he nurtured those favorite shoes of his, the chukkas with the genuine-leather uppers and the breathable Cambrelle lining. He'd tried other brands that were cheaper. But none of them offered the heel stabilizer cup or the posiflex rubber soles with the slip resistant coating. He always went back to his old kind. *Besides,* he told himself whenever he shelled out an extra ten bucks for a quality pair, *where else can I get the speed-lace* D *rings and the back tab that makes them so easy to take off at the end of the day?*

And when all that was done, and when he could hear Donna typing in the guest room, Walter moved to the card table where he'd put the scale model of Ellenbach he'd built with Popsicle sticks. He mentally traced his route. Here was the important part of his ritual.

In the darkest months of his pain, an obsession had come over Walter. It was a pitiful one—as most obsessions are that occur when one's misery is so deep he believes he may never surface from it. Nevertheless, when he finally began to act upon it, Walter imagined it brought him comfort.

Each morning, Walter set his watch according to Greenwich mean time. Upon his first step from the Paradise Donut Shop, he pushed the stopwatch button on his wristwatch. From that point on, Walter's every stride was calculated, and he swung his arms in syncopation with his breathing.

Swing/Exhaaaaaaaaale

Swing

Swing

Swing/Puff Out

Swing/Short Inhale

Swing

Swing/Short Inhale

Swing

Swing/Exhaaaaaaaaale

When he got to Springdale Avenue, Walter cut across the Widow Spradling's lawn and jogged to the first mailbox on the route. That particular box had a rusty hinge on it, and Walter had begun carrying WD-40 for the sake of shaving seconds off his time in future days.

The next house got mail through a slot in the front door. Walter had to choose between navigating a garden and a split-rail fence or going around to the sidewalk. He gauged his choice on the initial hundred yards of his journey. If, for instance, the wind was stiff and from the north on a given morning, Walter deemed the time lost as due cause to hop the fence. On the other hand, if the weather was calm, Walter much preferred to lose a second or two if it meant he wouldn't have to scour the garden mud from his shoes that night. Those days, he took the sidewalk.

On he went with geometric precision—sometimes following wide arcs to avoid sprinklers, at other times transecting property lines as straight as any human being can walk.

At Troost, he took the mace from his pocket and rounded Fig Pemberley's privet hedge. If Fern, the Airedale terrier, wasn't in sight, Walter sprinted as fast as his fifty-six-year-old legs could carry him to Fig's mailbox before proceeding down Troost. It was an easy block because everyone had boxes on the street and little zigzagging was involved.

Bedford, however, was a different story. That street alone cost him nearly six and a half minutes compared to all the others. If it weren't for the fact that some of Ellenbach's most influential people lived on that street, Walter would have boycotted it a long time ago. He would have told its residents plain and simple that unless they wanted to have their mail sent to a P.O. box they had better line up their boxes on the curb, ASAP. But he never did that because Foster Jenson III, who lived at 517 Bedford, owned the bank, and therefore, in a roundabout way, Walter.

Consequently, Walter made sure he got Mr. Jenson's mail squarely down his slot at eight thirty-seven every morning, because that was when the perfectionist banker liked to read his *Wall Street Journal* and drink his coffee. Mr. Jenson was a foppish and finicky man. And he was a miser with his money, even though his father, who had died and left the bank to him, had been surprisingly benevolent for a man of means and thus far happier than his son. At any rate, Foster's stinginess was a point of gossip around town and an enigma, as well, since most people thought he should have got at least a little kindness by way of genes.

If Springdale, Troost, Bedford, Cistern, Birch, and Hampton Way were not all done by nine twenty-eight, Walter knew he was slightly behind schedule. On those days, he stepped up his pace for the rest of his morning route and arrived bushed and blotchy at the mailroom in time to collapse in the corner and devour a turkey and Swiss on rye sandwich, his favorite. Walter stopped his watch during lunch.

Afterward, there were only three trouble spots in his afternoon route. One was Mrs. Suggs on Pine Bluff, who baked cookies for Walter and talked and talked and talked and stole his time without even knowing it. So on Mondays, Walter consciously walked that street first thing after lunch, because that was when she got her hair combed and colored blue. Another was the Travis boy on Montclair, who always wanted to play catch. And finally, Fern again.

The quickest way to end his route was to cut back down Troost at the end of the day and head for the Paradise Donut Shop. And Fern was always there in the afternoons. The awful terrier stood by the privet and waited for Walter. Two lawns away, Walter could see her wheaten body through the holes in the hedge.

"Good girl," he'd say as he drew nearer, his trigger finger itching on the nozzle of the Mace can. The dog would show her yellow teeth and lunge at him, and Walter would run, spraying the Mace wildly over his shoulder in the hope of hitting his target.

If anyone had ever insinuated to Walter that Fern was a blessing in disguise, Walter would have disagreed. But that's exactly what Fern was. Fern got his tired legs moving at just the right moment and sped him on his way. And if Walter were honest about the matter of Fern, he would admit that she was responsible for many of his beatifically precise days, allowing him to mash his stopwatch with a sweaty thumb and stroll into Paradise acting as if the whole world were his plum.

Patrons in the shop would look at one another and shake their heads, for they remembered a time when Walter was not so possessed by his job. They missed the days when he lingered over coffee at the end of someone's driveway. They missed his easy smile and the sparkling slits his eyes became when someone told a joke. Back then, he brought heaven into conversation as naturally as he brought the mail. Some said there wasn't a man in the county with so much Bible in his veins, nor a preacher with half so many converts. The irony is that the people who missed those days the most gained the greatest satisfaction from Walter's sad changes.

For instance, Mr. Jenson wanted his *Wall Street Journal* and his petroleum royalty checks on time. Aldo Cobb required insulin from the drugstore in Laird. Junior Withers waited vigilantly for his social security check. Beth Fitzgerald watched for her LSAT scores and hoped to be the first woman from Ellenbach to go to law school. And an excited Suzie Parsons counted the days until Walter delivered her prom dress. All in all, the greater amount of energy Walter expended in avoiding the pain he felt, the faster the townsfolk got what they wanted.

But on this particular morning in May, when Walter Conniston closed the door quietly behind him and left Donna sleeping, he had on his mind something besides the stopwatch.

*If Donna can do her writing, then I'm entitled to a little happiness, too,* he convinced himself, and he set his face toward Cistern Street, where an extraordinarily beautiful woman had just moved in. As he walked, his conscience seemed to poke at him. Nevertheless, he shrugged off his conscience, just as he'd done countless times since resigning his position as deacon at Ellenbach Community Church.

*Besides,* he told himself, *if God really cared a whit about me He wouldn't have let Muriel and Bent die.*

On his way, he passed the Ellenbach Community Church where he had once served. Being so early in the morning, the front doors were still locked. But it was obvious the caretaker had come by, for a sprinkler spit diamonds near the rose beds, and all the petals wore jewels.

COME HEAR THE GOOD NEWS THIS SUNDAY! OUR DOORS ARE ALWAYS OPEN! read the white-and-green sign on the corner of the property.

"Hmmph," said Walter as he passed the sign. "A lot of good the place did me." He quickened his step toward the woman on Cistern, and his heart quickened, too. Through the window of the doughnut shop, two men spied Walter as he walked by.

"Now there goes a man who takes his job seriously," said one to the other.

## ~ 2 ~

*Neither snow, nor rain, nor heat, nor gloom of
night stays these couriers from the swift
completion of their appointed rounds.*

—Inscription, New York City Post Office,
adapted from Herodotus

FAR above Walter, a messenger of another kind went
about his job. Seen from the ground, he was a tiny, darting speck struggling upward through the heavens. The
little demon mail carrier was invisible to human eyes.
But all around him his former angelic peers and play-
mates turned their faces away, trying not to look upon
his shame for sorrow's sake.

"How did I ever get this lousy job?" Ripskin muttered
to himself as he flew under the enormous weight of the
daily mail. "And what did He think He was doing, building His throne so high and mighty far from decent folk?"
Already he had traveled over a trillion miles to make this
delivery.

The angels parted to let Ripskin pass. As they did,
they covered their noses with their wings, for the demon
stank of soot and fury.

"Give him room," said the most muscular angel. "Move
aside. It's the least we can do for our brother. He'll suffer

double if he's late in his return. Make way, there. Quick. Here he comes. Can we help with your load, brother?" asked the angel.

"Get away from me," grumbled Ripskin. "And save your brotherly slop for someone else. I'd rather be a page in hell, than a prima donna in this place you call home. Besides, you fools don't know what you're missing."

The dirty imp smirked, and the look in his eyes made it seem as if he'd love nothing more than to launch into a tale of hell's lewdness, just to taint the ears of his listeners. But the angels had no option except to love the little fiend. "Godspeed," they cried in the direction of Ripskin and his bulging mailbag.

Ripskin set his face toward the great East Wall of Heaven. Above him loomed the wall in all its splendor, so bright that Ripskin would have shielded his eyes with his hand if he could have done it without dropping his bag. Instead, he kept his grip and squinted, approaching the wall with caution. He scanned the towering expanse of jasper and glass, firmly founded on its twelve-tiered base of jewels.

"Hang the fool who built this place! Where is that rotting mail slot?!" he hissed.

Ripskin could feel his strength waning. He beat his wings harder, and slowly he ascended the foundation of the city, past jasper, sapphire, agate, and emerald. Onward he flapped, his black talons scraping hard against onyx, then carnelian, then chrysolite and beryl. He could just make out the three massive gates miles above him. But when he reached the layer of topaz, he could fly no farther. There he found a little flake of stone jutting out from the otherwise sheer surface of the wall. Reluctantly, Ripskin pressed his precious load tightly against the foundation, crammed the bag in his mouth, and clawed the wall for some semblance of a grip.

Just beyond his reach, there was a narrow crack in the pink silicate mineral. Ripskin knew if he stretched his hand toward it, the bag would pull away from the wall and be torn from his teeth. The letters would spill. They would flutter away on the winds of paradise. And he would be left there gasping, scratching the sides of heaven, too weak to go on, and too scared to go back to hell without completing his assignment.

Then, by a stroke of luck he found another hold with his foot. Ripskin pushed upward and knifed his right hand into the crack above him. The wind howled cold around Ripskin's ankles. His hand flared hot against the stone, yet held. Beneath him, planets wheeled and black deeps called him homeward. Ripskin stared at his ragged reflection.

He was handsomer once, he thought—a full foot taller than this stunted demon he'd become. Satan had made him that way—made them *all* that way, actually. So determined was Satan to tower above every other citizen in hell, he outfitted them all with shirts of heavy metal and decreed that they be worn until every knee bowed and every shoulder stooped to his liking. Ripskin hated what he saw.

Three-quarters of the way to the top of the wall, Ripskin reached the gates. He found rest there on a ten-inch ledge of pearl. Quickly, he attached his bag to the silver handle of one door and looked around. All around him the East Wall loomed, that wall to beat all walls. It is 216 feet thick at every place but one. Someday, even that one thin place will be filled with molten jasper, like a colossal cavity that has ached for as long as Satan has tempted. Then the temptation will cease. But it is precisely at that thin place that God's golden mail slot exists.

Ripskin took his bag in his two fists and eyed the spot. Its opening, perhaps no wider than a small package, would have to do for his purposes. He tied the leather bag into a knot—something he should have done before ever leaving hell—and compared its dimensions with the object of his long journey.

"Yes, yes. It should fit nicely," he assured himself.

He flung himself at the mail slot and rammed the leather knot inside. As Ripskin had hoped, the knot held. With a white-knuckled grip on the neck of the bag with one hand, Ripskin reached behind himself with the other and drew a knife from his back pocket. Then he plunged the knife into the side of the bag and cut a slit slightly larger than his hand.

One by one, he removed the letters and packages—all 213 of them to be exact. Some letters were handwritten requests from Satan for permission to tempt souls on earth. Some were propaganda designed to incite heaven-dwellers to another universal riot. The packages held pictures of wraiths in pornographic poses, tiny bottles of booze, handguns, ammunition, vials of hemlock, order forms for subscriptions to suicide societies, and a variety of literature crying out for civil disobedience. But alas, for the intemperate in hell, temptation in heaven is moot.

With a vengeance, Ripskin shoved each piece through the golden mail slot with his right hand, while he hung on with his left. Finally, when he was too tired to have noticed return addresses anymore—or to have cared, for that matter—Ripskin lifted the last letter from the bottom of his bag, thrust it in the slot, and finished the job.

Yet Ripskin hesitated.

As he delivered the mail, hanging above all creation, Ripskin thought he heard the sounds of children playing on the other side. The sounds were faint at first—not much more than the clumping of a stick horse, or the whine of a toddler's three-wheeler. But he was sure he had heard them. And when the sounds grew louder, becoming testimony to the joys just a yard or so away from his grizzled head, Ripskin resolved that he must see inside.

When Ripskin had discharged himself of the last letter—the one he would have done well to notice, but didn't—he did something quite opposed to better judgment. Rather than swinging back down upon the ledge and resting himself properly for a slow descent, Ripskin hoisted his tired body up to the golden mail slot until his eyes were even with the opening in the wall's thin place—and he saw the children.

"Ohhh, you sweet little tots," Ripskin breathed through the slot. "Come here, dear ones. Come here to Uncle Ripskin for a treatie-poo . . . a cherry cordial . . . a lemon tart right here, inside my bag. Won't you come? Won't you come to Uncle Ripskin?"

A child pedaled toward the slot.

"Yes, that's it. That's a dear. And ohhh, how blue your eyes are."

"Hello," said the boy. His hair was black and fine. He wore a sailor suit and a bright red cap. And he sat on his trike like a captain at the wheel of his ship.

"And hello to you, too," Ripskin replied. "Just as I imagined. You speak with the tongue of an angel. So dignified. So mature for a boy your age. A big boy, no doubt. Yes, that's what you are. A big boy. What is your name, big boy?"

"Edward Louis Robinson."

"Ho, ho! My! Such a fine name. A royal name. A great big name for a great big boy."

"Thank you, sir," said Edward.

"Now Edward Louis Robinson, the biggest and best boy in all of heaven, wouldn't you like to know who I am?" asked Ripskin, his dark eyes peering through the slot at the child. All the while his teeth were grinding, and his feet madly clawing the wall beneath him. But this little ploy was worth the extra effort, he told himself. After all, there were perks in hell for those who brought back information from the enemy's camp.

The boy nodded.

"Well now," said Ripskin, "I'm a friend of Jesus, a long lost friend, no doubt. Nevertheless, a friend. Have you been here long, Edward?"

"What's *long,* sir?"

"What's long? Well, it's . . . it's . . . oh, never mind. It's not an important word."

Ripskin's sweaty hands began to slip down the neck of the bag. His right thigh had a deep burn on it from bumping against the wall. Still, he tightened his grip and continued his deception.

"By the way, son (and at this point, Ripskin told an enormous lie), I've only just returned from the blue planet on a mission for our Lord. And I was wondering . . . of course, you may not know the answer to this since you are just a young lad. I mean, it's clear you *are* a big boy—and probably much cleverer than these other children with you—but still, I've never met a child who knew much about anything when it came to certain . . . er . . . battle strategies?"

The boy cocked his head naively.

Ripskin's grip was slipping again.

"Call to arms? Crusade tactics? Mobilization? Do you know a thing or two about these matters . . . er . . . uh . . . Edward Louis Richardson?"

"*Robinson,* sir," said Edward.

"Listen, you," and then Ripskin caught himself, "you dear, intelligent child. Has Jesus made any new announcements concerning his . . . uh . . . his return to the blue planet? Surely, you realize I've been gone from home a long time. And it would be helpful for me to—"

"Please, sir. I'd like my candy," interrupted Edward.

"And so you shall have it," said Ripskin, curtly. He was certain now he would get nothing of value from the contemptuous brat. "Here it is. Can you see it in the slot? Just feel inside right here. Then, I'll be on my way."

The child reached his hand toward the opening to receive the promised sweet. But just as his chubby fingers touched the gold, and just as Ripskin's lips curled back across his teeth in anticipation of the baby-fat flesh he fully intended to bite . . .

. . . the knot came loose.

Ripskin's cry was pithy. It told of a painful fall. As he tumbled, the footings of heaven rose up to meet Ripskin. Millions had fallen before him. And not one had fallen with greater agony, for Ripskin had dared to trick a child through the mail.

But had he known what would happen to him when he finally reached hell, and were it possible for demons to utter prayers, Ripskin would have prayed to go on falling. For the last letter he stuffed in the slot should never have reached the enemy.

# ~ 3 ~

*Let us establish a royal courier service that will be known of all men.*

—Urduk, servant of King Sargon, 3000 B.C.

ON the other side of the wall, not far from where Ripskin met misfortune is the Cloud Cafe.

Just outside the back door of the kitchen, there runs a river. It is a laughing, singing chorus of living water, said by all to have sprung from beneath Jesus' throne long years ago, though few have ever tracked it to its source. There is a place in the river where the bank cuts sharply toward the Cloud Cafe, then back out again. Here an eddy is formed. Out of the center of the eddy grows a tree so thick with fruit in every season that a host of entrepreneurial children could not pick it all in a year if they tried. The tree's laden branches hang until they nearly touch the ground on either side of the river.

The fruit is thick-skinned, drawn to a point on one end and fat on the other. It is usually described as golden, but a more accurate description notes its ability to change colors depending on the angle light falls upon it. Concerning the fruit, however, two things remain constant.

The first is that the fruit is never in shortage. No tree is more bountiful than the one outside the Cloud Cafe's kitchen door. And second, the fruit's taste is—and always will be—ecstasy to those who sample it, for it imitates the favorite foods of the saints.

And that is why Jim Bob can order biscuits just like his wife made on the day he drove off to work, and was struck by a train before he ever reached the plant. And Ramón can have his five-alarm breakfasts, Günther his brats, and Ravi his curry. And even the little Thompson girl, who has arrived fresh from her short life on earth, can have the thing that will soothe her tummy most—a hotdog and a Coke.

OH, TASTE AND SEE THAT THE LORD IS GOOD!

From where she sat at table 10, Muriel Conniston Robbins studied the banner over the kitchen door, agreeing with its message.

"Yes, You are," she sighed, looking across the table at Jesus, who heard her quiet praise and acknowledged it with a smile. Even after twelve years of being in heaven, she was still awed whenever the Lord invited her to breakfast.

"Did you hear that scream a moment ago?" He asked her.

"A scream? I thought it might have been an angel taking speed practice."

"No, it was a scream," said Jesus. "It means the mail is here. Would you collect it after breakfast, please?"

"I'd be honored," said Muriel.

Then she folded her menu, placed her napkin in her lap, and boldly told Sam who stood waiting with his pen and pad that she'd be having the crabmeat and eggs New Orleans as well as the prosciutto blintzes with the marmalade glaze. Encouraged by the fact that Jesus didn't bat an eye, she added the crêpe suzette and a large glass of guava juice.

"Oh, and could you bring margarine instead of butter, please?" Muriel asked.

"Butter is all we have, Muriel," said Sam. He was a huge angel with wings that folded neatly down the backside of his well-pressed tuxedo.

Muriel blushed, and Jesus chuckled inwardly. He was always amused to find citizens of heaven still counting fat grams in the butter.

"You can take cream with your coffee, too, you know," said Jesus, as He pointed to the porcelain cow pitcher in the center of the table.

Muriel smiled, poured the cow's contents into her cup, and stirred until the brew was beige.

"And what will you be having today, Sir?" asked Sam.

Jesus raised two fingers to his lips and eyed the menu. Behind Him, and far below the cloud upon which their table perched, a blue-green ball hung against a background of deepest indigo. To the left of the tiny planet, a shooting star streaked away into the darkness, and Jesus eyed it knowingly. Above them was the bright sky. And all around them were the inhabitants of heaven taking breakfast at their leisure.

"I believe it's a waffle morning, Sam," said Jesus. "And would you put some berries on the side?"

"Done," said Sam, unfurling his wings and rushing off to the kitchen.

As soon as Sam was gone, Jesus leaned toward Muriel, and took her hands in His. She tried not to stare at the cylindrical nail prints just above the lunate bone in each of His wrists. But she was drawn to them.

"You're going to learn a great deal about My love in the coming weeks, Muriel," said Jesus. "Your lesson starts today with the gathering of the mail and will not end until your father learns it, too."

"My father?"

"Yes, Muriel. Walter Conniston of Mulberry Court. He has been on your mind more than usual in the last few days, hasn't he?"

"Yes, but—"

"Well, he's about to receive some love letters," said Jesus with a twinkle in His eye.

"You mean—"

But before Muriel could say another word, Sam returned with their meals, and Jesus was folding His hands in prayer.

"Would you?" He asked, with His eyes closed and a tiny smile working at the corners of His mouth.

Muriel bowed her head.

"For the fruit of the tree, and for Your love unfailing, I thank You, Father. Amen. Now, what is this all about?" she asked.

"My child," laughed Jesus, no longer trying to stifle His joy, "if it will make you feel any better, you can go get the mail now."

"But—"

"Go on," said Jesus.

Muriel draped her napkin on the table's edge and hurried toward the far end of the Cloud Cafe. Out on the sidewalk, she turned left and ran the short distance to the mail slot. She could see the boys and girls playing on their tricycles, and to their rear, a jumble of assorted envelopes and packages were scattered at the base of the brilliant wall.

"Hello, children," she said, as she rushed past them and approached her task. A small, cloth sack hung on an iron peg. Muriel took it down and began to gather the morning mail. Her eyes raced from envelope to envelope, trying to find some clue that would help her make sense of Jesus' words.

"Fine day," she offered. And the children agreed with her, happily nodding their heads and ringing their handlebar bells with gusto. A boy with a handsome cap rode up to Muriel and spoke confidently for a child his size.

"I'm Edward Louis Robinson," he said.

"Pleased to meet you, Edward Louis Robinson," answered Muriel, without looking up. "Oh! Whatever could Jesus be talking about?"

"I'm five," said Edward, flashing a fistful of fat fingers.

"I could tell by the way you rode," said Muriel. "So much like a five-year-old. Now be a gentleman, please, and we'll play as soon as I'm finished."

Undaunted, Edward dismounted and walked closer.

"An angel came by with lemon tarts," said Edward, motioning toward the mail slot. "He had cherry cordials, too."

Muriel paused and glanced at the boy. Immediately she understood that the offer of sweets had been a ruse. How many times would an angel from hell attempt to breach heaven before realizing that good *always* triumphs over evil?

"Well, thank God He keeps us all from danger, children. Ride along now. Go on. Have fun." Muriel watched the children pedal off and round a corner in the distance. Then she returned to her work, loading the sack with a tune in her heart and an eye for any unusual correspondence. When the sack was full to bursting with communication from the underworld, Muriel pulled the drawstring and rose to go.

It was then she saw the letter.

She might have missed it had she not reached up to close the little flap on the mail slot. But there it was, lodged diagonally in the opening, as if its deliverer had lacked the strength to push it all the way through. Muriel pulled the heavy stock envelope from the slot and turned it over in her hand. On its front, the address read:

Muriel Conniston Robins
Heaven
c/o Saint Peter

Her heart began to race. She held the envelope up to her face, and looked closely at the typing. She blinked. She looked again, and it occurred to her that nobody outside her family ever used her maiden name. And nobody but her older brother spelled her married name with only one *b*.

"Dear Bentley. Can it be you?" she said, as she tucked the letter inside her gown pocket.

Trembling with excitement, Muriel flung the sack over her shoulder and raced to the Cloud Cafe. At the table she found Jesus had left His own meal alone, preferring to share the breakfast with her when she returned. He glanced at the bulging bag. When Muriel released it and it fell to the floor with an ominous thud, He winced at the sound.

"Well now, let's have a look at what flotsam has floated up from the deeps today. Care to guess, Muriel, before I spill it on the table and the two of us sort through it?" said Jesus.

Muriel said nothing. The letter in her pocket seemed to burn a hole into her thigh, and she wondered if this breach of policy would go unnoticed. But Jesus went on talking between bites of waffle, and all the while He worked His fingers against the enormous knot Muriel had tied in the drawstring.

"No doubt, there'll be sad tales in this bag. There always are, you know. Some will say it's too hot down there. Others will claim it's too cold. Have you ever wondered why I was called a Man of Sorrows in the Bible, Muriel?"

Muriel shook her head.

"The reason is before you. A Man of Sorrows always aches for the ones he loves, no matter how far they've fallen."

Then Jesus turned silent. He ran His hands down through the opening of the sack and plunged them deep into hell's communiqués, as if He were reaching down to those who'd penned them far below.

"Before the Rebellion, we used to throw the ball together, you know," He said quietly. "Before any of you came here, I taught them all how to fly, how to read, and how to write."

Muriel watched as Jesus pushed His breakfast aside and dumped the contents of the sack on the table. Then ever so slowly, she reached into her pocket, retrieved the letter, and laid it on the table with the address face-down.

"Thank you," said Jesus. "You're a ray of light for Me in this gray bit of business. Thank you for not concealing your brother's letter from Me."

"Then it *is* from him?" asked Muriel excitedly.

"It is," said Jesus. He watched Muriel reach for it and clutch it to her breast. "But I wouldn't rush to read it just yet," He added. "Not without considering the pain it might contain."

Muriel's fingers were poised to tear the seal.

"What do you mean, *pain*?" she asked.

But Jesus did not respond immediately. He sorted letters and whistled, and several stacks of common correspondence began to form.

"Let's see," He said, "*grievance, grievance, grievance, request, grievance, request, threat,* oh, dear," He laughed. "Where was I? Oh, yes, *grievance, grievance, request, contraband, grievance . . .*"

The stacks grew until some of them began to lean precariously and it was necessary to begin new ones. When the task was nearly done and Muriel had proceeded no farther in the tearing of the seal, Jesus' hand ran across a certain letter in the bottom of the sack and He paused. Without lifting it out, He cocked His head to the side, as if He could hear the message through the sides of the envelope. He breathed slowly, whispering to Himself.

"'There are always one or two in every batch," He said. "Ones that are known simply by their touch."

"What's that?" asked Muriel.

"Oh, nothing worth troubling yourself about," He replied. "Just little projects, special endeavors Satan ruminates over and fancies only he can attend to."

"Satan?"

Jesus pulled the letter from the bag. "Shall we read our mail aloud?"

"Let's," chimed Muriel.

Muriel poked her finger under a corner of the envelope flap and slid it slowly along the fastened seam. When it was completely undone she saw the folded edge of her brother's letter inside and looked across the table.

"Pain?" she asked.

"The distinct possibility of it," said Jesus.

Cautiously, Muriel lifted the letter from its confines, unfolded it, and began to read.

# ~ 4 ~

Dear Muriel,

I'm not sure if this will ever reach you, but if it does I want you to understand two things. First, I never killed Tom Caudell. I was at the commissary at the exact same time Private Caudell got the daylights beat out of him. That's a fact. I just could never prove it. Whatever else you may think of me, I don't want my own sister thinking I'm a murderer for the rest of eternity.

Anyway, when I got here I saw this one moan—that's what they call the demons here, "the moans"—anyway, I saw this one moan act like he was going to give the heartiest handshake to a guy ahead of me. And when the moan grabbed the guy's hand, he kept on squeezing until everyone in the line could hear bones breaking.

The registrar told the guy he was guilty of stealing, and that he could expect an eternal punishment. Then the registrar laughed and told him he'd be eligible for parole in a trillion years if his behavior was good. But that's not all. When they stripped the guy and went through his belongings I noticed there was a bone sticking out of his wrist and that he was bleeding. However, by the time they got finished, his hand was all healed up. Not a scratch.

Just as soon as this guy came out on the other side of customs, another moan grabbed him by the hand and did the same thing. Busted bones, and all! And the moan sort of grinned when he did it and said, "Welcome, Stan."

I've run into that guy a dozen times since I've been here, Muriel. Sometimes he has a broken hand and sometimes he doesn't. The moans make Stan go everywhere barefoot. And believe me, Muriel, it's as hot as you've always heard it was down here. Stan's feet are in pretty bad shape.

Anyway, when I got up to the desk, the registrar looked up at me and stopped everything he was doing. "Well, well, well," he said. Then he looked at a huge mess of papers and started reading out loud for everyone to hear all the bad things I did on earth. Everything he read was true. I just wished he'd have skipped the part about me and Janie Jenson in the barn, though. Of course you remember her. You lectured me enough when she got pregnant. I laughed about it then, and called you a prude. But it's not funny anymore, and I'm sorry about all that stuff. If you see Janie Jenson ever (she'll probably be up there someday), tell her I said I'm sorry.

Anyway, when the registrar started reading the part about me murdering Private Tom Caudell, I don't know what came over me.

"I didn't kill him," I screamed. The registrar sort of reeled back in his chair with his eyes all round and everything. And a ton of other moans raced to shut me up. Before they could grab me, I started running trying to find some doorway where I could escape or wake up and find that this is all a bad dream. But the moans tackled me and marched me right back to the registrar's desk and made me listen to the whole thing again, including the part about Janie Jenson. And this time when he got to the murdering part, I begged him to listen. But he told me to shut up. Then he said, "I know good and well you didn't kill Caudell, you sniveling idiot!"

He went on to say that I may not have killed Tom
Caudell with a pool cue, but that I had killed him a
thousand times in my head and half as many times
with my mouth.

Then he laughed and told me what my sentence
was. He said that if I was so good at coming up with
cruel images in my mind and spewing them out on
people that I hate, then I could just spend eternity
thinking thoughts and typing words.

So, that's what I do here, Sis. I sit all alone in a
little room (about as big as your old closet), and
type on an ancient typewriter. I don't get paid for it
or anything. And <u>deadlines</u> have their own special
meaning here.

Twice a day, they let me out of my room to go to
the field. It's always great to leave my tiny space
for a while and stretch my legs. But the little side
rooms can really get to you. They are what I report
on. In fact, my whole job is to go into those rooms,
find a seat in the back, and just take notes on what
goes on in there. Then I'm supposed to go back to
my stinking closet and prepare an article for the
<u>Chronicle</u> in time to go to evening press. Oh yeah,
the <u>Chronicle</u> is hell's daily newspaper. So I guess
you could say that I'm working for Satan.

I've never met Satan, but I'm constantly
reminded about the type of article he likes to read.
It saves my neck to write with a particular slant
every time I sit down at this lousy machine.

On my first assignment, I was sent to report on
the room where I would have been stuck if I hadn't
gotten this job. The rooms are called <u>sanctums</u> here,
which is really just a fancy way to say <u>torture cham-
ber</u>. The sanctums are divided according to different
kinds of sins. So if you did mostly klepto stuff like
Stan, you end up in a room with all the other klepto-
maniacs. If you're a sex offender like Barty Schindler
used to be—remember him?—then you go to another
room. If you cheat, you're with the cheaters. If you

kill, you're with the killers. And so forth. Every now and then, some pretty decent people wind up here, too. They're the saddest ones of all.

Sometime in the morning of that day a message was slipped under my door: "Satan wants you to go to sanctum 909 in the east sector. Now."

So I went. And when I got there, I was given a briefing by the sanctum's warden, "You better take good notes, sonny, because this is where you're going to be if you ever lose that cush job of yours!"

Inside the room were all the souls whose crummy thoughts and words were their greatest sins.

The souls walked in a circle to the one point where the warden stood with a bucket of coals. Each time a soul came to him, he reached into his bucket with long tongs and pulled out a red hot coal. He made the soul open his or her mouth and he shoved the thing inside. The souls couldn't shout or spit the coal out or anything, because if they did, they'd have to turn around and get two more coals placed in the mouth. The souls suffered until they reached the far side of the circle, where another moan waited with a bucket of water. At this point, the souls opened their mouths, the moan splashed water down their throats, and the souls headed off toward the warden again to get another coal. Around they went for hours, Muriel, until they were finally allowed to stop for lunch, which was something like hot coffee and chili.

But the worst thing about it all was when I saw Tom Caudell walk by in the circle. I thought for sure he wouldn't be here! I mean, I hated him, but I always thought he was a much better person than I was when he was alive! At least he went to church. When he walked on by, I thought about all the times I killed him in my heart for stealing Janie Jenson from me, and all the times we both spread rumors about each other at school, and especially the time I swore to Tom's face I'd cut his throat for talking

Janie into having an abortion. That was <u>my</u> kid he murdered, you know—not his!

But seeing him here, Muriel—somehow all those old feelings disappeared and there was only one feeling left. I felt sorry for him. And I had to write this stinking little blurb on the whole thing as if it was grand and good and wonderful. So I did, because I didn't want to be in that horrible sanctum. But the entire time I was writing, I felt as if my tongue, brain, heart, and body were on fire anyway.

Satan liked the article, so I got a promotion, which I'll tell you about tomorrow when I write. I'll send the article along, too, if I can get a copy.

I mentioned there were <u>two</u> things I wanted you to understand. First, I didn't murder Tom Caudell. We were soldiers together. But that's about as far as our relationship went after high school. And second, I miss you, Muriel. I miss you and Mom and Dad, especially Dad for some reason. Maybe it's because I know he's got a lot of time on his hands, walking around that town, wondering about you and me. I think of him when I'm typing at night. I've almost forgotten what he looks like, along with all the other faces of people I knew when I was on earth. But I promised myself I wouldn't forget. Sometimes when it's late and I'm pretty sure the moan outside my door has fallen asleep, I try to draw your faces on pieces of typing paper. I don't draw for long because the moan would report me if he woke up and didn't hear my typewriter banging away. But at least I try. I try to hang on to my family.

I am sending my letters through Stan, Muriel. Somehow, he got a job in the mail room. He has agreed to smuggle these out with Satan's batch of requests that apparently go straight to God. A moan delivers mail daily to heaven and returns with correspondence from God. Stan is responsible for sorting the mail when it returns, so see if you can put a letter in for me from time to time. Just make sure

you address it to Moan B. I'll tell Stan what to look
for, and when he receives it he'll sneak it to me
whenever we see each other on the main path. Of
course, none of this may work, but it's worth a try.

I'll understand if you don't have time to write. I
mean, heaven's a great place, isn't it?


Love always,
Bentley


P.S. Tell me everything you can about heaven.

## ~ 5 ~

*A man he was to all the country dear,*
*And passing rich with forty pounds a year.*

—Oliver Goldsmith, *The Deserted Village*

WHEN Muriel finished her letter, Jesus placed His fingers on her eyes, and the sad thoughts that seed the tears faded away. "Oh, Bentley," she whispered. "Dear Bentley. But what does all this mean?"

"It means we have work to do, Muriel. I think you'll understand after I read my letter," said Jesus. He cleared His throat and asked Muriel if she was ready. She nodded, and He opened the letter from the former Archangel and began to read.

"It says, 'To Whom It Concerns.' That is so like him," said Jesus. "He can hardly bring himself to say My name. Ah, here it is," said Jesus as He scanned the letter, sparing Muriel the customary vulgarities that are Satan's manner of small talk.

Being the know-it-all that you are, you undoubtedly recall our deal regarding that insignificant mortal—that puny little letter carrier who lives in . . . oh, I've forgotten the name of the place. It doesn't matter. You know the town I'm talking about. And you know the man, too. Well, I want him! I demand permission to finish sorting his life

just like he sorts the mail for the rest of those
sorry citizens in . . . Ellenbach. That's it. That's
the place.

Jesus paused and looked at Muriel. Her head was notice-
ably raised, and her ear turned toward the sound of His
voice. The words, *Ellenbach* and *letter carrier* had jolted
her. She was beginning to understand.

Certainly, you didn't imagine I'd be satisfied
with just his older son, did you? I want his wife
and the other brat, too, and above all, the man,
himself. Oh yes, I know you've probably been
busting your buttons over him all these years,
what with his holding up so well under his little
darling's cancer. How terribly sad. Well, then, I'm
sure you've noticed how the bitterness has fairly
sprouted leaves in him. Can you hear them
rustling? But of course you can. You don't miss a
thing.
So, hear this.
You were lucky to get the woman. But I'm going
to take this pious little postal worker and show you
just how flimsy a former deacon's faith can be.
Faith?! Hah! In what?
In you? In the great shepherd of the heavens
who's done nothing but stand aside and watch one
of his own flock choke on a tumor and another
one go traipsing off to hell?
You humor me for eternity.
Now listen here. I've discovered a lovely, willing
soul on earth with whom to tempt this wretched
courier. Pay attention now. All you have to do is
keep your end of the bargain, and I'll show you
once and for all how weak this so-called Christian
really is. Piece by piece, I'll pull him down by way
of flesh. I'll have Walter Conniston. In the end,
there'll be no more meddlesome evangelism in
Ellenbach!

At the mention of her father's name from Satan's pen, Muriel sat straight up in her chair.

And his housefrau, Donna, as well. And the jock son. Dallas, I believe his name is. I'll get him, too! What do you say, coach? Do we play ball? Or do you fear this man of substance has grown a bit thin over the years?
As always, until I hear from you, I am

Disrespectfully yours,
Lucifer, Rightful Ruler of All Realms

P.S. Don't keep me waiting.

When Jesus finished reading, He crumpled the letter and tossed it toward the pile of correspondence.

"Why is this happening to my father? He was such a good man. He was a deacon."

"People's goodness neither damns nor delivers them. The same is true of badness. After all, heaven houses a great many 'kleptos' and 'sex offenders' whose only real distinction from Stan or Barty was that when they found they could no longer hide their deeds in the shadow of Golgotha, they came out into the Light. Your father, Muriel, stood in that Light since before you were born. In fact, he was one of the few who take My highest calling seriously by bringing everyone they meet a step farther from the darkness. Nevertheless, it has always been those brightest shining saints whom Satan tries to extinguish."

"Then my father's in danger, isn't he?"

"He's nearly blind with bitterness," said Jesus.

At that, Sam returned again with Muriel's warm meal and a basket of bread, which he placed in the center of the table.

"I'm not very hungry," said Muriel, when the angel had disappeared through the kitchen doors.

"At least have a slice of bread," said Jesus, as He reached toward the basket and uncovered the simple brown loaf. It appeared so ordinary in comparison to the other things on the menu, but there was a certain aroma to it that was hard to resist, even for someone like Muriel who ached with holy pain.

"All right. I'll have some," said Muriel. "But what about—"

"Shhh," said Jesus, tearing a handful of the dark bread and extending it toward Muriel. "Here," He said. "Take. Eat. This is My body broken for . . ." He hesitated briefly, ". . . the Connistons."

Muriel reached out and took the bread. When she did, her fingers came closer to that raised skin on Jesus' wrist.

"Would you like to touch them?" asked Jesus, seeing her stare at His scars.

Something welled up inside of Muriel. It was not fear, for she could hardly have gone through chemotherapy, radiation treatment, and the painful throes of cancer and still have much capacity to ever fear anything again. Instead, she felt an awe of sorts, a sudden kinship with all the doubting Thomases of time. With her left hand she grasped Jesus' wrist, and with her right she lifted the bread to her lips and placed it in her mouth.

"Extraordinary," exclaimed Muriel.

"Yes, it is," agreed Jesus. "It is good enough for kings and presidents, yet ordinary enough for a mail carrier. Which brings us to the matter of the letters. Any notion of what to do with them?" He asked with a smile. As He spoke, He motioned for Muriel to rise and come sit with Him on the cloud's edge, which was a yard or so from their table.

Soon the two were dangling their legs over the rim of the towering cumulus, upon which the Cloud Cafe perched like a jewel in heaven's bright crown. In and out of holes in the cloud, Muriel saw birds darting, bright swallows flashing their underbellies, buntings banking, and larks and finches yawing on the wind. And way down below she could see the blue planet when she leaned forward and looked between the tips of her sandals.

Muriel thought of her father there, living out his days on that distant globe, trudging through Ellenbach on sluggish December mornings, cursing the cold, cursing the loss of children, cursing the God whom he once loved. She thought of her mother alone at home. She thought of the threadbare relationship she'd had with her. She thought of Dallas on his paper route, and of Bent in hell. And finally, she remembered how things used to be.

"He used to be happy," said Muriel, feeling for some reason as if she needed to defend the bitter man her father had become. "He used to tell people all about You."

"You'd be surprised what he says about Me now," answered Jesus. "Everything will be all right, though. In no time he'll be as good as new. Now, about our letters. What shall we do with them?"

"What *can* we do?" asked Muriel.

"For starters, we could tear them up and throw them to the wind," said Jesus. "Or we could save them and file them someplace. Then, of course, there's always the option of answering them."

"Answering them?" said Muriel.

"Ah-ha! I knew you'd choose that one. It is the polite thing to do, you know," said Jesus. Behind Him, six angels stood at attention, but it was obvious they were having a hard time fighting the urge to smile, for they could tell another spectacular chapter of Jesus' sovereign will was about to unfold.

"You're quite serious," said Muriel.

"Quite," said Jesus. "I've been planning this for centuries."

"You mean I can write my brother in hell?"

"That's the plan. We can both start right away."

"And Bent will return my letters?"

"Yes, he'll return them. But he'll get caught."

Muriel looked at the letter.

"So, Muriel," said Jesus. "What would you like to say to your brother?"

"Well, I suppose I should try to comfort him. That's the least I can do for Bent."

"That's noble. Go on," said Jesus.

Muriel hesitated. It was one thing to declare what she'd write to Bent in hell. But imagining what Jesus was going to say in His letter to Satan, that was altogether different. She thought about Satan's threats to sort her father like the mail, and she wondered what *sort* meant.

"You've jumped ahead a bit, haven't you?" said Jesus, reading her thoughts. "Remember, I never lose," He said, holding up His wrists.

"Right," said Muriel. "Tell that treacherous serpent he can give it his best shot."

"That's the spirit," said Jesus. "I have few warriors at my disposal for the purposes of Ellenbach, however. Nearly all of them are in larger cities, presently, Chicago, L.A., London, New Delhi. So we're left to fight on different terms. Listen closely," He said. Muriel faced Him on the cloud.

"These are the best angels available to me," Jesus said, indicating the beings to His rear. "May I introduce to you Ace, Homer, François, Albert, Doc, and Chaney.

"Take a bow." The six angels bent low.

"They're civilians," continued Jesus. "You probably recognize them as waiters from the cafe. However, they're all experienced in field work and have merely been out of action for a while. Their skills are a bit rusty, Muriel. But they're as strong as angels come. Here's my proposal."

Muriel listened excitedly.

"Satan has no clue about your brother's letter, at least, not yet. But soon he will. And when he *does* learn of the leak, you can be sure he'll shut down the mail room. There'll be no more correspondence out of hell until he gets to the bottom of it. That's where Homer comes into play," said Jesus, pointing to a gangly angel with a surfer's tan. "He's the best flier of the bunch and the least likely to cause a stir in hell when he takes your letters back to Bent. After all, how much threat can one California Angel pose?"

Homer grinned.

"Next, when Homer brings Bent's letters back, François will make three copies. He knows the print shop inside and out, but he's most remembered for the years he spent in the French Alps."

A short, mustached angel with a checkered beret stepped forward and spoke in a thick accent. "I do as Monsieur says, Madam. I make one copy for you, one for Him, and one to go to the town of Ellenbach."

"Ellenbach?" exclaimed Muriel.

"Listen, Muriel," said Jesus touching her arm. "Every second is precious, so hear Me out. When the third copy is safe in Ace's hands, all six will fly like the wind to Ellenbach. Once there, they'll put the letters in your father's mailbag. And then we'll just have to wait."

"You *are* kidding," said Muriel, starting to grin. "How in the world will they be able to put supernatural mail into an earthly mailbag?"

"Trust me, Muriel. Matter is immaterial to Me, since I created it. But listen, please. The whole affair could get difficult for your father. Are you ready for that, Muriel?"

"Will *my* letters reach my father, too?" Muriel asked.

"Yes. The same as Bent's. Give them to François. He'll take care of the rest."

"So, You intend to help my father through the mail?" asked Muriel.

"Not *help* him, Muriel, *hound* him," said Jesus. "Some saints need more than just a little nudge to get back on the right track."

"And You've been planning this all along?"

"Yes. This is foreordained."

The angels nodded in the background.

Muriel's eyes widened. In an instant, she saw the significance of timing. She saw her own role in her father's sanctification from start to finish. She saw herself walking with him down a candlelit aisle to take the name of Jack Robbins. She saw her childless marriage, and through it all her father's kindness. She saw the grunt and groan of bedridden days. She saw her spirit lifted from the hospital bed amidst her husband's tears, her father's ashen stare, her mother's wailing. She saw herself today gathering heaven's mail from under the golden slot at just the right moment. Had Jesus not asked *her* to gather the mail, some other soul would've been there. And that last, forlorn letter in the opening might not have been seen. Bent's cry might have blown off into the universe and collected dust somewhere with all the other dead letters that are never delivered. Finally, Muriel saw herself sitting at a computer tapping out messages to her brother and, indirectly, to her family. A wave of happiness washed over her.

"When can we begin?" asked Muriel.

"Just as soon as Homer can locate a word processor for you," said Jesus, nodding to the angel to get cracking.

"I've got to cruise, ma'am," said the West Coast angel. He took Muriel by the arm, and they were off, leaving Jesus with the five remaining angels.

"Gather around," said Jesus, dropping to His knees. And the angels circled Him. "I don't expect any of you to return from this mission unscathed. The moans are thick in Ellenbach, up to no good."

"But Jesus, can't troops from farther north pitch in? Surely there are some on furlough," said Albert, an angel who loved and served Jesus faithfully but had a hard time doing so without the details.

"Out of the question, Al. I need every battleworthy

spirit I can muster in the big cities. That's where the majority of the children of the dust have chosen to live. That's where the moans strike the hardest."

"But why Ellenbach?" asked Al. "What possible interest could the enemy have there?"

"Y-yeah," chimed Chaney, a stuttering favorite of rural souls who found his country drawl comforting as they made the transition from temporal to eternal. "Isn't that j-j-just a hole in the road, anyways? Seems like Satan could get a l-l-lot more bang for his buck somewhere else."

"It does seem that way, doesn't it," said Jesus. "But the fact is, sometimes the impact of a common soul extends far beyond that soul's county line."

"Would that all Your followers were like that, Monsieur," said François.

"Muriel's father is one such soul," continued Jesus. "In fact, Walter was at one time quite a mouthpiece for My kingdom. I aim to make him that way again. But when Satan finds out about these letters, he's going to try to stop Me."

"Isn't there more You can tell us?" asked Albert.

Jesus stood up. "Thirty-six years ago," began Jesus, "a man moved to Ellenbach to take the job of Postal Carrier 1009. The man was Walter Conniston. His young bride was Donna. He was a simple man, with a heart that was pure and contrite. And in him was no guile. Some said it was a pity he didn't hold a degree. But I saw in him the tenacity of a Peter or a Paul. For up and down the streets of Ellenbach he told people of My love, and he had a way of making things plain enough for them to understand. Soon, the carrier had told everyone in town the good news of the First Coming. And even if some didn't believe it, they saw the works of Walter and gave a measure of credit to My Father.

"About that time, Satan saw what Walter was doing, too. He sent a messenger to me with a request to touch the man.

"'What pride is there in one who speaks for You, but has never tasted anything besides the nectar of life?'

read the messenger from a blackened piece of paper. 'Give me the man, and I'll have his tongue as silent as a tomb in no time.'

"Willingly, I permitted it. The rest is history. Muriel is here, Bent is below, and Walter thinks I killed his children. Consequently he hasn't spoken My name in years, outside of speaking it in vain. In his anguish, he pretends I no longer exist. And he is in anguish—perhaps not as much as Job was, but suffering never seems light to the one who suffers.

"It hurts to think how Ellenbach has taken its cue from Walter. Because of his joy originally, many of them came to Me. Now because of his bitterness, many have gone. How strange it is when I am judged according to one person's frown. Ah! But here is the happy part," said Jesus. "Satan knows the deal is off the moment Walter's tongue is loosed again for My glory. Therefore, he's doubling his efforts to destroy the man by destroying his reputation. But destruction was *never* part of My plan for Walter. You have heard it said that the testing of one's faith produces endurance. Not only do I have Walter's endurance in mind as I test him, but the well-being of an entire town, plus the salvation of a certain soul to whom only Walter can minister. And that's precisely why these letters must be put into his bag. Walter *must* speak of My love to Ellenbach once again."

"Excuse me, S-Sir," said Chaney. "But we're just w-w-waiters. You told the woman Yourself we haven't been to war in a while."

Ace bit his lip and looked away.

Jesus glanced at Ace, then smiled at the other four who knelt around Him. True, they had all been out of commission for a long, long time. But they had all fought for Him in that long-ago skirmish, the great Battle of Ascension in which so many of their peers had fallen out of heaven. They were strong angels, and adequate fliers at that. Consequently, He had no fear for them.

"You'll do just fine," He assured them. "Now off with you! Find Homer and Muriel. Don't forget to make the copies, François. And at all costs, friends, get those letters into Walter's mailbag."

"Jesus, what if we need You along the way?" asked Doc.

Jesus considered the question. In His hand was the envelope containing Satan's request to sort Walter Conniston like a piece of mail. And on its front was Jesus' proper name, or at least a rendering of it, scrawled in blood. It read:

Jesus' eyes narrowed and His lips drew thin across His face. Turning towards the angels, He said, "If you ever get into trouble, just say My name and I'll be there."

Muriel and Homer returned with her letter.

"Back so soon?" He said, as He took the envelope from Muriel. "You must have known exactly what you wanted to write."

"It wasn't hard my Lord. Twelve years is a long time to go without saying I love you."

"True," said Jesus. "And can you imagine how long it must seem to the one who hasn't *heard* those words? But move along now," He said to the angels as He pressed the letters into François's hands. Then, just before their takeoff, Jesus pulled Ace aside.

"You're My headwaiter, Alistair. I'm putting you in

charge," whispered Jesus. "Above all, I want you to remember these four words: *One soul in Ellenbach.*"

"One soul in Ellenbach," repeated Ace.

"Yes," said Jesus. "Say them over and over, night and day. Teach your troops to do the same. For even as we speak there is one quite ordinary soul living in Ellenbach who will perish before the north wind blows if the Story is not told. Death always prevails where the Story is forgotten. I know of nothing more dismal than a kingdom whose bards are silent, and the only noise at bedtime is the grate of the evening news. It is My will that Walter tell the Story once again. Make that your will, as well. And Alistair . . ."

"Sir?"

"There is no trial so great that you and I can't face together. Do you understand? Not even that one you fear the most."

Ace closed his eyes at the suggestion of his archenemy.

"I might as well let you know. You'll meet him on the first day out. And you will do just fine, My friend. But there is no more time for talk now," said Jesus, turning toward the others and spreading His arms to embrace them. "Go in peace, faithful servants," He said, smiling. "Go with healing in your wings, and a most unusual surprise for the mailman of Mulberry Court. But go quickly! At this very moment Walter is closer to disaster than he's ever been."

## ~ 6 ~

For I dipped into the future, far as human eye
  could see,
Saw the Vision of the world, and all the
  wonder that would be;
Saw the heavens fill with commerce, argosies
  of magic sails,
Pilots of the purple twilight, dropping down
  with costly bales;
Heard the heavens fill with shouting, and
  there rained a ghastly dew
From the nations' airy navies grappling in
  the central blue.

—Alfred, Lord Tennyson, *Locksley Hall*

AFTER securing his load at the post office, Walter skipped breakfast and walked toward Springdale, his windburned face parting the air as he went. Mindlessly, he shoved mail in boxes along the street. Troost and Bedford were equally uneventful. But when Walter reached Cistern his pulse quickened. Halfway down the block he saw the sign.

It was ordinary, white, square, with two words printed on it: FOR SALE. It had been in the yard of 602 Cistern for only a day when a third word appeared across the top: SOLD.

Walter walked slowly and kept his eye on 602. Four weeks ago a moving van had come gliding up in front of the house. A man got out and walked around to the passenger side of the truck. He helped an extraordinarily lovely woman step lightly from the cab.

Even now, Walter's jaw hung slightly open as he thought about the woman. He recalled her walking up the driveway, through the front door, and out of sight. And though Walter's vision of her was brief, he still held an image of her. He had seen her a long time ago, it seemed. But he would not allow himself to remember when or where.

Walter had stayed up the night before, staring at his scale model, staring at *her* house, and wondering why he hadn't seen her for a month. The moving van driver, it turned out, was not a boyfriend, which made Walter glad. The driver was simply an employee who left as soon as he and another worker had unloaded the contents of the truck. Walter found himself thinking about the woman, wondering whether she had a man in her life, and wondering if . . . *No! That wish would never come true,* thought Walter.

Nevertheless, the wish kept coming. Already unseen principalities were sorting Walter, skillfully sowing thoughts of lust and guilt until the mailman could no longer admit that the woman in 602 looked a great deal like Muriel, for fear that his interest in her was either morose or incestuous.

As he approached the modest board and batten home on Cistern, Walter took inventory of himself: fifty-six years old, graying temples, spectacle-dependent for reading purposes, trim from all the walking, and handsome, in a limited sort of way. "What's the use?" he told himself. "I'm crazy to think something might become of us."

He was standing in the woman's front yard like a codfish with its mouth open, when a blast of wind caught the lip of his mailbag and—*kafooofutta!!* A loose bundle of letters came shooting up out of the bag and across the lawn. For the slightest moment, Walter felt as if something more than just wind had hit him. Something almost solid. Walter raced to retrieve the letters. Just as he was bending over to pick up the last two, which had landed in the woman's begonias, he got the urge to look inside the window. It was only a foot or two from his forehead. If he brought his head up slowly and gazed through the top portion of his glasses, he could appear as if he was just pausing to think, not actually peeping into her quarters. As Walter was pretending harmlessness in the begonias, the front door suddenly swung open and the woman stepped out onto the porch. Her hair was gold and shining, and her cheeks wore the rose of summer.

"Hello," said she of high cheekbones and golden hair. "May I help you?"

Walter froze. He felt the earth beneath his feet moving on its axis. He saw that memory again, of a child's face long ago, coming clear, overlapping itself with this person in front of him. It faded in and out so fast that he could not pin it down in time to see that it was Muriel's face he was remembering.

"Uh, I . . . I guess I made a mess, ma'am. Uh, spilled my, well, anyway, I won't be long," said Walter, as he bent to retrieve his letters. "There," he said, holding up the last two letters for the woman to see, "Here're the last of them."

Walter stuffed the letters in his back pocket and snatched the bag from the ground.

"Are you all right?" asked the woman. "You look as if you've seen a ghost."

"Who, me? What makes you say that?" said Walter, backing out of the garden and tripping over a masonry border. He landed with an *ooof* on the woman's lawn.

"Hard to figure, isn't it?" said the woman, smiling.

Walter grabbed his bag and rose to leave.

"Look," said the woman. "I was just putting groceries away in the kitchen, and I saw you in my flowers. I was curious, that's all. By the way, I appreciate the hard work you do. What's your name?"

"Walter Conniston, ma'am. I wasn't trying to cause you any trouble. I would've been halfway down Birch by now if it weren't for this wind," he stammered, trying hard not to gawk at the woman when he answered.

The woman felt the stillness of the morning, glanced at the leaves in the trees, then back at Walter with suspicion. Feeling the weight of her look, Walter stuck his finger in his mouth and held it up to the air.

"Well, it was windy a minute ago. I swear it was, ma'am. I wouldn't make up a thing like that. Why, I . . . you do believe me, don't you?"

"Of course, I believe you. It must have been just howling to send your letters all over my yard. Would you like a pop to take with you?" the woman asked.

Walter relaxed and allowed himself a smile.

"You're from the north, aren't you," said Walter.

"How'd you guess? Was it my accent?" asked the woman.

"No ma'am, it wasn't that. But you ought to know that down here folks call them *Cokes*. That's not to say it didn't sound all right the way you put it."

"So, Mr . . ."

"Conniston. Walter's fine, though. Just Walter."

"Okay. Walter it is. Would you like a Coke for the road, Walter?"

As Walter stood there on that patch of lawn, he seemed to be retrogressing, reeling backward under the powerful influence of this woman's charm to a time when life was less complex and to a memory that was pleasant. He was happier then. And he saw again in his mind's eye the flaxen waif waving a cold drink in his direction and calling to him as he passed by the porch with his lawn mower. *The smell of fresh cut grass . . . the sound of machinery humming . . . and Daddy! Daddy! Do you want a drink?!*

"Walter?" said the woman a second time.

"Hmm? Oh. Right. Fine. A Coke would be fine. Thank you very much, ma'am," said Walter, snapping forward to the present.

"I'll be right back," replied the woman as she disappeared into the house.

In less than a minute she came back with a bottle of Coca-Cola, the top having only just been removed and the specter of carbonation still curling from its frosted lip.

"My mother always told me to treat strangers with care, Mr. Conniston. She said that some of them are angels and that you never can tell when you're going to actually meet one. Judging by the way you deliver the mail, you might as well be an angel. In all my years in Detroit, I never once saw a man quite so prompt as you. And they use Jeeps up there to get the job done."

"Thanks," said Walter.

He took the Coke, lifted it to his lips, and turned it upward in the sun. A bead of condensation dripped slowly down the sweating bottle and then flattened out where Walter's mouth met the opening of the soft drink.

"I bet you tell that bit about angels to your own kids," said Walter, lowering the bottle and wiping an errant drop from his chin. He was gaining confidence steadily. Now, he was interested in the details of this woman.

"As a matter of fact, I've never been married," said the woman.

"Is that so. I wouldn't have guessed it by looking at you."

"Oh? I didn't know it showed on a person."

"Not like wrinkles or anything. Not in that way," said Walter, quickly. "What I meant was, you're about all a fellow could ask for. And, well, I imagine there're a lot of fools out there still kicking themselves for not asking."

"Why, Walter Conniston, that's the nicest thing anyone ever said to me," exclaimed the woman, blushing.

Walter blushed, too, and took up his bag from where he had set it on the grass during the conversation. He had forgotten about everything for a moment—his race with time, the loss of children, his reputation, the investment of over half his life with the same woman. All seemed to vanish with the coming of this glorious creature and her ice-cold pop.

And then before he could ask her name, she vanished, waving good-bye, saying thank you again for the compliment, and shutting the door behind her softly. Walter pulled 602's only letter for the day from his bag and looked around for the mailbox. There was none.

"Nuts," he said, when he saw it was addressed to Occupant, and that the beautiful, nameless occupant of this house had a P.O. box instead of a mailbox at the end of her driveway.

Walter wanted to run straight up and ring her doorbell. He had to know the woman's name. It wasn't fair that she knew his. It wasn't right that she could take leave so easily from his presence. But he checked himself. He turned slowly, head down, and his feet shuffled heavily back through the grass to the sidewalk. When he reached the edge of the property, Walter took off his watch and put it in his pocket. He reached in his mailbag and reorganized the jumble of letters that he himself had created in his attempts not to be caught snooping in the woman's flowers. When he was certain he had everyone's letters back in order again, and his heart rate had returned to its normal condition after having soared to such heights, Walter took one last inventory of his belongings and discovered two letters in his right back pocket.

They were the ones he'd been reaching for in the begonias when the woman came to the door. And now when he took them out to check their addresses, he saw that they were smeared with dirt from where he'd tripped, fallen, and made a perfect clod of himself.

"Just my luck," he muttered at the soiled envelopes. "Oh, well. At least they aren't Jenson's *Wall Street*."

Walter's consolation was short-lived, though, for when he turned the letters over and read the return addresses, his eyes became round and wild looking. Immediately, he took his watch back out of his pocket, placed it on his wrist, punched the button that set his stopwatch in motion, and started running. And farthest from Walter's mind as he ran was that the woman in 602 Cistern might be running from something, too.

"Did they see us? Do you think they saw us? Oh, ephods and omers! What if we've been seen?" said Doc as he flew skyward from the woman's yard on Cistern.

"You d-did just fine," called Chaney, in support of Doc.

"Quiet!" commanded Ace. And the knot of angels obeyed.

"What are you talking about, Doc?"

The weathered angel was more than glad to make himself heard again, for he was certain he had seen Satan's forces lurking on the chimney of the woman's house just before he collided with Walter's mailbag.

He began excitedly, "They were there. They—"

"*Who* where there?"

"Big, beasty moans, Ace. And hairy, too. With fangs and flappers and pointy ears. It was all I could do to keep from running into our client."

"All right Doc, take it easy," said Ace.

"I saw four moans in all," said Doc emphatically. "Alpha Order, maybe. I'm not sure. But they were big chaps. One had on a leather jacket with a patch on the left shoulder, I think. The patch was red like Alpha. And his sword was an Alpha sword. And his teeth . . ." Doc paused and swallowed hard. "His teeth were filed to points, just like they do to all the Order. Tell me it's a dream, Ace. If these are Alpha moans, I can't go on."

Doc sat down on the cloud as if he intended not to budge another inch. His wings settled around his face, hiding from the others his fearful eyes. And in his lap, Doc's hands shook. They were famous hands, for they belonged to more than just a decent medic. They belonged to heaven's oldest and most renowned surgeon. Throughout time, those hands had swabbed and severed and sutured some of history's best-loved figures—both mortal and immortal.

Back when the Rebellion started, Doc had served valiantly. The hours had been long and tedious, but his hands kept working. And often, the thanks given in return was little more than a nod as the mended warrior flew back into the fray.

After the Rebellion, Doc's hands were seldom idle, for the war wasn't over yet. It had simply shifted locations. That's when Jesus told Doc he was needed down on the round battlefield.

And so he went. He served. He plied his trade on earth until he was called to work on humans. A boy named Abel was his first.

"You're needed back in heaven," the note from home had read. So Doc hurried upward as fast as his wings could carry him. When he arrived at the East Wall he was shown the body of a young human. It was impossible not to stare at the gash on the back of the boy's head. It was so wide, so slippery—so red. Angel veins coursed with a clear substance called, *zoe*. But human veins were full of a crimson liquid. The line of bodies that started arriving in heaven demanding Doc's attention was endless.

Hour upon hour Doc labored next to Jesus, watching as the Great Physician of heaven breathed life into the various casualties. Then Doc used the skills that Jesus had given him to put their earth suits back together and make them fit for eternity.

It was a hard line of work, and the work had taken its toll. Consequently, Doc, the greatest angelic surgeon of all time, sat trembling on a cloud.

"Come on, Doc. You can't fall apart. We need you on this one," said François. "Besides, you heard Jesus. He said it could get rough. Where are we going to find a better doc to take care of us than you?"

"He's right," said Albert, trying to sound supportive. "This is your big chance. You know as well as the rest of us that you've been itching to make your mark again in some way."

"Haven't we all," nodded Ace. "What do you say, Doc? We need someone along who can fix our injuries."

The semicircle of angels drew tightly around Doc. Secretly, even Albert revered this colleague of theirs. For as far as he knew, Doc was the only one among them who had heard the clash of swords and breathed the smells of war, while the rest of them waited tables. Doc had done what they had dreamed of. He had fought the enemy.

"Well?" asked François, anxiously. "Can we count on you, monsieur?"

Doc rose on one knee. His friends were right. If not him, who would assuage their wounds?

"I told myself I'd never go active again," said Doc, standing now at his full height of five foot six. "I said wild unicorns couldn't drag me back. Give me one good reason why that's got to change now."

"Because you're the b-b-best doc this universe has ever known, and we'd b-b-be lost without you," twanged Chaney.

"Give me another one," said Doc, unmoved by the compliment.

Suddenly, a voice boomed from behind the crescent of angels.

"Because without your little nursemaid along, we're going to make stew out of you poor, lost angels!" screamed the leader of the Alpha squadron. The moans had sneaked stealthily up the leeward side of the cloud and stood bristling with the sun at their backs and their great wings billowing above their heads.

Doc's knees buckled.

"Weee-hah-hah-hah," the demon guffawed, slapping his knee and clutching his sides with mirth. "There's nothing better than catching an angel unaware. Looks like Doc doesn't do well with house calls anymore," laughed the demon, whose name was sewn in loud, red letters across the breast pocket of his leather jacket. At his side hung a zoe-crusted sword sheathed in a rusty scabbard. His feet were shod with combat boots. In an instant, the demon's face turned foreboding. "You thought you were being mighty sly. But we surprised you, didn't we? Why don't you start by explaining what business you have with that mailman back on Cistern Street," the demon growled.

Ace shook at the sound of the demon's voice. He stared at his eyes. They were different from the ones he recalled, more sinister and smoldering. He allowed his gaze to travel down to a familiar cleft chin, then over massive shoulders until they reached the embroidered name on the demon's jacket. He whispered the word to himself as if it held some personal meaning.

"Colonel Sky," he mouthed.

"Yes. I see you remember who I am—or used to be. The name's Citizen Pogromme now," said the demon to Ace. "It's nice to be remembered after all these years. Don't you agree, Captain?"

Citizen Pogromme seemed to relish this last word. He bit it off sharply with a toothy grin and talked on.

"By the way, Captain, there're rumors that you've adopted a more civilian ideology about life. Might that be true? Are you seeing things differently now?"

Ace didn't answer. His silence prodded Pogromme and put him in a sparring sort of mood.

"I can't say I blame you for not wanting to comment on your past. But I must say there are those in the under-world who have mixed feelings about your retirement.

Most feel lucky to be in one piece. However, a fair number of them would have liked another chance to run you through. You were good, you know—at one time, that is," said Pogromme, laughing.

Seeing that he'd failed to provoke the big angel, Pogromme turned to introduce his squad members.

"This is Moan Greedo, Private First Class. He is a biter. Keep your wings trimmed, gentlemen," Pogromme warned. "If you don't, he's apt to snatch a feather or two. Show them your pearlies, Greedo."

Moan Greedo opened his mouth and threw back his head. Straightaway everyone could see why Greedo liked to bite. Teeth like his demanded exercise.

Pogromme continued.

"To his left is Moan Spleen. He's mean as Satan himself. But he does what's he's told, so we bring him along on the less vital missions where the odds are already insurmountably in our favor—like this one," grinned Pogromme. "Spleen should behave himself, though. Then again, he might not. It's hard to tell from day to day what sets him off. I suggest a wide berth around the brute whenever possible. That way, we'll all get along much better.

"And last but not least, there is Moan Pater Mordo," said Pogromme. When he said the name, the ugly lout, who was by far the biggest in the squadron, showed no sign that he'd been recognized. Instead, he drooled and stared at the world through bleary eyes.

"Charming, isn't he?" noted Pogromme. "He's a boob. A dunce. But Pater Mordo does know one good trick. We like to demonstrate it whenever there's a volunteer."

Throughout his introductions, Citizen Pogromme had been pacing, sometimes toward one of his squadron as he singled him out, and at other times a step or two toward his opponents. By the time he had made his allusion to Pater Mordo's inconspicuous talent, Citizen Pogromme had circled around behind the angels. When he said the word *volunteer*, Pogromme gave François a shove that drove the gentle waiter right into the fat demon's arms. Immediately, Pater Mordo, whose name means "Father Death," began to squeeze.

François's eyes bulged and his face paled. At his side, he clutched the small satchel in which Muriel and Bent's first letters had been carried to earth. Had he realized he'd forgotten to give Jesus the copies He requested and that at this very moment those same two copies were still inside the satchel, François might have maintained his grip on the bag. Instead, he let the bag drop with a soft sploosh to the cloud, at which time Citizen Pogromme snapped his fingers and Pater Mordo dropped François with a more substantial sploosh.

"What do we have here?" exclaimed Pogromme, snatching up the satchel and peering inside. He dumped the contents into his hand and cackled at his findings. "Satan will be quite interested in this bit of correspondence, quite interested." Behind him, Pogromme's three stooges howled with delight, though they had no inkling as to what they were howling about.

Ace clenched his fists and took a step toward Pogromme.

"You've got me shivering, Captain Evermore. Captain Alistair Conrad Evermore," said Pogromme with obvious contempt for the angel's name. "You, of all angels—glory's finest working in a restaurant. What's the matter? Wouldn't they let you back into the line of fire? Or haven't your friends heard the story?" spat the demon.

Ace wasn't afraid of Pogromme. But he couldn't hide from the questioning looks of his own angels. So far as they knew, he was—and always had been—a headwaiter. Ace took another step toward his ancient nemesis. In a flash, the two were chin to chin.

"I could have rid the skies of you for good back then, and you know it, Pogromme," seethed Ace.

"Yes. But your reach exceeded your grasp, didn't it? And now, the only thing these friends know of you is that you set a mean table and look proper in a formal tux. Imagine that," snorted Pogromme. "The great Ace Evermore, former hero of the Imperial Host, shuffling about like a penguin with a towel on his arm. How pathetic."

"What do those letters say, boss?" asked Moan Greedo.

"Shut up, soldier! I'll do the talking here," snapped Pogromme as he began to read. "Hmmm . . . mmm . . . ahhh-hah," he added. "Just as I surmised. There's been a leak in the mail room, and some soul has succeeded in sneaking his poor, little sob story to his sister in heaven. Wait until Satan hears of this."

François's heart sank with the discovery. But as Pogromme continued to scan the letters, the demon's eyes flashed with every paragraph. And by the time he'd finished reading, his eyes were glowing slits of amber.

Pogromme bellowed, "Some meddler has blotted out the most important name on these documents!"

François smiled, inwardly. Jesus had said there wasn't any use in incriminating Stan, who was simply doing a good turn for Bent. So, François had borrowed an indelible marker from the Palace Laundry and deleted Stan's name along with Bent's.

The smile broke out on François's face, and Pogromme noticed.

"You think you've pulled a fast one, don't you little angel? You think you've fooled old Citizen Pogromme. Let me tell you, I've coughed up bigger things than you before. I could swallow you whole, without so much as a sip of water."

Pogromme gave another signal for Pater Mordo to work his magic on François. But before the command could register in the mind of the enormous dullard, François darted out of his reach and took refuge behind Ace.

Ace stood with his feet apart, grinning at Citizen Pogromme.

"Who'd have thought we'd ever see each other again, Sky," laughed Ace.

"That's not my name!" screamed the demon.

"I know how bad it must feel to be reminded that you were once one of us. And now look at you," said Ace, reaching out to touch the smoke-damaged sleeve of Pogromme's jacket. "It must be terribly hot where you live."

Citizen Pogromme hissed and yanked his arm away.

"Hand me the letters, Pogromme," ordered Ace.

With a snarl, the demon balled the sheets in his fist and threw them at the feet of Ace.

"Now, Citizen," said Ace, fingering his sword, "either I can put you out of action for a very long time, or you can agree to go peacefully without further interruption."

"You haven't heard the end of this, Captain. I can assure you of that," seethed Pogromme. "Satan will know there's been a leak of sorts. It won't be long before he finds the source. Whatever you're up to can be stopped, you know. Surely you recall the number of troops we can muster. Surely you've not forgotten the pain we can inflict."

Ace looked away for a fraction of a second, remembering. The break in eye contact was just long enough for Pogromme to assume he could gain a foothold.

"Thaaat's right, Captain," crooned Pogromme. "You're not quite so young as you used to be. Wings don't work so well now as they did at the Beginning. Sinews aren't so supple. Legs aren't quite so capable of *running* as they once were."

"You forget, we don't age," said Ace.

"Ahhh, but sometimes courage has a way of breaking down. And when that happens *retreat* becomes an option, doesn't it, Captain?" replied Pogromme.

Ace's shoulder seemed to stoop at Pogromme's mention of the *r* word.

Citizen Pogromme moved in for the kill.

"Now, Captain, I'll have those letters back," he barked, motioning to the wad of paper at Ace's feet. "Then, you'll be free to go back to that cush job of yours and live out your days serving crème brûlée to all those self-righteous do-gooders who just happened to sneak into heaven by the skin of their teeth."

"They're in heaven because they know Jesus," said Ace without moving.

"Perhaps you didn't hear me, Captain. I said, bend over and pick up those letters *now!*"

All was still. Not even a breeze blew across the cloud. Creation had held its breath for a moment to watch the showdown, as if it were loath to exhale again without some resolution.

"*Now!*" screamed Pogromme even louder.

Ace looked the demon squarely in the eye, and, without a trace of malice or condescension, calmly told Citizen Pogromme, "Go back to hell."

Citizen Pogromme bristled and charged. But before he had covered half the distance between himself and his opponent, Ace met Pogromme with a terrific blow to the jaw. For a second the demon's legs wobbled, and a glassy look came across his face.

"Get him!" screamed Moan Spleen to his superior. "Break his nose. Pound his pretty face."

Pogromme's eyes cleared and he charged again. This time Ace stepped into his punch with all his weight and sent Pogromme sprawling over the side of the cloud, out into the wide arena of the earth's atmosphere. Behind him—as closely behind him as three demons can follow without appearing to be cowards—went Moans Greedo, Spleen, and Pater Mordo, taking with them their bad breath and their bad temper, all the while vowing their swift return.

"That was really s-s-s-something, Ace," exclaimed Chaney.

"A coup d'état, monsieur," said François.

"Let's not stand around gloating over past victories as if there's nothing left to do today," said Ace, his voice trembling. "François, there'll be more letters for you to copy back at home. And I don't want to hear another word about the mistake you made. So far as I'm concerned, what's done is done. But from now on, make sure you bring only one copy. Okay?"

"Oui, monsieur."

"Anyway, it all ended well."

"Uh-uh," warned Homer. "They'll tell everything they know just as soon as they touch down in Hot City. It's lights out for the mail until Jesus sends a runner to pick it up."

"Right you are, Homer. And Jesus has already chosen *you* to be the runner. I suggest you catch up on your sleep before you make the trip. In fact, I *order* you to get some sleep. It's a long way to hell, and I'd hate to see this mission botched for lack of shut-eye. We've got to keep those letters flowing. You all heard Jesus. There's a soul in Ellenbach who will die if Walter keeps the gospel to himself."

"Right, Captain," said Homer.

Homer rose from his spot on the cloud. But he lingered over how he had just addressed the angel he'd always known as Ace the headwaiter. The other four seemed to have caught upon it, too.

"I never knew you served, monsieur, I mean Captain," said François.

*Captain.*

The title was new to them, definitive in some way of the bright golden angel who stood before them now on the cloud. No one begrudged Ace the name that had somewhere in ancient history fallen upon him and not themselves. They saw his muscles rippling beneath the covering of his wings. They saw the love of heaven in his eyes. And they had seen the way Ace calmly met Citizen Pogromme with the most reliable of punches, the jab, and sent him somewhere into the Pacific. They each knew secretly that if they followed this angel, none of them would ever be the same again.

Without a word, five angels rose to salute their leader. Even Doc, who had only recently recovered from his swoon, followed suit. They were lined up on a visible body of mist dispersed in the atmosphere at ten thousand feet above a lonely globe, five waiters at attention and one proud yet abashed captain.

Something in the way the troops stood—with the light photographers often refer to as *god light* slanting from openings in clouds farther up and coming to rest on the crowns of their heads—brought a certain feeling swelling up from Ace's gut into his windpipe. But when the captain tried to apply words to the feeling, a great and rasping croak was all that came from his throat.

"Any orders, s-sir?" asked Chaney, coming quickly to Ace's rescue.

Ace cleared his throat and tried again.

"Ummm . . . yes. At ease. François, I want those next copies in my hand by the time the planet Venus rises in the northern hemisphere."

François nodded.

"Well, I suppose that about does it. Excellent first mission," concluded Ace.

The sky was at its brightest. Clouds had thinned and floated away to other regions of creation. Above them the sun was burning hot when Captain Alistair Conrad Evermore finally sent the other angels off to their appointed rounds, reciting the mission objective as they flew.

"One soul in Ellenbach. One soul in Ellenbach. One soul in Ellenbach. One soul . . ."

Ace smiled and shook his head until the five were scarcely pinpoints in the wide sky above, and he could no longer hear their voices. He thought of Jesus, and he grinned upward.

"Thanks for the second chance," Ace said aloud. As an afterthought he added, "But if You had asked me, I'd have chosen warriors over waiters."

Ace turned to preen his wings for his own flight home. But just before the pinpoints disappeared into the distant haze of heaven, a voice came bouncing down from the clouds with such clarity that Ace could not have mistaken it for a trick of the mind.

"Captain Evermore," boomed Jesus' voice. "Where in all the universe is there one more fit for taking orders than a waiter?"

"You have a point there," said Ace as he lifted off from the cloud. For if ever there was a soldier most valued in combat, it is the one who obeys. And Ace knew that as soon as Satan caught wind of the leak, there'd be no room for anything *but* obedience.

*"Satan the envious said with a sigh:*
*Christians know more about their hell than I."*

—Christopher Marlowe, *Doctor Faustus*

ALEAK?" roared Satan. Above the gritty island where the Prince of Darkness kept office, stalactites quaked from the power of his voice. He had always wanted a domain to call his own. Had he known, however, he would wind up with a plot of sand in the middle of an oily lake, he might never have issued the challenge in heaven. Oh! How biting jealous it made him to know his long-lost home was peopled with mortals. He shouted again, and the bank of blue-gray surveillance monitors, which had been recently installed, blinked rhythmically from their position just inches from Satan's face.

"I'll throttle the fiend who's responsible for this! I'll vivisect him! I'll poach him like an egg! I'll—"

"Careful, your excellency," chided Citizen Pogromme. "We wouldn't want you to get too upset. Remember the last time you—"

"Don't talk to me about getting upset," Satan thundered. "What the heaven is wrong with everybody in hell these days? Can't a simple bag of mail be delivered without some saboteur botching it to high heaven? Confound it, Pogromme. You're my chief of staff around here. *You* manage these brainless underlings for a change! I'm much too busy!"

"But, sir—"

"Yes, Insolent pixie?" screamed Satan.

"I . . . I was concerned about your health, sir."

"How dare you interrupt my train of thought with such petty concerns! I could have you skinned in an instant."

"Of course, sir. I was just—"

"Brimstone and blast furnaces! Where is that chuckle-headed rube who used to deliver the mail? Can't we get him back? What was his name? Howl? Howles?"

"Howler, sir?"

"Yes. That's the one. He was at least competent enough to carry a bag of letters. Where is Howler?"

"You sent him down to sanitation to muck the waste pit."

"I'm well aware of that," raged Satan.

"Sir—" Pogromme ventured again.

"What is it now, Pogromme?"

"I hope you don't mind my saying so, sir, but, well, it was just one letter."

At that, Satan ground his teeth.

"Just one letter! Would you like to know what *one letter* can do, Citizen Pogromme? Well? Would you?" he screamed.

Pogromme cringed and shook his head to no avail. Once again, Satan's voice was like a bludgeon.

"I've seen what happens when humans latch on to a letter and read it and revere it. It gets stuck in their minds that the things are more than just pulp and pen ink. But do you know what's worse?" cried Satan, his eyes protruding from beneath his shelflike brow.

Pogromme shook his head again.

"What's worse is that the ones who sent the blasted things in the first place finally die, and the ones who received them rummage about in their drawers until they find it. Then they put it in a scrapbook of sorts, along with other worthless letters from other worthless dead people, and they call the collection their *Scriptures*, and they begin to study it and memorize it and live their lives by it. And then, where does that leave us, Pogromme? Do you know, Pogromme? Do you know? Well? Do you?"

Pogromme tried to answer.

"Well, sir, I—"

"AAAGGGHHH! Blast that holy scrapbook!" roared Satan. "Have you any idea how long I've toiled to get those wretched earthlings to drop the whole matter? To end their love affair with those dead letters they call their Bible? To simply see the entire compilation as legends bound in leather? It was on the verge of working, Pogromme. We were mere whiskers away from complete global disinterest in the writings. But now, nowww!"

Hell's walls shuddered. Satan grew suddenly quiet as if he imagined that his own rantings might very well tip the world to his presence and his agenda. That's why he worked so hard at keeping souls' letters from leaving the mailroom. That's why he watched the monitors like a hawk. He was not about to stand by and allow another letter campaign like the one Peter and Paul and the rest of those infernal disciples pulled off in the first century. Even if there was a wealth of difference between the Bible and this alleged leak, he could not be too careful. Oh! How he hated those holy letters.

Great, angry tears welled up in Satan's eyes. His tears ran freely down his cheeks, mingled with saliva blubbered from his cracked lips, and finally dripped off his chin into a puddle of spit and sorrow.

In vain, Pogromme tried to redirect the subject.

"*Now,* sir?" he asked. "You were saying something about *now*?"

"Yes, Pogromme," hissed Satan. "Once again they'll suspect we're really down here. They'll hunt around until they find those *other* nasty testaments, the ones they call holy. And then they'll take their Bibles from the shelves, dust them off, and refamiliarize themselves with all that drivel."

"It was just a small leak, sir. Not enough to cause a revival. Not more than a few pages, I'm sure."

"They'll teach their children to take me seriously again."

"But—"

"That I'm mean and dangerous and ought not to be trifled with."

"Excuse me, sir," said Pogromme. And here is where the chief of staff always saw the opportunity to help his boss, for nothing worked better on Satan than to remind him how good he is at being bad. "Excuse me," he said again, when Satan finally looked up through soggy eyes and seemed to be listening to Pogromme. "You *are* mean and dangerous, sir. And so am I. And so are all the devils who inhabit this great and wonderful kingdom of yours, my lord."

The flattery worked like a magic potion. It soothed Satan and brought him around to a semblance of sanity. It medicated him for the task at hand, the running of this vast inferno. Pogromme healed his master with a wag of his tongue.

"Spoken eloquently, Citizen," said Satan. His eyes were drying, and already his cheeks appeared less puffy.

"You are the worst of your kind," coached Pogromme. "You're the foulest, most hurtful, pernicious, mischievous, noisome, noxious, sinister serpent I have ever met, your excellency."

"Thank you, Pogromme. You always seem to rally me."

"I try, sir. I really do."

"Well, find who sent the letter. I want the fool roasted. The same goes for whoever delivered the mail today," said Satan. And here is where he noticed for the first time that Pogromme's nose was slightly askew from its normal appearance. When Satan dried his tears, he saw clearly that the demon's eyes, as well, were not their usual selves. They were swollen with a network of yellow streaks traversing the sclera.

"What the heaven did you do to your face, Pogromme?" asked Satan.

"My face, sir?" said Pogromme, stepping back into the shadows. "I . . . well, I . . . fell, sir. It's just a scratch, really. I've been through worse."

"Fell?"

"Yes. I took a horrid fall from which I haven't quite recovered yet."

"You're lying to me, Pogromme. I know a lie when I hear one," warned Satan with his brows turned upward. "Nevertheless, you ought to be more careful where you're going next time."

"Yes, sir. I'll do that, sir."

"Now, where were we?" asked Satan. The fire had returned to his eyes, and once again Citizen Pogromme breathed a sigh of relief at seeing his boss return to the subject.

"I believe we were discussing the letter, sir, the one that happened to find its way to heaven from our mail-room," answered Pogromme.

"Exactly, and who was the fool that replaced that last idiot, Howler?"

Pogromme paused and scratched his head.

"If I remember correctly, sir, the replacement came from somewhere near the new projects by the waste pit."

"I don't care where he came from, Pogromme. I simply want to know his name!"

This was a good sign for Pogromme. The resurgence of Satan's rage told him he'd done his job as chief of staff. After all, of the many hats he wore, this particular one entailed very little responsibility for managing Satan's subjects. It required Pogromme to be more of an image consultant than anything else, someone to keep Satan's spirits up and his mind from wandering down to the fact he'd been foiled long ago by the low King of heaven.

"I believe his name is Ripskin, sir," Pogromme said finally.

"Yes. I remember now," roared Satan. "Ripskin!"

The sound echoed down the passageways of hell until it reached the little hole in the wall that Ripskin called home.

The address read 121 STYX BALD RIDGE above the doorway in the wall. Inside, Ripskin was curled up in fetal position on a filthy bed of rags. He had been waiting for this call. When he heard Satan's voice, Ripskin felt his stomach twist one more complete revolution. He propped himself on his elbows, wincing at the wounds of his fall.

It had been a half day's tumble from the East Wall to the sidewalk outside the gates of hell. Upon impact, there had been such bursting of bone as well as laughter from his peers. Ripskin felt sure his frame and reputation had been shattered beyond repair. With no one's help he crawled the distance to his little hollow and collapsed in the heat to assess his wounds. His right leg was broken in three places. His pelvis was cracked. His ribs were bruised and bulging. And though he'd not had occasion to use a mirror since his ill-fated landing, Ripskin could tell by passing his hand across his head that a great deal of his hair had been burned in the reentry.

"Ripskin!" came the voice again. This time the demon moved as quickly as his ailing body would allow him. From underneath the rags, Ripskin pulled a rude crutch that he'd fashioned from the only piece of furniture in his room, the table where he ate his breakfasts. He leaned against it gingerly at first. Then, slowly, so as not to faint from the bone-splitting pain in his leg, Ripskin placed the full weight of his frame upon the crutch. Right away he recognized the thing would not do nearly the job he'd expected of it.

"Scratch," he muttered. "And to top it off, my table is more tottering now than myself. Double scratch. I suppose it doesn't matter. I'll be boiled in my own juices before the evening's over. Why worry about a stick or two of furniture?"

Quickly, for he didn't want to keep Satan waiting any longer, Ripskin hobbled through the dark, arterial passages of hell. He clumped past bottomless chasms, chambers, and smoking tar pits, through spiderwebs spun fresh across the corridor, and twilight toadstools growing thick as weeds.

Far, far ahead, somewhere in the labyrinth of veins and capillary detours, his name was being muttered over and over and over again, along with all the heinous crimes Satan himself was vowing to do to a certain Ripskin of 121 Styx Bald Ridge.

## ~ 8 ~

*Where there's marriage without love,*
*there will be love without marriage.*

—Benjamin Franklin, *Poor Richard's Almanac*

AT precisely six o'clock, Walter stepped across the threshhold of 333 Mulberry and gave Donna the usual obligatory kiss that signaled the end of his day and the beginning of the evening's silence. But instead of heading straight to the utility room and placing his bag above the dryer where it normally rested during supper, Walter took it to the bedroom. Donna waited until the door was closed before she went quickly to it and listened with her ear pressed softly against the wood to see what she could gather of her husband's day. Dallas hadn't returned from his last afternoon at school yet, so she was alone in the hallway wondering about Walter's strange behavior and listening.

It was not his silence that was strange. That was painfully normal. It was the way Walter had looked at her when he came through the door tonight. And the kiss, too. Something in its quality was different. It was not quite right, or perhaps it was perfectly right. It had given a hint of love gone by. She *had* felt something in those wooden lips, she thought. And his eyes seemed to remember how good his marriage used to be.

*Could it be that he's changing? Coming back to us?* began Donna in her mind. But she let the hope subside. She had thought those thoughts before. She knew where they led.

If her girlfriends saw her eavesdropping through her own bedroom door, they would swear she was crazy, especially Emma. Emma had often told her, "Donna, twelve years of mourning isn't normal. One way or another, it's got to end."

"But he needs me," she would say.

And Emma would remind her in return, "When a man doesn't have the sense to let his woman help him, then it's time for her to find someone who does."

At first, it sounded wise. She had tried it for a while with substitute loves: the cat, the house, the Junior League in Laird. But the payoffs were scarce, and so she quit trying and went back to waiting.

Waiting for Walter.

That had become her full-time job since Bent and Muriel's deaths. She waited for a man to love her. Many of her urban friends seemed to have fascinating jobs: IBM executive, interior decorators, pediatrician, attorney. Even her Ellenbach friends found jobs to do in town once their children were away in school. But Donna? She was just a waiter.

Donna leaned against the door and waited for a clue. She heard the front door bang open and then shut again, and she knew her son was home.

"Mommm," called the voice.

"Dallas? Is that you?" Donna replied, as if she was still a mother of three. She hurried away from the door when she spoke so that Walter would think she'd just been passing.

Immediately, the bedroom door swung open behind her and she turned to see her husband. In his hands was an old boot box.

"Mommm," Dallas shouted again, as seventeen-year-old boys often do when they're hungry or in pain. For Dallas, the two were synonymous. Grown-ups, on the other hand, are much more self-controlled when it comes to personal affliction. A man's heart could be eating a hole in his chest, and his neighbor might never know it until the man left his wife or quit his job or put a bullet through his head.

Keeping her eyes on Walter, Donna anticipated Dallas's request for orange juice and addressed it.

"Behind the milk on the top shelf, sweetheart. It's already made."

"What?" shouted Dallas.

Walter was retreating down the hall.

"Walter?" said Donna.

"Mommm," Dallas cried.

"*I said,* if you're looking for juice, it's behind the milk on the top shelf. Don't drink it all, though, honey."

Walter was nearly to the doorway at the end of the hall. How natural it had become for Donna to call to loved ones from a distance.

"Mom, I still can't hear you," said Dallas from the kitchen. "Can I have some crackers?"

"Don't spoil your supper, sweetheart. And don't forget to clean up your mess. I'm glad you're home, Dallas."

Walter and his boot box were almost gone.

"Wait, Walt. Please. Can we talk?" said Donna, almost begging.

The boot box stopped in the doorway.

Donna watched her husband's shoulders rise and fall one time only; the telltale sign of a tiresome day. Walter pivoted slowly to face her.

"I thought something might be wrong," said Donna, swallowing dryly.

Walter shifted his weight and clutched the box with both hands.

"It's been a long day, Donna, that's all," he replied.

Donna wanted to shout that it had been much more than a long day, that it had been the longest twelve years of her life. Time itself was weak measurement for the ache in her breast and her screaming desire to be touched in the way Walter used to touch her. It wasn't fair that death could stroll twice into her house, take its pick of the living, and leave her with a corpse for a spouse. But she bit her tongue as always, saying, "I'd like to help."

"Help?" said Walter. "It's nothing but a boot box. It isn't heavy enough for the two of us to fuss over. I'm just going to put it in the attic to get it out of the way."

Before Donna could explain that it wasn't the boot box she was concerned about, Walter disappeared around the corner. She could hear him pulling down the attic stairs and ascending into the darkness. Down the hallway came the sounds of Dallas still searching for his orange juice. Donna paused to look at herself in a mirror and said to her reflection, "Does anybody love me? Or do they just need me?"

"Mommm," came the voice from the kitchen.

"Coming Dallas," said Donna.

She gathered her hair at the nape of her neck and let it fall behind her shoulders. Then, she went to the kitchen to locate the orange juice behind the milk on the top shelf, where she'd said it would be.

The lightbulb at the top of the attic stairs was burned out. He used his pocket flashlight, but even so it took a while for Walter's eyes to accommodate the darkness of the dust-filled room. But after a minute or two things close at hand took shape, and Walter could grope his way about without hurting himself or stepping through the ceiling. He looked for a place to set the boot box down where it wouldn't get covered with insulation.

There were several large sheets of particle board he'd nailed to the two-by-eights some time ago. But because it had been so long since he'd come up here, Walter had to reorientate himself to certain objects in order to find that hard, flat surface. Right away, he remembered why he avoided coming up here. To his left was that galloping pony on springs—the one that drove him batty at midnight whenever Bent refused to stay in bed, the one that rocked the house to sleep with its squeaky lullabies.

The horse's plastic mane gleamed at Walter; it reflected the slivers of moonlight that streamed through the attic vent. Springs twangled at Walter's intrusion. He ignored the horse, feeling his way along the joists with one hand on the rafters and the other cradling the boot box firmly under his arm. He passed a collection of old corsage ribbons and remembered, reluctantly. He sneezed insulation. He found himself looking at his feet. All around were the dolls his daughter cherished. He was ankle deep in memories.

Walter spotted the particle board behind a stack of suitcases. He waded through the dolls, careful not to tread too heavily and equally careful not to look at them either. He squeezed his sweating body around the suitcases. He pushed, panted, and balanced himself so he wouldn't go crashing into the living room. Finally he came out into a rectangle of gray light that fell softly on the particle board and bade him to sit down.

Walter's heart ran a footrace with logic.

"Only a fool would think these are real," he told himself, squatting down with his box in the fading sunlight. With trembling fingers he opened the lid, pulled out the strange letters from Cistern Street, and read them for the third time.

Behind the cinder-block chimney that rose through the floor and disappeared between the rafters sat Moans Greedo, Spleen, and Pater Mordo. After their superior's embarrassingly short round with Captain Evermore, they had followed Citizen Pogromme from the cloud as far as the island of Tutuila in the South Pacific where Citizen Pogromme had landed abruptly in a mangrove thicket.

Immediately, Pogromme had ordered them as far from his presence as possible, saying, "No. I do *not* need your athithtanth. My noth ith juth fine." And he sent them to keep an eye on whoever Ellenbach's mail carrier was, just in case they could learn something more about the letters. Now, as the three moans squatted in the attic, they were eager to do more than just watch.

"Greedo thinks he wants to bite the man," said Moan Greedo, who usually referred to himself in the voice of an innocent bystander.

"Let's not rush things," said Moan Spleen. "I say we scare him first. And then you can bite him. What do you say, Mordo?"

Pater Mordo only drooled.

"Never mind," said Spleen. "Stay close to me, and we'll circle behind those garment bags to the right there."

"Greedo says the man can't see us, so why are we sneaking?" said Greedo.

"Because it's fun to sneak," hissed Spleen. "Why don't you stick to what you do best and let me do the thinking. In a minute or two, if you behave yourself, I'll let you chew on the man's instep or something. Agreed?"

Moan Greedo acquiesced.

"Besides," added Spleen, "I'm the one Pogromme left in charge."

That was not at all true. Nevertheless, it might as well have been. Between the three, Pater Mordo was too dumb to lead and Greedo was too preoccupied. Naturally then, it was only fitting that Spleen lead.

"Come on, now. Follow me, and keep your fat backside down, Pater Mordo," rasped Spleen. "As I said, we'll crawl behind those garment bags. Then, let's see, we can pop our heads up by that footlocker. The man will never suspect a thing. He'll go right on reading as if he were alone. Anyway, I've been wanting to get a look at that letter ever since we saw those goody two-wings put it in his bag," whispered Spleen as he belly crawled along.

"And then Greedo gets to bite the man?" asked Greedo.

"Yes, Greedo. Then, you get to bite the man."

When the three moans reached the footlocker, Pater Mordo was breathing hard. He plopped himself down and let his fat hang between the ceiling joists.

Spleen and his comrades didn't sneak for Walter's sake, because humans can't see matters of the immaterial world. On the contrary, they did it just in case the enemy shared the attic with them at this precise moment. Nevertheless, Greedo was tired of playing Spleen's childish hiding game. He perched himself in plain view on top of the footlocker and filed his teeth as loudly as he pleased.

"You're very careless, Greedo," said Moan Spleen. "I'll have to report this, you know. I can guarantee Pogromme won't like it one bit. What if this very moment the enemy were with us in this attic? What would you do then, hmmm? Make the same kind of racket you're making right now? Flash your greedy little incisors like a flare of sorts? I think not."

Greedo snorted. "Greedo would bite them, too!"

"Oh, what's the use. You've not got room for brains in that head of yours with all those teeth. Just shut up and sit still."

Using the sleeping Pater Mordo's flab as a chair, Spleen positioned himself behind Walter's shoulder so he could read. He was angry at what he saw, because the human had removed Muriel's letter first from the boot box, and Spleen was not at all interested in *that* letter. Nevertheless, he moved from side to side until he got comfortable on Pater Mordo, and he began to follow along with Walter as he read.

Walter shuddered as he opened Muriel's letter, just as he'd done when he found it for the first time on Cistern Street. When he saw the addressees' names, he had run for several blocks disregarding Fern, traffic, and the remainder of his morning mail route. He had arrived at the Paradise Donut Shop in record time, ordered a cup of coffee to steady himself, and read the letters away from prying eyes in the corner booth. What he read made him spill his coffee. Now Walter glanced at the text again, which had parts of several lines blacked out. If he wasn't a sensible man, he might have believed the letters were actually from his son and daughter. That was ridiculous, though, he told himself.

Nevertheless, he unfolded the letter, and began to read.

Moan B.
517 Hell Place

    Dear _____,

    I couldn't believe it when I received your letter! I knew it was from you when I saw my last name spelled <u>Robins</u>. You always forgot the other <u>b</u>. Is your cheek okay? Are you taking care of it? How about the food there? Do they feed you well? Can you have a well-balanced meal? How about sleep? Is that allowed? Are you getting enough of it?

    Forgive me. I must sound twice the mother to you as I ever was. What can you expect when your sister is so much older than her kid brother? I guess I'll always fret over you in some ways. I love you, _____. I love you. I love you. I love you. Tomorrow I'll write you a letter with just those three words on it and you can tape it up on your wall.

    That won't work, will it? The moans would see it. But I'm going to send it anyway. You can fold it up and tuck it away somewhere. And then at night when you're lonely you can pull it out, look at it, and remember how I feel about you. Forget tomorrow! I'll send it today, on the last page of this letter. I can't bear to keep you waiting.

    Oh, _____, I just don't know what to say to you. I can't preach at you now, because it's all over and words wouldn't matter anymore. I can't tell you a joke, because there's nothing to laugh about. I can't send you a care package because you'd get caught and sent to that room. And I couldn't bring myself to write to you of heaven for fear that it would break your heart.

I'll write again when I know what to say. For now, I'm going for a walk to think. Please respond as soon as you can. Until I hear from you, I am . . .

Eternally yours,

_____

At the end of the letter there was a separate page with just the words *I love you* arranged in columns. And at the bottom of the page were the initials MC with a tiny heart adjacent to it.

"Ho-hum," said Moan Greedo, rolling his eyes and yawning. "Greedo says to wake him when it's time to bite."

"You moron! Don't you see it?" gasped Spleen.

"Greedo sees a silly woman's letter, that's all."

"No, not that one. There!" shouted Spleen, pointing to Bent's envelope, which Walter had now taken from the boot box and was holding in his hand. "Don't you see it?" Spleen repeated.

Greedo stared blankly. He saw the letter but not the significance. From a mound of insulation came the sound of Pater Mordo's snoring.

"The *i*'s, idiot! Look at the *i*'s," ordered Spleen. Before him was the obvious work of a *Chronicle* typewriter, complete with sticking keys and faded ribbon.

"Greedo's overwhelmed," yawned Greedo again.

Spleen ignored him.

"This is a stroke of luck. Oh, I should get a pretty promotion for this," said Spleen. "Just wait until I tell Pogromme, and he tells Satan that old Spleen was the one who discovered the mysterious i that sticks and raises and fairly shouts the name of the author himself, who is, no doubt, a reporter," he concluded.

"Yes. But Greedo thinks there might be thousands of those."

"Oh, sour grapes, Greedo. You know good and well that every reporter doesn't have a sticking i. You're just sorry you didn't discover it. That's why you're a biter and I'm a thinker. Let's see, I must get word of this to Pogromme right away. I can hardly believe such good fortune."

"Yea, for Spleen," said Greedo. "Now, can Greedo bite the human?"

Walter sank back against the footlocker with his bosom cradling the letters and the back of his neck feeling eerily exposed to the blackness behind him. His hands were shaking, and he grabbed the right one with the left to make it stop. But it kept on.

"There isn't a hell. And there isn't a heaven. I was wrong to think so back then," Walter shouted up into the shadows. He no longer cared if Donna heard him. The letters were a joke, a sick prank perpetrated by God knows who. He *had* been working long hours. But they weren't real. They *couldn't* be real. Bent was in the ground at Ellenbach Cemetery. So was Muriel. And he had buried God a long time ago, as well.

Still, whether trick or truth, the letters certainly sounded like his poor, dead children on paper here in his hands. He held them gently, kissed them, then tucked them back into their envelopes, as if he were tucking Bent and Muriel into bed. And all the while Walter wondered if he were going mad. In a moment, he had his wits about himself again, and the bitterness within him sprang forth afresh.

"Moans, my foot! Wild-haired punks is more like it. And if I get my hands on whoever did this thing, I'll give him what Johnny gave the drum," seethed Walter. He placed the letters in the boot box and rose to leave.

But something held him there in the moon-spattered attic, something both real and intangible at the same time. Walter could have struggled all he wanted, but it would not have helped him. Even if the lightbulb had not been burned out, and if the entire attic had been flooded with the brightness of the universe, Walter could not have seen the thing that held him by the footlocker. And if by slimmest chance he *did* see it, he would have wrongly named it. He would have called it *nerves* or a *figment of his imagination.*

"Walter? Are you all right?" came Donna's voice from the bottom of the stairs.

"I'm fine," said Walter.

"What are you doing up there?"

"Just picking through things. Straightening up. Nothing much."

"A minute ago, it sounded like you were talking to someone."

Walter clutched the boot box tightly. His hands were sweating, and the back of his neck was damp. *I will not believe in God again,* he told himself. *And if I do, I won't trust Him. Not in a million years.*

"Nobody here but me," he answered. As he heard Donna's footsteps fading down the hallway, he wished that she was with him, if not at his side in the attic, at least at the bottom of the stairs where he could sense her presence and wouldn't have to be all alone with the strange, unearthly letters.

Walter curled himself into a ball, whispering over and over, "Nobody here but me . . . nobody here but me . . . nobody here but me . . ."

# ~ 9 ~

*Children begin by loving their parents;*
*as they grow older they judge them;*
*sometimes they forgive them.*

—Oscar Wilde, *The Picture of Dorian Gray*

IF ever there was a son who loved his father, it was Dallas Conniston, who was waiting to be loved in turn.

By the strength of his right arm, Dallas had fared well enough growing up in Ellenbach. He eventually had earned the respect and attention of everyone in town except his father. Like his father, Dallas was a deliverer of sorts. He was swift of foot, devoted to timing, and committed to defeating the clock by reaching his appointed goal before the sweep hand aimed skyward. The townspeople depended on him, too, much as they depended upon Walter to put mail in their boxes. Dallas was tall, tan, and handsome like his father. But that is where the likeness ended.

Unlike his father, Dallas was happy at the beginning of that particular summer. And all the world was his to court, which is not unusual for the quarterback of a rural high school football team. He had learned to throw as a result of the paper route he'd inherited from his brother before Bent went bad. And he had risen to stardom in spite of the fact that he'd been born with only one kidney.

Dallas came to Mulberry Court when he was prunish, red, and fresh from the Laird General Hospital. It was a dead-end street . . . without much warning at the "live" end. Consequently, folks from out of town started down it all the time, thinking they'd discovered a novel way to get from one side of Ellenbach to the other. They always had to turn around, and some of them would cuss the inconvenience. Others would slow their cars, smile, and gesture at the country homes, like lovers do at a rib of silver moon. But all of them drove away unaware of the glory and the gloom that resided at the home with CONNISTON printed boldly on the mailbox.

Dallas had the vaguest memory of being there that September when news of Bent's court-martial was official. He remembered eating Bomb Pops by the curb with the other kids; following the Royals on his transistor radio; listening to the cicadas buzzing in the trees; and wondering where brothers and sisters go when they die, why mothers quit smiling, why fathers quit throwing the ball with their sons, and why everyone quit talking about Jesus.

Perhaps back then Dallas was too young to mourn his siblings properly. Or perhaps that was the secret to his mourning, that he was a child. As soon as his brain registered the loss, Dallas had cried. Then he broke a window at the Apco, flung all the bad words he knew at the sky, pitched his papers in Coon Creek, stole, lied, and cheated at school. And he never once felt guilty for his transgressions. After a month or so of lamentation, Dallas went back to being good. He moved his things into Bent's old bedroom—because it was bigger than his—and carried on with his life as if he and his brother were closer than they'd ever been.

Meanwhile, his parents grieved by purchasing a pair of end-table lamps for the living room.

On the morning after Walter went to the attic, Dallas rose earlier than usual to throw the *Ellenbachian.* Donna

Conniston was in the kitchen making coffee. She looked as if she'd been there all night waiting for Walter to come down from above. She brightened when she saw Dallas in the doorway.

"Hey, Mom," said Dallas, smiling.

"Morning, Dally. Off to work so early?"

"Yeah. There's extra stuff to insert today. Any OJ?" asked Dallas as he stepped toward the refrigerator.

"Top shelf. Behind the milk."

"Thanks."

Donna stirred a stream of sugar into her coffee and watched her son. He moved so effortlessly, like a cloud or a bird or something that Donna couldn't quite put her finger on. She knew she'd find the word for it someday, and it would all make sense to her.

There was a lot Donna didn't understand about Dallas. His navigation of grief nonplussed her and left her wondering if something was wrong with Walter and her. She had asked him once if he missed his brother and sister. He had told her, "No. It's hard to miss someone you think about so much." And that was the last they'd talked of Bent and Muriel. It was a far cry more than her husband had ever said.

Donna was closer to enjoying life again than Walter because her writing had given her a safe place to deposit her grief. Still, she saw specters in the hall from time to time. Whenever she did, she'd hurry to the bedroom where she'd take down one of Dallas's pictures and hold it to her breast. She clutched it there until it felt as if the image itself was beating with life.

She stirred her coffee and watched her son.

"Not too long before the season starts," Donna declared. "You know, just the other day I heard the Laird game was first on the schedule. Is that true?"

"Mom, it's May. What's the rush? I have the whole summer before football," grinned Dallas. He knew how much the sport meant to his mother.

"You watch out now, Dally Conniston. August will be here soon, looking to punish boys whose arms are stiff. Besides, Ellenbach's counting on you."

"Yeah, well, you wouldn't know it by the way folks act around town," said Dallas. "I remember when Bent was . . ."

Dallas shot a quick glance at his mother, who was studying herself in the surface of her coffee.

". . . when Bent was quarterback, everyone in Ellenbach talked about the Laird game two months ahead of time. It hardly makes the papers now. I don't know. Sometimes I think the town don't like my style."

"Not *don't*, dear. *Doesn't*. *Doesn't* like my style," said Donna, who found it difficult living with men who murdered the English language.

"Well, however you say it, they've lost their faith in me, or something."

Dallas paused for a moment, then lifted the juice from the refrigerator.

"Mom?" he said, searching for a glass in the cupboards.

"Hmm?"

"Am I as good as Bent was?"

Donna rubbed her eyes and squeezed the bridge of her nose between her thumb and forefinger.

"Dallas," she began, "you know we loved you all: you, your sister, your brother. Muriel and Bent had things they were good at that made us proud and glad to be their parents, just like you do now."

"Yeah, but—"

"Let me finish," said Donna, raising her hand. "Bent threw with his arm, son. But you, Dally, you throw with your heart."

"You think so?"

"I do."

"Then, how come Dad doesn't throw with me like he used to with Bent before the big games?" asked Dallas. His words fell at Donna's feet with a thud.

"Because he thinks . . ." started Donna. But she took a long sip of coffee before she began her sentence again. And when she did, it was a good thing she had not put on makeup that morning, for her eyes dewed over with the kind of tears that don't fall right away. Instead, they collect there, making a mess of one's appearance.

"Because he thinks that if he ever threw with his heart again, it might crash to the ground, break into a million pieces, and lie there for an eternity. So he doesn't throw at all," said Donna, her tears trailing slowly toward her chin.

Dallas set his juice down and crossed the kitchen to the table. He put his arms around his mother and stayed that way until Donna's shoulders stopped shaking and her breathing returned to a normal cadence. Then he turned, went back to the counter where he had placed his canvas bag, picked it up, and headed for the door. He felt awkward not knowing what to say, as many seventeen-year-olds might feel in his position.

"Uh, I have to go now, Mom. I love you," he said. Then he took one last sip of orange juice and walked out the door, closing it softly behind him.

When Donna looked back up, she thought she saw Dallas still standing there, so she ran a robed wrist across her eyes to dry the tears. When she looked again, she saw Walter by the doorway, sullen and disheveled. His hair was unkempt from spending the night in the attic. Bits of insulation clung to his cuffs and his chukka boots. His mailbag had not been oiled. And he looked tired.

Across the linoleum, Walter and Donna stared at one another. Walter's lips parted. Then, he drew them thin again and averted his eyes.

"I missed you in bed last night," said Donna.

"Slept on the couch," answered Walter, embarrassed to admit he'd spent the night in the attic.

"Well, anyway, I thought you'd already gone to deliver the mail."

"Nope. Still here."

"Guess so."

"Uh-hm."

"Coffee's on. Would you like a cup?" asked Donna, wondering how much he'd heard of her conversation with Dallas.

Walter eyed the pot on the stove.

"I'll take a cup with me."

The warm mug felt good in his hand when Donna placed it there. Out of nowhere he asked, "Are you . . . will you be writing today?"

The question rattled Donna.

"I don't know. I mean, I hadn't thought about it, yet. Did you have some other plans or something?"

"No. No. Just wanting to know. That's all. You know, just curious."

Walter noticed Donna's bathrobe. It was his favorite and he almost smiled. He shifted the mug of coffee to his left hand and reached for the door. Donna moved toward him ever so slightly.

"What time will I see you tonight, Walt?" she asked.

"I don't know. Late, maybe. You and the boy go ahead and eat without me," said Walter.

And he went out into the world, propelled toward Cistern by an ungodly force.

At the live end of Mulberry, Dallas sat in the grass and folded papers. Ever since his ninth birthday, he had thrown the *Ellenbachian*. Twice daily, he loaded down his blue Stingray and made his rounds. Bragging aside, Dallas could throw the paper with either hand, true as the Bible both ways. He got paid double by some folks for pitching it on their porch. And only on two occasions was his judgment off a little. One paper he judged right through Jenny Dunn's dining-room window. The other one landed in Betty Potter's science-fair roses. After that neither Jenny nor Betty ever gave him the time of day at school. His name might as well have been mud for the rest of his sixth-grade year. But older folks said he'd make a good Bulldog quarterback someday if he kept at it.

So Dallas kept at it.

He always threw his own street last, starting with the Commons's place, which all the kids in Ellenbach said was inhabited by a mole and not by a man, on account of Henry staying inside all the time and never seeing the sun. Dallas got a whipping once for writing "mole" on Henry's toolshed. Afterward, Walter sat him down and explained things that made Dallas feel terrible inside.

"Henry Commons has had a hard life, son," Walter said. "His dad died when Henry was two, his mother when he was four, and the woman he loved became ill and died the morning of their wedding and never even saw the ring Henry bought for her. Right then and there he made up his mind he was not going to be happy in this life. As far as I can see, he has stuck to that decision. Vandalizing his property can't change that. But we can pray for him."

And Walter did pray, for years and years until his own life became a thing of pain, and his happiness eventually faded away like the unkind word on Henry Commons's toolshed.

After the Commons place, Dallas always worked his way around the north side of the cul-de-sac, pitching the Allisons', the Edgerleys', Emma Sanger's—who was Donna's best friend, and a writer also—and then along the south side, where the Demings and the Lundys lived, until he got to the Ravelles' house. He usually skipped his own home, which came in between the Lundys and the Ravelles, and brought the paper in with him after he'd completed his route.

The Conniston house was a modest dwelling, mostly because Walter earned a modest income, but partially because the Connistons had always elected not to improve a house that bore the weight of three very active children. The lot was flat, as most of Kansas is except Flint Hills or east of Lawrence. Throughout the years, various grasses vied for dominance of the lawn. At one point before Dallas was born, Bermuda boasted superiority. Then Johnson grass made a show of it, around the time Bent left for the military. And finally, when Muriel had married, moved, and had a yard of her own, and it was Dallas's turn to mow the lawn at last, there were mostly crabgrass and dandelions left, which didn't bother Dallas any. He was determined to get good and grown-up like Bent. He didn't want to enter high school not having passed the rites of mowing a lawn and holding a girl's hand. He figured the Conniston lawn was as good as any, and Eddy Lundy's hand more than suitable for holding.

Dallas had only realized one of those goals. The other one, the one that meant more to him than the state record in touchdown passes, was somewhere on the campus of Kansas University serving her sentence as a Jayhawk.

*And she'll be home for summer soon,* thought Dallas, as he folded the last of his papers and stuffed it in his bag.

Already he had begun to think of the summer as *the* most important three months of his life, *the* all-emcompassing season, *the* test, *the* measure of his manhood, for by fall Eddy would be gone again. She would be a senior in college. And after that, who knew? She might never return.

Dallas slung the bag across his handlebars, mounted up, and pedaled out the mouth of Mulberry. He rode along the main thoroughfares whistling, running over worms that warmed themselves in the gutter puddles, and thinking of Eddy. Beneath his wheels the road tar softened, signaling a hot day ahead. It was quiet except for the footsteps behind him and the voice that brought a smile to his face. Even before he looked around, Dallas knew that, next to Eddy, it was his favorite person in the world.

"Top of the morning, Dally," called Coach Larry Ravelle as he came puffing parallel with Dallas. "Can I tag along?"

"All right by me, Coach," said Dallas.

"Much obliged, son. Whoa now. Call the law. Now that's a load. Looks like you got some throwing to do, pal. Wouldn't happen to be limbering up for Laird, would you?"

Dallas grinned at this second reminder in just thirty minutes of how obsessed Ellenbach was with its Bulldogs. But he said nothing.

"Not a bad idea, you know. Never hurts. It nevvver hurts," said Ravelle, eyeing the fat bag of papers.

Larry himself had been a stellar athlete at one time. In '52 he had quarterbacked the Bulldogs to the championship game but had lost in overtime on a goal line end around when his shoe came off and he fumbled the ball straight into a Laird player's arms. The Plainsmen went on to win that night, 23–21. And a lot of folks said he'd never get over it. That shoe would come back to haunt the boy the rest of his natural life.

Country folk are known for talk like that, extremes, that is. They speak of "corn as high as an elephant's eye," and "never meeting men they didn't like." And, of course, a wind doesn't exist that behaves itself. Wind comes "sweeping down the plains," "snatching chickens," and "pulling pants off the clothesline."

In Coach Ravelle's case, however, the people were right. The shoe did come back to haunt him a long time afterward. But the details of that haunting are a different story. What matters is that when the shoe resurfaced and caused Larry to stumble far worse than what he'd done on the gridiron that night in '52, he was not destroyed by it. True, he lost his job as pastor of the Ellenbach Community Church, and he nearly lost his family. But in the end, he gained something that had never been his. He gained peace, peace with that part of him that wished like mad to have the Plainsmen on their goal line again. Peace with his fellow Ellenbachians. Peace with Rose, his wife. And peace with God.

Eventually, he gained another job, too.

Luck and a losing season brought Larry's name to mind when it came time for the school board to hire a new football coach. They wanted someone who could lead the Bulldogs back to prominence. So once the administration dismissed its fears about "that Sunset Grille mark on Larry's record," they hired him to teach English and regain the state championship pennant. His feet were back where they belonged—planted firmly on the turf of Foster Jenson II Memorial Stadium.

Some say there's nothing so good as seeing people go all the way to the brink of sin, over it even, only to find themselves downstream, prosperous, and in one piece. But it's a better thing when, from that point on, such persons conduct themselves a safer distance from the water's edge. After all, many are those who disappear over the falls and wind up sinking in pools farther downstream. Fortunately, Larry had felt the tug of certain diversions and was glad to be out of their current.

"Ahhh," breathed Larry, filling his lungs with May air. "Good morning, Ellenbach," he shouted.

Dallas rolled his eyes. This was the one thing about Coach Ravelle that everyone tolerated. He was like a child who had become an old man and then somehow got to be a child again. He went jogging and splashed through Jefferson Fountain in the town square. He wore sandals until December. He brought doughnuts to class and taught grammar with a glass of milk in one hand and a maple bar in the other, punctuating a sentence from time to time with a thrust of his sugary pointer. Once, he even sneaked his family to the top of the chamber of commerce building to watch for shooting stars.

But when it came to football, Coach Ravelle's record covered a multitude of eccentricities. Come game day, not a snicker was heard when Larry painted his face maroon and gray and sang the "Star Spangled Banner" at the center of the field before the kickoff. When he followed with prayer, a hundred chins were lowered. Ellenbach gleaned more from those sacred moments than they ever did from one of the Reverend Ravelle's sermons when he was bloated with the glory of himself.

Truly, the second shedding of his shoe was the greatest thing that ever happened to Larry. For with it went the weight of secret sin, pride, fear, and sorrow. And that's why he kept a cordovan loafer on his mantelpiece at home. A plaque above it read: HE WHO WALKS LIGHTEST WALKS BEST.

The sound of Larry's feet and the Stingray filled the morning. The fragrance of freshly-cut grass wafted over the stockade fences. Martins swooped from lofty, green-roofed houses, crossed paths with man and boy, and darted off to find breakfast for their children. As they went along, Larry seemed to be thinking, and his smile grew wider with every thought. At Dunbar, where Dallas normally turned to begin his route, the coach reached over and touched the boy's shoulder.

"See the third house down, Dally?"

Dallas nodded and reluctantly took a paper from the bag. He knew what always came next. Normally, he would've jumped at the chance to impress his mentor. But with Eddy coming home, there was a lot on his mind.

"Okay, son. Three seconds left in the Laird game. We're down by six. See if you can hit the lamppost in the end zone. Down . . . set . . ."

"Hold it, Coach," said Dallas.

But Larry continued. "Blue! Ninety-eight! Blue! Ninety-eight!"

"That's Percy Fink's house."

"36 out!"

"Coach?"

"36 out!"

"Coooach?!"

"Hut! Hut!"

"Coach!"

"What is it, Dallas? What could possibly be more important than finding that lamppost alone in the end zone with no time left and our team in need of a touchdown?"

"That's Percy Fink's house, sir," said Dallas.

"Fink schmink. Throw the ball, son."

"He ain't taking the paper anymore."

"He what?"

"Mr. Fink ain't—"

"I know. I heard you. And you ought to know by now that *ain't* isn't a word, Dallas Conniston. Besides, you can throw the ball and we can pick it up when we get to his driveway. What's the matter with you, son? You've been acting funny since I caught up with you. Is something on your mind?"

"Welll . . ."

"Come on, champ. I can't have my star player moping around so close to game time."

"First game is three months away, Coach," said Dallas.

"Come on now . . . spill it."

"I don't know, Coach. It ain't . . . *isn't* anything important."

"Spill it, Conniston, unless you'd like to fetch water for me this season," said Larry.

Dallas spit and scuffed his tennis shoe against the pavement. When he spoke, his chin was on his chest and his voice was barely audible.

"It's just . . . it's just that my dad's been acting kind of sad lately."

At the mention of Walter, Larry stopped in the middle of the road.

"If you don't mind my saying so, son, your dad's been acting sad since you were five. People miss the way he used to be. I miss him. Sometimes I fear what might happen if he ever lost you, too," said Larry, shooting a glance at Dallas. "I've been meaning to talk to him, lately. This town really needs him, you know. Believe it or not, a lot more things revolve around Walt Conniston than just the mail."

Dallas looked perplexed.

"What I'm trying to say is, your dad has a way with certain people in Ellenbach whom I can't seem to get close to. He could sell Jesus to anybody, back before things changed. Why, there were nights he couldn't sleep if he hadn't shared the gospel that day. The message burned so hot in his heart he couldn't hold it in too long, for fear of catching on fire. But come on, son," said Larry. "That's only half of it. What else is bugging you?"

Dallas kept his eyes on the ground until he couldn't stand the coach's pressure anymore.

"Do you think I have half a chance of winning Eddy Lundy from Thane Edgerley?" blurted Dallas.

Larry grinned and looked away toward Percy Fink's house.

"Eddy Lundy," he repeated the name slowly. "So that's it. She's coming home soon, isn't she?"

"Uh-hm," Dallas nodded.

"Well now, she's a trifle older than you, but I don't see why it couldn't work out. Anyway, what makes you think she belongs to Thane Edgerley?"

"I don't know," said Dallas. "She's more his age, I guess. And I've seen him looking at her before."

"He's only older than you by a year," said Larry. Then he asked, "Can Thane throw a tight spiral?"

"No. I don't think so. I ain't . . . *haven't* seen him do it."

"Can he read the coverage? Do a five-step dropback? Throw across the field to a man on the sidelines and hit him in a pinch?"

"Nah, Coach. Thane pretty much just hands off. You know that."

"Well then, does he hunt his own night crawlers like you, Dally Conniston? Does he crappie fish at midnight when the bugs are swarming and the moon is full?"

"No, sir."

"Does he dove hunt? Frog gig? Noodle for catfish? Any of those?"

"Coach, I don't recall. But he's older, and he's bigger than me, and—"

"Just answer the questions, Dally," Larry chided like a lawyer. Then he closed his case with a final query.

"Is there any way possible in the great, wide world that Thane Edgerley could pitch a Sunday edition of the *Ellenbachian* at full-clip on a bicycle and hit Eddy Lundy's front door every time?"

"No, sir," Dallas said confidently. "I don't believe he could."

"There you have it, then," Larry concluded. "A man's got to win a woman some way. And if Thane Edgerley can't do any of those things, then he doesn't stand a chance. If you ask me, I'd say barring some cataclysmic accident, you and Eddy Lundy will be practically married by August!"

Dallas blushed and studied his spit on the pavement, satisfied with Larry's assessment of the situation.

"I guess I ought to learn how to talk to her first," he said.

"That always helps, son. Do you have plans for doing it before the turn of the century?"

"Ah, Coach. I can't help being shy."

"And that's exactly why you'll stay that way, too, son. Dallas, you couldn't hit the broadside of the universe when I first got hold of you. Now look at yourself. You can roll left or right, stop on a dime, connect with a man coming out of the backfield, even take a shot from the blindside, and still get up with a grin on your face. And you know why?"

"No, Coach, why?"

"Because you've been taught right, son. You've been told how to do something, and now you believe in yourself. There's a lot of power in words, Dallas, a lot of power."

"What's that got to do with Eddy?"

"What's that got to do with Eddy? It's got everything to do with Eddy's heart, because every woman wants to hear the words that make her heart feel good. You may be able to throw a football like Fran Tarkenton, but you don't know diddly about words. It's all in the delivery, son. It's all in the delivery."

"So?" said a red-faced Dallas.

"So I'm going to teach you."

"Teach me?"

"That's right, Dallas. When words are strung together to make a sentence, and then that sentence is put into a heart, well, that heart can't help being changed one way or the other, for good or for bad. Understand?"

"Not completely, sir."

"I'm going to teach you how to write a letter, Dallas, a proper love letter."

Dallas washed white and tilted precariously on his bicycle.

"I thought you said I'd win Eddy if I could throw a football and shoot doves and catch fish."

"You missed the point, son. That was just to build your confidence, to remind you of the things you do better than any boy I've ever known. Those aren't the things that really win a woman's heart. It's what's inside you that counts."

"But Coach, I've never even asked her for a date. I can't send her a love letter."

"Who said anything about sending it? Just practicing it on paper is half the ball game. Besides, like I was saying before, if a message stays inside you for too long, it doesn't do you, or your dad, or anybody else a bit of good."

"That's different."

"Yep. But not by much. The gospel of Jesus and the language of love will never change the world or win Eddy Lundy's heart if they're kept inside. They're bigger than shyness, Dallas. Bigger than Thane Edgerley. Bigger than those two graves with Bent and Muriel's names on them."

"But . . ."

"No buts, son," said Coach Ravelle as he plodded off down Dunbar. "Just be at my house on Sunday nights, and I'll have you waxing eloquent in no time."

As Dallas watched Larry jogging away from him, he wasn't sure if he wanted to wax eloquent, much less write a love letter to Eddy. But if it helped him reach that other goal, if it helped him get the nerve to stretch his trembling fingers to actually touch the hand of a woman, then he would do it. In the distance he heard Larry yelling something.

"Tell your father I'll be talking to him real soon."

Dallas signaled back with a thumbs up, as he pedaled along his way, tossing papers into the teeth of the defense, hitting porches on post patterns, dreading the writing of a letter and never once imagining that across town on Cistern Street his father was about to fumble.

# ~ 10 ~

*What men call gallantry, and gods adultery,*
*Is much more common where the climate's sultry.*

—Lord Byron, *Don Juan*

SOME men pace when they consider doing evil. Others prefer to be still. Walter sat on the curb and stared at 602 Cistern as if it were some emetic he was loath to take but could not avoid. For him, the elimination of pain had become everything.

The neighborhood snoozed in the midmorning—its breadwinners long gone, garage doors winked shut behind them, dogs napping soundly on a cool May mattress. A cat tiptoed across the hood of an Oldsmobile. And in the tops of elms, cicadas snored sonorously.

Across the street from the woman's house, Ace and company crouched behind a clump of junipers that pressed against the side of a neighbor's garage, and they watched the man. It was the second morning of the mission, and conspicuously absent from them was Homer, who had gone on orders from Jesus to retrieve the day's mail from hell. None of the developments surprised Jesus. He had known forever that Satan would halt all postal activity at the first sign of a leak and that He would need a runner of His own. Throughout the host of heaven a better flier could not be found than Homer Windkook.

And today he was late.

"What's taking him so long?" said Albert, searching the sky from his position in the junipers.

"Patience, Albert. He'll be fine. Homer's a first-rate flier, not to mention the fact that Jesus has confidence in him," said Ace. But he was beginning to wonder himself.

"He did leave for hell nearly a day ago, monsieur," offered François.

"Look here," Chaney interjected, "when was the last t-t-time any of us had to f-f-fly there? It isn't easy, you know," continued Chaney. "Those Alpha Order t-types are p-p-posted everywhere down there."

Doc flinched at the reminder.

"Chaney's right," said Ace. We should be praying for our brother rather than worrying how late he is. After all, he has to fly all that way. Then, he has to observe the tray-out, ask a few questions to appear official, make the contact, secure Bent's letters, and travel back through the moans all under the disguise of a postal inspector, which, by the way, can't be too easy for an angel like Homer. Which of us would be so brave?"

"I hope he doesn't forget to swing by home to make the copies and the necessary changes in the documents," said François.

"I thought that was your job," said Albert.

"I forgot," said François.

Albert turned his attention to Walter on the curb.

"How in the world is he ever going to start telling the town about Jesus again if all he thinks about is his pain and this woman?" said Albert.

"That's not our concern," said Ace. "We were only told to get the letters in his bag. And as soon as Homer gets here, that's what we're going to do."

"Excuse me," said Doc, who was sitting on a splash block at the base of a rusted piece of gutter. "Might we all be safer to move inside somewhere? In a chimney? A shed? Anywhere but here in this open place where we can be seen, and—"

"Shhh! Be quiet! He's getting up! Walter's g-g-getting up," said Chaney. Had he stopped to think, he'd have remembered there wasn't a need for secrecy, for humans are as unaware of angels as they are of those who chose a fouler master. At times, angels are barely perceptible in the snapping of a twig or in the puff of wind in a mother's face as she strolls her baby or in the fortunate start that wakes a man who has forgotten to set his alarm clock and is in danger of missing a business presentation. But at other times, angels raise a regular ruckus. They make such a din that the dead are roused; demons curse and angels clash their broadswords. Ironically, the sound escapes the living. People tilt their heads skyward as if they heard thunder, and they comment . . . "Hmm, left my umbrella at the house."

The sky pours rain; and the lords of the air do battle; the earth spins on.

In Walter's case, he wouldn't have recognized an angel if one stood up fully visible in a juniper bush and waved. He hoisted his bag over his shoulder and was slightly cognizant of being an hour behind his schedule already. He walked in a daze toward the woman's front door.

*I'm just going there to see if she's still happy with her post office box,* Walter told himself as his foot made contact with the curb on the other side of the street. *Lots of folks come to town and take a long time putting up a real box. She might just need some help, might just need someone to remind her to do it. So I'm reminding. Nothing wrong with that. Nothing in the world to hide. Nothing at all.*

Nevertheless, Walter had taken extra precautions that morning to reach Cistern *after* Eunice Honeycutt had started her walk, Clyde Culvert had left for the John Deere distributor in Laird, the Pickleman twins were laying out trotline in the swollen parts of Coon Creek, and the Finches, the Shacklefords, the Peets, and Judge Roy Pickens were all too busy reading their newspapers to notice Walter's waywardness.

Suddenly, Doc gasped and pointed toward 602's roof.

"Get him down!" ordered Ace, at the sight of the Alpha Order squadron coming over the roof's edge. There were ten in all, three of which were moans Greedo, Spleen, and Pater Mordo. On Pogromme's orders, the three had tailed Walter from his home on Mulberry, merging unexpectedly with their peers from hell at the eastern end of Cistern. Even before they reached the roof, the usual sense of client ownership had sprouted among the motley crew.

"What business do you have with the human?" growled the leader of the new Alpha Order.

"Who wants to know?" countered Spleen. Behind him, Pater Mordo waited for a fight. His meaty hands twitched uncontrollably at his side.

"Moan Dice, that's who. Five Slash commander, in case you hadn't noticed," said the moan, tilting his head toward the corresponding insignia on the shoulder of his jacket.

Spleen eyed the crimson marks that verified the moan's place in Satan's chain of command. Seeing he was outranked and outnumbered, he fabricated a more respectful answer.

"Citizen Pogromme sent us on reconnaissance."

"Well, aren't we special. That must make you feel terribly significant," replied the moan. "Perhaps you'd like to know that it was Satan himself who sent us several days ago to tempt the man. Judging by the looks of him, this assignment's not big enough for both of us. I'll permit you to watch, but no more."

"How kind of you," said Spleen.

"I knew you were the sensible type," responded Dice. That brought a chuckle from his cronies. "Now, little demon . . ."

"The name's Spleen."

"All right, Spleen. Observe the fine art of temptation. Pigweed!"

"Yes, sir," said a runty, red-eyed demon.

"Take Toad and Teasel to fetch the man."

"He's already heading this way, sir."

"I can see that, Pigweed. I want you to speed him up a little. Make the procedure excruciating for him and entertaining for us. Use your expertise. Goad him with a lusty thought. Make him fairly rush to ruin his marriage, as well as his reputation in this former missionary field of his."

At that Pigweed scampered off the roof with Toad and Teasel in tow. The trio of tempters arranged themselves around Walter, casting suggestions into his mind.

"The woman's a beauty, isn't she?" whispered Pigweed into Walter's ear.

Walter touched his temple at the sudden throb he felt there.

"If you play your cards right, she could belong to you," continued Pigweed. "Then again, she may have belonged to you in the past. You have noticed the resemblance, haven't you?"

A single frame of Muriel flashed across Walter's cranial screen. *What am I doing here?* he thought to himself. But the suggestions would not subside. It was Teasel's turn.

"You're looking for love," cooed Teasel. "A kind that won't leave you—a safe love, a love that wants you as much as you want it, a love that will last until you choose to terminate it."

"But what about Donna?" said Walter aloud, in seeming conversation with the unseen world.

"She'll understand," said Toad with a grin. "She'd do the same if the tables were turned. Who knows? This very minute she too could be somewhere trying to soften the blow that tragedy has dealt her heart."

Walter winced.

"Yesss," said Pigweed. "Who said anything about fathers and daughters? This is just a visit to a patron on your route. Now, get moving."

"Oh! This is perfect," said Dice, looking down from the roof. He turned toward Spleen. "Do you realize how long a demon must study in order to tempt and accuse simultaneously?"

Spleen humored his superior by shaking his head.

"Mark my words, there's no one better at it than Pigweed," continued Dice. "Listen to him. Have you ever heard a finer command of the language? Heh, heh. We'll have the evangelist before the sun goes down."

And so, with *a great deal* to hide and with reasons not completely known even to him, Walter crossed the woman's lawn, ascended her steps, and stood there trembling on her porch and willing his hand to reach for the knocker when again the door opened wide in front of him. The woman was wrestling with a galvanized mailbox nearly the same height as her.

"Mr. Conniston! I mean, Walter. What a habit this is becoming. Imagine my opening this door and finding you standing there. Twice in one week. Must be destiny. I was just about to plant this," puffed the woman. She dragged the mailbox past Walter onto the porch where she leaned it against the iron railing, wiped her brow, and closed the door.

"Phew," she gasped. "I never knew so much work went into communication. I always thought these things just sprouted from the ground. Sort of a backward abiogenesis."

"Pardon, ma'am?" said Walter, grabbing the rail to steady himself. The woman's features were staggering.

"You know, like spontaneous generation in reverse. Didn't you ever study that stuff in school?"

"Uh, I've heard of it," said Walter.

"You okay, Walter?"

"Yes ma'am."

"I mean, I don't want to sound nosy. But both times we've seen each other you haven't looked so well. Must be all those hours in the hot sun," said the woman.

"Must be," said Walter, limited to a two-word sentence by his shortness of breath.

"Say, it just occurred to me that I've never introduced myself. My name's Marla Coe."

She offered her hand to Walter, and he took it, enrapt with its childlike softness next to his own rough skin.

"Well, don't just stand there," she said. "I'm a damsel in distress and without an address. Help me get this thing down the stairs and across the lawn, will you? It weighs a ton."

Walter set his bag aside and took the heaviest end of the mailbox. Inwardly, he groaned under the load. But he smiled to hide the strain. At the end of the driveway they set it down, and Walter straightened slowly.

"This thing *does* weigh a ton," he said. "Did you buy it at the hardware store?"

"No sir. I made it," said the woman.

"Well, if that doesn't beat all. What did you make her out of?"

"Sheet metal and sweat. My father showed me how."

"He must be a fine man," said Walter. "I bet you make him proud."

Marla didn't answer. Instead, she bent over and loosened the nut on the mail receptacle so that the pole could slide free. When she did, the collar of her shirt fell slightly open, and Walter turned away from the view.

On the roof, Dice elbowed Spleen. "Ho! Ho!" he chortled in his joy. "See how deeply confused our client is? Ruin is a step away."

"I should have thought of this before we hauled it down those stairs," said Marla as she tugged at the pole until it came away from the box and she landed with a thud in the lawn. She stood, brushing grass from the seat of her jeans. "My father's dead, if you're wondering," she said. "He worked himself into the ground before I started high school."

"I'm sorry, ma'am," said Walter. "I really am. What was his line of work?"

"I don't remember. Say, there's a posthole digger in the garage if you can stick around for a bit. I can pay you by the hour. One Coke for every hour of work. It's the best I can do without a job."

Walter eyed his bag on the porch and gave in to his desire to help. "It's a deal."

"Good," she said. "Let's get busy. And stop ma'aming me. My name's Marla, remember?"

"All right, Marla," said Walter, following her up the driveway. His eyes grew heavy with the hypnotic swing of her hair. All thoughts of his responsibilities to the postal patrons and his family were fading in importance.

At the same time, Homer was about to meet the challenges of hell's mail room.

# ~ 11 ~

*That's the greatest torture souls feel in hell:*
*In hell, that they must live and cannot die.*

—John Webster, *Duchess of Malfi*

IN hell's mail room that morning, business was bustling. Some souls trayed mail with burnt black hands. Others strained against canvas carts loaded to the brim with correspondence. Behind them moans clacked over mottled tile and muttered their intentions. They poised their whips. They gripped their gaff hooks and waited, watching for the unsuspecting loiterer. The wheels of the carts screeched horribly across the floor. And over it all, the blades of the ceiling fans, which were never switched on, slowly rotated in the rising heat.

In the middle of the room a grisled foreman sat high up in his glassed-in booth giving grief to the souls over his microphone. A moan came by with a heavy box of tools and a purchase order in his hand.

"Camera's fixed in the bathroom, sir," said the moan. "I'll need you to sign off for some parts, so I can put in another one."

"Give me that PO," snarled the foreman. "It's always fix this and fix that. You just watch, kid. I'm the one who'll get raked over the coals at the end of the year for over-spending. Who comes up with these cockeyed projects?"

"I think this one's from the top, sir," said the moan, scratching the back of his neck.

The foreman blanched and checked to see if the microphone had been on. Fortunately he had turned it off. "Why didn't you say so in the first place?"

The worker shrugged and wandered away, and the foreman returned to his favorite pastime.

"Get them letters sorted faster, or I'll file a report," he shouted over the microphone.

One soul who ran the meter machine by the loading dock popped off bravely, or foolishly, however one chooses to look at it.

"What's the hurry? This stuff's not going anywhere soon," he shouted. His back was to the foreman, but his voice was just loud enough for the old moan to discern above the din.

"What do you mean?" asked another soul nearby.

"Oh, it's all over hell. I heard it from a secretary who said she was close to the top. She said they're shutting us down for a while. Why, she—" Suddenly, he felt a hot pain in his shoulder.

"Aaaiieee!" he screamed, falling face-first into his machine. He slumped heavily toward the floor, smearing the counter and the custard-colored cabinets with his blood.

"Please," he begged the moan with the hook who straddled him, "please . . . aagh . . . pleeeaaase . . . I'll be good."

But the moan just lifted him like a piece of meat and dragged him to the foot of the foreman's booth. He gave the hook a sharp shake, and the soul came off in a quivering heap.

"Uuuppphhh."

"Smart mouth won't get you far in this place," said the foreman, peering down.

The soul nodded slightly.

"So you may as well be a gentleman while you tell me

about that secretary, because I just might let you off. I just might forget about the whole thing, depending on your attitude."

Eagerly, the soul rose on one arm to tell what he knew.

"Well," he began, fingering the wide cut on his upper lip where he'd fallen against the machine. "I happened to be in central files, and I heard this secretary—she was one of those good-looking ones from the main office pool—anyway, she was on lunch break and she was standing there, smoking a cigarette, and—"

"Ooo, yes. I know her. Red hair? Long legs?" said the foreman, leaning down toward the soul.

"Yeah, yeah. That's the one."

"Hmm," grinned the foreman. "But I can't recall her name. Can you?"

"Carol. Her name is Carol Jones," said the soul, quickly. He saw the foreman's face light up, and he was certain he'd be back at his post in no time. The foreman took a pencil and scratched the name on an envelope. Then he leaned again toward the soul, his pencil ready and his dark eyes winking.

"You were starting to say something about Carol in the file room," he began.

"That's right. Okay, where was I? Oh. She was standing there, smoking a cigarette, and I was going through one of the drawers looking for the address of someone in Cleveland. I think I was in the *T* files over by the fireplace—"

"Just get to the point," ordered the foreman.

"Sorry. Sorry. Okay, let's see, yeah, that's right. Just as I closed the drawer, Carol Jones swishes over next to me and says, let's see, uh, she says in a whisper (and at this point, the soul cupped his hands to his mouth and craned his neck toward the foreman), she says, 'Hey, Mack. You heard about Satan closing the mail room?' I just told her no. But I really wanted the conversation to continue—"

Right in the middle of the soul's sentence, the foreman gave a nod to some moans who'd stolen quietly up behind the worker, and another hook swept down into his back, catching him squarely in the lumbar section and sending spasms along his spine.

The soul convulsed, wide-eyed. Something was wrong. He'd been ordered to speak. He was following orders.

"Now," said the foreman, "you can begin again any time you want."

A thin whisper blew between the soul's teeth.

"The secretary, sir—"

A second hook came down.

"Uuuoowwrr . . . but . . . the secre—"

And a third.

"There isn't any secretary," hissed the foreman.

The hooks held fast. The soul dangled and wheezed.

"Say it, mister. Say, 'there isn't any Carol Jones,'" shouted the foreman.

"There isn't any Carol Jones," the soul complied.

"And you don't know anything about the mail room closing down."

The soul twitched on the hooks.

"Say it," repeated the foreman.

"I don't know anything, sir."

"That's better," said the foreman, smiling. "Now, that wasn't so bad, was it? You're behind, though," he added, pointing to the meter machine. "You'd better get back to work."

At that, the moans carried the soul back to his position and shook him loose. He fell like a rag to the ground, but the moans hoisted him up again to start the machine. No one took much notice of the unfortunate worker. Souls went on licking stamps for the non-metered local mail and loading sacks and hardly glancing at their colleague's slick, red torso. These occurrences were commonplace, just hell as usual and no more extraordinary than an argument over a postal rate or a tiff in the men's room.

When the machine operator's lamenting was finally lost in the whir of the machinery, there came a knock on the broad metal doors of the loading dock, and a hundred heads yanked toward the sound. The foreman came down from his booth and clicked across the floor, spitting orders this way and that. His brow was furrowed, and his fat little legs pumped in staccato-fashion to see who'd come calling.

"Get back to work," he said to the lickers and to the loaders. "I'll punish the first idle man or woman I see. You heard what happened to that Ripskin fellow, didn't you? He's working graveyard in C-storage now."

Another knock came, this time, louder.

"No one is supposed to come here today," grumbled the foreman to himself. "At least, I wasn't notified of it. Why I'm always the last to hear things, I'll never know."

At the door he pressed his head against the metal, and one more sharp knock rang out in his ear.

The foreman winced.

"Yeah, what do you want?" he said in a gravel voice.

"Postal inspector," came the curt answer.

"It's a PI!" rasped the foreman, turning to survey the condition of his workplace, for there is nothing more feared in a mail room than a postal inspector. "You," he said, pointing to the meter machine operator. "Get a rag and wipe that blood off those keys. What do you think this is, some sort of slop house we've got going here? This is a place of business. Now, get going."

The soul scurried to find a rag, and the knocks came louder.

"Just a minute," said the foreman, and he whirled again on his employees. "Hurry," he spat. "Line those dollies up over there! Get those carts out of sight! Everybody, comb your hair! Tuck your shirts in! Just keep your mouths shut!"

The foreman turned back toward the door and took a deep breath. Then he cracked it half an inch and squinted into the darkness.

"Yes, sir. May I help you?" he said, cordially.

"Name's Wetterman. Horace P. Wetterman," came the reply. A hand shot up with a business card.

"Come in. Please come in, Mr. Wetterman," minced the foreman. And though it probably went unnoticed to those inhabitants of hell, the room became a lighter shade as the inspector entered and closed the door behind him. No one thought it strange that he kept his sunglasses on.

The foreman began to talk rapidly.

"We're glad to have you, sir. Can't say we were expecting you, though. Place might need some tidying up, you understand. It's usually much cleaner. But on such short notice, well, you know, it's easy to let things get out of control from time to time, things like order and neatness and what not. But I like to think we run a pretty tight ship around here. Yes, a pretty tight ship," he said, just as three rolls of packing tape fell from underneath a moan's jacket and came wobbling over the tiles.

Homer chuckled to himself and shook hands with the foreman. He had practiced dropping the surfer accent on his long flight to hell. Most of it was gone. Now as he looked around the room, he hoped his audience would be too rattled to notice either the bulge of his great, white wings tucked neatly beneath his postal jacket or that part of his dialect he couldn't seem to shake.

"Horace Wetterman," he repeated, still pumping the foreman's hand, energetically. "I've got a few questions to ask these workers if you don't mind."

"No. Of course not. Be my guest," said the foreman. Then he shouted to his charges, "Keep working, folks. There's no reason to slow the mail on account of Mr. Wetterman's being here."

In the far corner of the room stood a thin soul without any shoes. He kept his face to his work as his feet shuffled on the hot floor and his hands sorted envelopes deftly. Once or twice his eyes darted in Homer's direction and then down again. Homer spied the soul and repeated the name he'd memorized.

*Stan,* he said, inwardly. *So there's the dude with the guts.* Homer started down the first row of workers, checking various work stations and scribbling things on a clipboard. As he went, he prayed for proper recall of all the statistics he'd crammed in his brain. And all the while he moved toward Stan's corner.

When he reached the meter machine operator, Homer asked his first question. "You with the colorful back," he shouted. "What's the express rate for a half-pound parcel?"

When the soul turned around there was pain in his eyes. "Would that be to the addressee? Or to a post office?" asked the soul.

"The addressee, you smart aleck," said Homer. And it hurt him deeply when he said it.

"A hundred and seventy gorms, sir," said the soul (which is just a nickel shy of ten dollars in U.S. currency).

"How about priority?"

"Almost three and a half times less, sir. Flat rate, all zones."

"All right, wise guy. You pass. Keep busy," said Homer. Then he whispered as he went by, "I'll be praying for you, man." And the soul gazed after him with a hint of smile as Homer moved on with his interrogation.

"What's the zone number for three-day select to zip code prefixes 496–499?" he shouted to no one in particular. When none of the souls could answer, a handsome moan with a gold ring in his nose took a crack at it.

"Thirty-five, sir," chirped the moan, arrogantly.

"Lucky guess! How about ground delivery to 612?"

"That's easy. Zone three," said the moan.

"I bet you think you're really something, don't you?" said Homer, leaning so close to the moan's face that he could smell his rotten bridgework.

The moan allowed himself a smile.

"All right, Mr. Brimstone-for-Brains. No one outwits Horace Wetterman," sneered Homer. "I'll eat my briefcase if you can tell me the zone for next-day air to Goat Creek, Alaska."

"Twenty-two, I believe, sir," said the moan, apprehensively.

"You believe, do you? You believe?" bellowed Homer. "Well, down here you're not paid to believe."

"It was an educated guess, sir."

"Educated or otherwise, it was incorrect," said Homer. He was on a roll now. "Suppose you got a coworker on assignment up in Goat Creek. And that coworker of yours is in a pinch one morning. Enemy troops all around him darting in, slashing at him, giving him a taste of wrath like he's never known before. And suppose that coworker of yours didn't have to be there in the first place, and he wouldn't have been either if it wasn't for the fact that a certain partner in hell sent his notice of furlough to some other zone because he didn't know the difference between Goat Creek and Kotzebue!"

The room was silent. Heads were bowed. Black hands feigned interest in their work. Eyes blinked leadenly at the wall. But inwardly, each soul laughed along with Homer, for it wasn't often a member of hell's staff was publicly barbecued. However, Homer wasn't finished.

"That coworker of yours doesn't care whether you 'believe' or not, mister. He wants you to *know*! And you better know next time I come calling! Do you understand?" yelled Homer.

"Yessir," snapped the moan.

"That's better. Now, since we're on the subject of the proper zone number for Goat Creek, Alaska, why don't you try twenty-three."

"Twenty-three, sir," said the moan.

"Wrong," shouted Homer. And a volley of titters rang out in the room. "I suggest you do your homework next time before you try to go to the head of the class. The correct answer is twenty-four. Now, get out of my sight. Go on. Get."

The moan with the gold ring in his nose slunk away as if led by an unseen hand, and Homer carried on in the same way until he was standing in front of Stan. The little, barefoot postal worker cringed like a schoolboy who is ill prepared for an exam. Homer's back was to the rest of the room. He could hear the men and women working; he could feel the faint rumble of steel wheels throughout the room. He knew there was little time to make the transaction, and that one slip could bring a host of moans from the maze of hallways that surrounded the mail room.

"Letter for Moan B," whispered Homer, as their eyes met.

Stan turned pale and fumbled with the envelopes in front of him.

"Man, don't you go chicken on me now, Stan," said Homer, leaning close to the soul's sweating face. Stan swallowed hard. When he finally began to talk, he was talking to the wall.

"It's in the men's room, up inside the ceiling above the second stall. Feel around for it. There's only one today. Bent said there's not been much time to write. Be careful, though. Can't be sure when they'll have the cameras on. Watch for the red light."

"Thanks. I'm sorry I was so harsh with you," said Homer.

"It's okay," said Stan. "It's just that I've never seen an angel before."

For a moment, Homer looked at the soul.

There is a bitterness to many of hell's residents. One can see it in their faces, and in the way they carry their shoulders when they walk, and in all they do. Like a shroud, it comes across them the moment they enter the underworld and is accompanied by the circular logic that says, "How did I end up in hell? I'm not that bad. I'm a pretty good guy. I didn't murder anybody. I didn't steal. I didn't whore around. Come to think of it, Don Robard did all those things. And I haven't seen his face around here. How did I end up in hell? I'm not that bad. I'm a pretty good guy." And after about a hundred years of going round and round like that, the logic ceases because the soul finally figures that it won't do any good, and that it was godlessness rather than bad behavior that got him there in the first place. Then the bitterness disappears, and misery replaces it.

"Stan," whispered Homer, "if you had received Jesus, things would have been different."

"I didn't think it would end up this way," said Stan. For a second the cold gaze disappeared from Stan's face, and he looked at Homer with the most desperate of eyes. "Is there any way you could give me a second chance?"

"I can't give you that. I'm sorry. I really am," said Homer.

Then Homer shook his leg, and a pink envelope dropped from the cuff of his gray cotton postal trousers and settled next to one of Stan's blistered feet. The smell of paradise was heavy on Muriel's letter, and Homer looked around to see if anyone would notice it. Fortunately, hell's stench drowned the scent immediately.

"Take care," said Homer, though he knew the words were empty ones. "Now, play along with me here, and everything will work out."

Stan looked confused.

"You fool! You absolute fool," screamed Homer at the top of his lungs. "Any bonehead knows the maximum weight and size of a priority mail package. Well, for your information, it's—Oh! Never mind! You've got a brain, slight though it may be. Look the thing up yourself. Is that too hard for you?"

"No, sir. I'll do it right away," said Stan.

"See that you do. Now, is there a bathroom in this place? Or are your manners just as awkward as your

work habits?" roared Homer, glaring toward the foreman's glassed-in booth, where the corpulent demon
mopped his brow and bit his nails.

"Men's room is down the hall and to the right, Mr.
Wetterman. It isn't hard to find," said the foreman.

"I should hope not," said Homer, spinning on his heels
and storming off down the hallway.

Outside the mail room, Homer ran as fast as he could.
The awfulness of hell crept in beneath his feathers and
made him shiver. But he was driven on by Jesus' orders.
"At all costs, get those letters into Walter's bag!"

Along the walls hung portraits of moans in somber
settings; diabolical CEOs sitting motionless for the
artist, founding fathers breaking ground with forks and
shovels, hell's politicians posing pompously, and, as
always, the nauseating array of consignments wherein
Satan smiled beatifically. For the average worker on his
way to relieve himself, the pictures were patriotic
reminders. But to Homer, they were a peripheral blur.
When he reached the men's room, Homer threw open
the door, and . . .

. . . his zoe froze.

At the sink there was an Alpha Order moan washing his
hands. He muttered angrily as he clawed the soap with
his talons, then fairly flew into a rage when he went to dry
them and ended up shredding the paper. The more he
pulled on the roll, the more it came off in little ribbons.

"Blast these hygiene codes!" growled the moan, his
huge neck bulging with hostility at being called back
from the field just when he was beginning to have fun. "I
don't care if Management does hear me," he added,
thumping his chest. "I know what's going on. I know the
score. It doesn't take a genius to understand that Satan
amuses himself by running everybody's lives like they
were puppets. He could have sent for Pigweed or Toad
or Teasel. But nooo, he had to send for me. Well, I'm sick
of it," he concluded, turning his attention back to Homer.

"I'm sick and tired of it, and I don't have to stand for it anymore. What are you staring at, anyway?"

Homer steadied himself and took a chance.

"Must be difficult trimming your nails," he offered with a grin.

The moan's brow pinched together at the middle.

For a moment, Homer wondered if he might be torn apart right there in one of the stalls, and flushed away into oblivion. He widened his stance and clenched his fists for a fight. Then the moan's lip twitched upward at the corner. His black eyes twinkled. And deep down, something like laughter began in his diaphragm.

"Harrr-harrr-harrr," he wheezed. "Name's Dice," said the moan, extending his hand.

Homer gripped the huge thing, which was more like a paw than a hand, and breathed an inward sigh. "Never can tell when Satan might need a good stand-up comic."

"I know what you mean," said the moan. "If I wasn't out tormenting souls and tearing the wings off angels, I think I might like to do something else with my life, too. In fact, you know what I'd like to be someday?" asked the moan. He slapped his hand good naturedly across Homer's broad shoulders.

"No. Tell me," grimaced Homer, as the moan's talons pierced his jacket.

"I'd like to be one of those ferry operators down at the river," sighed the moan, with a distant look in his eye. "You know, one of those moans who takes souls across from life to death. Anyway, I can see me now—standing at the tiller, a mist sort of rising from the water. And I'd start singing, 'Should auld acquaintance be forgot'. . ." The men's room rang with rich baritone. When the moan was finished, he dried his eyes with the back of his hand and apologized to Homer.

"Need's work, I know. I could be decent on a banjo, if it weren't for these lousy nails of mine," he said, holding his hands up in the dull, fluorescent light.

The thought occurred to Homer that he'd seen the moan before, many long ages ago in heaven, with a handsome, smiling face and a banjo on his knee. Then the thought vanished.

"So, why don't you just do it, Dice?" said Homer.

"Do what?" asked the moan.

"You know, quit the Alpha Order and apply for the job?"

A scowl returned to Dice's face.

"It's like this," said Dice, pointing to a corkboard on the wall that was covered with photographs and memos. "You see these pictures?"

Homer's heart raced when he saw Ace's face there, along with Albert's, Doc's, Chaney's, François's, his own, and four others. Beneath each picture were the words AGGRAVATED ASSAULT. Casually, Homer adjusted his sunglasses on his nose, and nodded.

"You're looking at the ten most wanted angels in the heavenly host," said Dice. "There're perks for the moan who kills one of these chumps! But I still don't call the shots. Do you understand, postman? Satan tells me to kill so-and-so on this list, and I kill. He says to wring some little angel's neck, and I wring. You see? I don't have time for singing. I don't have time for anything as long as Satan keeps putting me on assignments and jerking me back home and sending me off again," said Dice, starting for the door. But the edge was gone from his voice, and he seemed more pathetic than intimidating.

"Whatever," said Homer. "But I thought your voice sounded good."

Dice paused on the threshhold of the men's room with the door open and his head leaning against it.

"No kidding?" he asked, without looking back.

"Straight up," said Homer. "You're as good as any I've ever heard."

"Hmmph. Well, thanks for the compliment. Good luck to you."

"You, too," said Homer.

Dice nodded and closed the door, and Homer listened to him whistling away in the dark.

Then Homer went to the second stall and glanced up at the camera on the ceiling. Checking that its red light was off, he climbed up and pushed on the acoustic panel directly above him. It moved easily, just as Stan had said it would. But he had to stand on the tank to feel inside. Soon his fingers came to rest on the rough envelope. He took it down from the ceiling, repositioned the panel, and smiled at Muriel's name on the front of the letter. The cameras rolled and recorded his moves, even without the red lights, which the worker had removed that morning, just as Satan had ordered.

"Smooth sailing," sailed Homer, as he stepped down.

Suddenly the door to the rest room flew open. There stood Dice with a queue of moans behind him.

# ~ *12* ~

*Look homeward, Angel, now, and melt
with ruth.*

—John Milton, *Lycidas*

Aᴌᴌ right, postal inspector. Let's see some identification," ordered Dice.

"ID? What for? Is there a problem?" said Homer.

"Yeah, there's a problem! Whoever you are, you weren't in there to powder your nose! We have it all on tape, pal," said Dice, nodding at the camera near the ceiling. "Who are you?"

A sudden wave of courage swept over Homer. "I'm an angel from the city of God," he said defiantly, ducking just as Dice swung a sharp left hook at his head. The big moan's claws stuck fast in the corkboard, and in a rage he yanked the cumbersome thing from the wall. Homer darted at the first moan in the doorway. He hit him in the chest with such force that the moan fell back against the one behind him, which caused that one to fall into the next. The others scattered just enough for Homer to squirm through their midst, and he was off and running.

"Catch him, fools!" roared Dice.

At the first corner, Homer darted right and traveled up a long hallway. "One soul in Ellenbach, one soul in Ellenbach," he said to himself as he ran. He was panting hard, and the smell of tar and sulphur was almost over-whelming.

Soon, there were other moans around him in the hall. Dozens of them, dozens of dozens, all coming the other way, and all of them leading souls downward to some unspeakable agenda for the day. The darkness was to Homer's advantage as were the sunglasses. But he could hardly see to fly. Dare he take them off? Surely, he'd be recognized in an instant.

*What can I lose?* thought Homer, as he flung the glasses from his face. "Come on," he shouted over his shoulder at his pursuers. "You have to act fast, if you want to catch me!"

That drew attention. Instantly, other moans joined the chase.

"Who is that? Who are we after?" came the voices from the shadows.

"Don't ask me. I've never seen him before. But he isn't one of us."

"Yeah, he's smiling. Like he was happy."

"*That* doesn't sound like a moan. Come on. We had better check him out."

Considering his options, Homer peeled off his postal jacket and tucked it under his arm. His wings were free, and he could put some distance between himself and the moans. At the same time, it became quite plain to all that he was not an employee of hell in the least, but a former brother from the enemy camp.

"Catch him. Beat him. Crush him. Stop the angel," everybody shouted. Homer flew on.

At a curve in the hallway, Homer saw the flicker of a torch advancing on the hard, stone floor and walls. He touched down, skidded to a halt, and came nose to nose with a blond-haired young soul. Under other circumstances, Homer might have recognized the soul's Deadhead jean jacket, the scar on his cheek, and the bright orange lapel button that read PRESS and known exactly who he was. But alas, it is difficult enough to identify anyone in the darkened hallways of hell, let alone when one is being chased by demons.

"You . . . you're an angel," said the soul with a look of surprise on his face. "Don't you know who I am? I'm the one who—"

"You're . . . you're . . ." In the excitement of the chase, Homer had forgotten his client's name. He snapped his fingers next to his ear, hoping to awaken his memory.

"Bent. I'm Bentley Conniston," said the soul.

"Bent! It is you," said Homer, wrapping his arms around Bent, and squeezing him to his chest.

"Is Muriel getting my letters?" asked Bent, his voice muffled by Homer's feathers.

"She got the first one," said Homer. "You might say the second one's cruising that way this very minute."

The sound of angry moans came bouncing along the floors, and Homer had to make a decision. "Sorry, Bent, I have to go," he said. "Don't worry though. We're going to help your father."

Bent's brow wrinkled questioningly.

"Oh, I forgot. You don't know about that. Well, never mind. Don't forget to write."

"Hey! Not that way!" cried Bent. But it was too late.

Homer collided with something that felt like a wall, but was really the chest of a mammoth moan. Fortunately the moan's intellect was not nearly so imposing as his body, for it gave Homer time to pull what he later described as one of his best stunts ever.

"Hello, sir," said Homer, quickly. And the moan merely stared at him. "I'm taking a survey this morning concerning pre-Rebellion wingwear. I'm sure you've heard of it. It's the latest fashion rage. Would you mind answering a few questions?"

"You look like an angel to me," said the moan.

"Why, I happen to be modeling part of the new line today! Stunning, aren't they?" minced Homer, turning to admire his wings. "On the other hand, *you,* sir, look like you could use a new set of flappers yourself. Oh, but for someone with shoulders as broad as yours, it could be a difficult fit. Here," said Homer. And he held up the clipboard. "Let's skip the questions! Why don't we just have a look at our sizes."

And when the big moan glanced down at the clipboard, Homer slammed it hard into his face.

"Sorry. We're out of XL's," he shouted, dashing off through the low doorway behind the bellowing moan.

Once he was alone again, Homer realized he'd made a grave mistake. He was no longer in the labyrinth of halls, where he could drive the devils crazy with his superior maneuvering. He was in a vast cavern. In the center of the cavern was a lake. Upon that lake was an island. On that island were two figures. Homer stepped between two boulders and turned his ear toward the voice that slithered across the water.

"Citizen Pogromme—it was a stroke of genius to have this thing installed," came Satan's voice from his office on the island.

"Thank you, sir. I trust you find it useful."

"I do. And then some. Why, I believe it's paid for itself in a single morning."

"Oh, really? How's that, sir?"

Satan paused and relished the moment.

"For starters, Pogromme, we have the true identity of the leak—his name, his occupation, his motives for such treason. *And,*" punctuated Satan by raising his voice a notch, "dear Pogromme, we have him on video. He was caught red handed in the middle of his treachery. His name is Stan, and he's a mail clerk. I always did suspect those bathrooms," he added.

"That was a good idea to remove the lights, your excellency," said Pogromme. "But, sir, we closed the post office last night. How did the fool expect to get a word to heaven?"

"Oh, this is the part I like the most," smirked Satan. And he clicked his teeth together. "It seems the low king of heaven has sent one of his fliers disguised as a postal worker to carry the letters back to heaven in the absence of our own couriers. He's being hunted as we speak. I have him on tape, too, if you're interested. When I enhanced the image with my voice activator, I saw his wings protruding from his jacket."

From his hiding place between the boulders, Homer heard the words. He pulled the uncomfortable postal garment back over his wings and hunkered farther down in the dark.

Back on the island, a light had gone on in Pogromme's dark mind. He thought of Spleen's telegram from Ellenbach just that morning—the part about the *i*'s that stuck and Spleen's theory that the letters were being written by someone in the press. *How unfortunate that Spleen will never receive recognition for his discovery,* thought Pogromme.

"So, you saw all this on the monitors, sir?" he asked, slyly.

"Of *course* I saw it on the monitors, you nitwit! Where else would I have seen it?" raged Satan.

"Then, you know everything," continued Pogromme. "Stan's part in it all, the angel's appearance, the . . ." And at this point, Pogromme chose his words carefully, to position himself for maximum reward should Spleen's hunch prove correct. "The *author* of the letters?" he asked.

"That's the *one* thing I don't know," screamed Satan. "And if I've told those numbskulls in the mail room once, I've told them a thousand times to never let a letter pass without a return address. If there's one thing I can't stand, it's incompetence!"

"Well, my lord," said Pogromme, "have you considered the possibility that Stan was merely passing them on for someone else, and that the true author's name will have to be discovered in some other way?"

"And how am I to do *that*, Citizen Pogromme?"

"Perhaps, *I* can be of some help. Did you happen to notice if the *i*'s on the envelope were slightly raised?"

"The *i*'s?" muttered Satan. "How should I—"

"Here," said Pogromme, moving toward a keyboard on the far side of the monitors. "Let me refresh your mind. Just tell me when to stop."

Pogromme spun the day's videotape backward until Satan shouted for him to go back a few frames.

"Warm. Warmer. Whoa," shouted Satan. And then his mouth fell open when he saw Muriel's letter in Homer's hand. There in the words MURIEL CONNISTON ROBINS were three distinctly raised *i*'s.

Pogromme beamed.

"You'll notice they're done on a stock typewriter, sir, which means the culprit comes from within your press corps. Does that help in any way?" asked Pogromme, as humbly as he could, considering he had stolen another demon's credit.

"How did you know this?" gasped Satan. "Why, if there were any place higher than chief of staff, I'd promote you today."

"A larger office would be nice," hinted Pogromme. "And maybe some extra sick days."

"Anything, Pogromme, anything," said Satan, elated. "With this stroke of genius, we've nearly solved the puzzle."

"*And,* I might add," said Pogromme, "we've nearly discovered what the Enemy finds so interesting about these letters."

"Pogromme, you're a god," sang Satan. "And to think, I was about to have poor Stan tortured for the information."

"Really, sir. It was nothing," said Pogromme. "But if you wish, I could follow up on Stan anyway, just to see if my hypothesis is correct."

"That won't be necessary," said Satan.

"Then I'll start right away, tracking down the author of these treacherous letters."

"No, no, no, Pogromme. I've got much more important work for a demon of your stature. Your assignment is to immediately join the chase for the intruder, whoever he is, though it's quite probable they've already caught him," declared Satan. He turned his face toward a small microphone on the base of the largest monitor and spoke in a monotone voice.

"Run a background check on frames 138 and 139, then print. By the way, Pogromme," said Satan. "Where are your three sidekicks?"

"Greedo, Spleen, and the Fat One, sir?"

"Yes, those are the ones."

"Well, sir, they're—"

"Wait a minute," interrupted Satan. "Something's coming up. Do pull those for me, will you Pogromme? Ah, yes, and here's the image enhancements on the screen. Let's have a look."

Pogromme walked to the printer, tore the pages from its teeth, then crouched next to Satan. The first image was of a blurred figure balancing on the back of a toilet bowl. The other one—a classified photo from central files—showed a grinning, golden surfer hanging ten on a cumulus cloud. And though the light in the cavern was almost too dim to make out any features, soon Satan began to chuckle.

"Homer S. Windkook. I remember him," he said. "He was—"

Satan stopped abruptly. He didn't like to think of his previous life, much less speak of it. Pogromme pointed to the background check and finished the thought for him.

"Says here on OldenScan he's still a waiter after all these ages. An obvious underachiever, no doubt, sir," offered Pogromme, seething at the sight of the angel who'd recently helped humble him on a cloud.

"Yes, and he's about to make the underachievement of all time, as soon as we catch him."

At that, employer and employee shared a good laugh. Then as Pogromme read farther in OldenScan, his smile became a scowl.

"Seems he's teamed up, also, with five others from the Cloud Cafe on some sort of assignment. The leader is a certain Captain Alistair Conrad Evermore," growled Pogromme.

"The infamous Captain Evermore?" asked Satan. "I didn't know he was still active. Do I hear venom in your voice, Citizen Pogromme? After all, he *has* bested you on past occasions," teased Satan.

"And he ran from me another time," hissed Pogromme.

"You know what they say. Once a runner, always a runner. I'm sure Evermore is still a coward. The way I see it, you have a personal interest in catching this Homer character. Why don't you join in the fun? What do you say? Hmm? Go catch an angel and chew his wings off. It'll be good for you."

"Let's just say I have a score to settle in Ellenbach first," muttered Pogromme.

At mention of the town's name, Satan nearly choked.

"What did you say?" he said.

"I said, I have a score to settle in Ellenbach."

"Ellenbach? What does Ellenbach have to do with this?" Satan demanded.

"That's where these letters are going. You see, your excellency—"

"That's where they're *going*? What do you mean, that's where they're going?"

"It's really very simple—"

"How long have you known this, Pogromme? You never said anything about this before."

"Well, on the day we first discovered the leak, sir, my squad was on a routine check of Ellenbach—"

"You've known this since the leak?" ranted Satan, who was beginning to get a very bad feeling about all of this.

"Yes, sir, I can explain, sir," said Pogromme nervously. "We happened to be on a routine flyby, when we noticed a disturbance below."

"A disturbance . . ."

"That's right, sir. So we decided to make a low pass for good measure."

"A low pass . . ."

"Yes, sir. For good measure. Anyway, that's when we saw Captain Evermore and his bunch interacting with some trivial mailman—"

"Trivial mailman?" screamed Satan. "You idiot, Pogromme. Show me that frame again."

"Sir?" said Pogromme.

"The frame, blast it. The frame. The one with that Muriel woman's name on it!"

Pogromme rewound the tape until he found the picture.

"AAACCCKKK!" shrieked Satan, when he saw her name again. When he had seen the picture the first time he had been concentrating on the raised *i*'s, and overlooked the woman's maiden name.

"I knew it! I knew it all along," said Satan.

"Knew what, sir?" asked Citizen Pogromme timidly.

"Use your brains for once," said Satan. "You don't suppose that dog in heaven would go to all this trouble lifting a ban on his own postal laws, jeopardizing the efficiency of his blessed Cloud Cafe, and sending waiters dressed as postal inspectors all the way to hell just for the fun of it, do you?"

"You have a point, sir. But I—"

"Of course I have a point!" screamed Satan. And here is where Homer began to inch ever so cautiously toward the opening through which he entered the cavern.

"You have no idea what you've done, do you, Pogromme?"

"Not exact . . . er . . . not . . . well, no . . . no, sir . . . I guess I . . ."

"You have just succeeded in paving the way for the

Enemy's insane gospel to spring afresh in Ellenbach through the mouth of Walter Conniston! What do you have to say to that?!"

"I . . . I'm terribly sorry, sir."

"You're terribly sorry. You're terribly sorry. No. That's not it. That's not what you are. I'll tell you what you are. Do you want to know what you are, Citizen Pogromme?"

"I'd rather not, sir."

"You're a greenhorn nincompoop. A dunderheaded ninny. A boob. A dolt. A silly, stupid, expendable duffer of a demon."

"Well, if you don't mind my saying so, sir, it can't be all that bad."

"It can't be all that bad, he says. It can't be all that bad. That's an easy thing for you to say," said Satan, who by now had begun to curse fluently. "Aaagh! The man's own *son* has been sending these letters!"

"Is there anything I can do, your excellency?" asked Pogromme, cautiously.

"You can catch that long-haired angel and boil him in the same pot with Stan and Bentley Allen Conniston."

"Yes, sir. Right away, sir," said Pogromme, as he crumpled the photos of Homer, whirled, and threw them as far as he could into the oily lake surrounding Satan's island. The first one sank almost the moment it hit the water. But the second one slowly unfolded and floated there like a brilliant sunfish.

"Don't let me down," said Satan. "Catch that angel—or this could be the end of a promising career for you, Citizen Pogromme," said Satan.

"Yes, sir. You can count on me, sir. There's not a single thing to worry about. Why, I'm sure when—"

Suddenly Dice and a hundred other demons came streaming into the cavern. Homer, who had been crawling on his belly toward the opening, saw them only just in time to back into the shadows.

"Your excellency," shouted Dice, as he came to the

edge of the water with the remnants of the corkboard still dangling from his wrist. "Your excellency," he repeated, "the intruder, whom you so wisely spotted on your monitors, has eluded us."

"Eluded you, has he?" said Satan from his island. "Well, perhaps the following bit of conformity will find its way into your thick skulls, and will not eeelude you again. You are to bow when you come into my presence," thundered Satan. Immediately the shores of that great cavern, which by now Homer could make out clearly in the light of Satan's monitors, became dotted with obedient moans.

"Now, little demon, what is it?" asked Satan.

"The angel has escaped, your highness," said Dice, with his face to the sand.

"He can't be far," said Pogromme. "I assure you, we'll—"

"Look," said Satan. "What was that? I saw something."

Then, as far as Homer was concerned, the cavern may as well have been flooded with the sun. For when a horde of yellow eyes turned in his direction, there was nothing in the room more obvious than his own bright, celestial wings.

"After him," thundered Satan. "Do whatever it takes to ruin that mailman. Tempt him. Harass him. Sift him. Sort him. But don't allow another shred of paper into Walter Conniston's bag! I will not have an evangelist delivering the mail in Ellenbach."

# ~ 13 ~

Roaming in thought over the Universe, I saw the
little that is Good steadily hastening towards
immortality,
And the vast all that is call'd Evil I saw hastening
to merge itself and become lost and dead.

—Walt Whitman, *Roaming in Thought*

THE stream outside the Cloud Cafe has an earthy tint
to it, not because it is dirty but because it is so thoroughly stained by the seeds, needles, nuts, and spores it
gathers along its run to the Crystal Sea. There it empties
into the larger body of water, sinking, mingling, merging
with a million other tributaries that have wandered
through the universe and finally found their way home.
From above, the sea looks blue, the traditional color of
water and the color schoolchildren are taught to use to
describe it. Consequently, this teaching leads to blue
lagoons, blue harbors, blue brooks—which babble, of
course—and bays, breakers, brimming waterways,
coves, gulfs, rivers, and rills, all rushing off somewhere
and always in the deepest blue.

But the Crystal Sea is more than blue. It is a rich,
translucent world of colors, much like the boundary

waters of Canada. Water there—as it is everywhere—is the color of whatever is in it.

In the shallows there are crawfish—hard, ocher-bellied, and enormous—spurting backward and stirring up a brilliant yellowish green cloud at the hint of a nearby swimmer. When they finally come to rest a yard or so away, all that can be seen are two long, vermilion feelers jutting from the cloud. Along the reefs go the goggle-eye. Their red orbs pierce the shadows. Lillies send their white shoots down into the mud, where the great pike cruise like subs. Between the rounded boulders live the smallmouth, black blips on a background of sienna. Nearby, the walleye patrol the yellow gravel bars. Their milky eyes roam to and fro. They are amused by the scarlet-headed mergansers who dive with their babies, teaching them to swim and hunt. All around there are the deepening shades that will not be defined by the single word *blue*.

The morning after her startling discovery, Muriel sat on a rock by the sea with Bent's letter in her hands. Beside her was Jesus. Above them spread the branches of a mesquite tree. Farther off on the beach was a group of men and angels playing volleyball in the sand.

"I've been meaning to tell You something since our breakfast yesterday," said Muriel.

"Oh?" replied Jesus, as if surprised. "My ear is an open door."

"I'm not sure where to begin."

"Why not the beginning? I find that best for jumping off into almost anything."

"Right. Of course," agreed Muriel. "Then, I should start with an apology. I really am sorry for the trouble my father has caused You all these years."

"Your father is no trouble at all," said Jesus. "On the contrary, I'm quite glad to bear him up. You see, Muriel, inside Walter is a gift of incalculable worth—*evangelism*. You know the meaning, don't you?"

"'Messenger,' I believe," said Muriel.

"'Of good news,' to be exact," replied Jesus. "Your father was given an irrepressible desire to bear glad tidings to his neighbors. He's tried to repress the gift. He's made himself miserable by replacing it with substitutes or ignoring it altogether. But in the end, he is—and always will be—a messenger of the kingdom. The real challenge is getting him to believe in the message again."

"I see."

"There's always hope," said Jesus, plucking a sprig of mesquite from an overhanging branch and handing the thorny thing to Muriel. "First, however, your father must get over the wrongheaded notion that pain and I are mutually exclusive. After all, I live quite close to pain— sometimes so close I feel the bite of it in My hands and feet."

Cautiously, Muriel turned the mesquite sprig with her fingers.

"Your father must accept his children's sudden departure from his life. He must come to grips with the fact that pain and I can *both* reside within him. No need to discard one for the other."

"But I can understand what he's going through," said Muriel.

"I'm sure you can," said Jesus. "But can you imagine if your own dear Jack had gone the way of Walter?"

Muriel thought of the man she once called husband, and she smiled.

"You loved him deeply, didn't you?" said Jesus.

"Yes. And I'm glad he has not been bitter."

"Or worse, cynical. Cynicism dines on the cynic, you know. In your father's case, it has nearly pecked him to the bone. Which reminds Me, Muriel. There was a certain blessing in your pain not being a lengthy one. Walter's, on the other hand, has been quite long."

"A quarter of his life, almost."

"Yes—almost. However, if you could look past your father's pain for just a moment, to a place in the universe where the fire is never quenched, and the worm never dies, then you will see what true suffering is."

"I can't stand the thought," said Muriel, closing her eyes.

"A thought or two of hell can cure a Christian's self-pity at a glance. And *that* is the cure your father needs."

"Which is to say . . . ?"

"Walter must stop hoarding the great gift I placed within him. He must see hell in all its severity and relinquish his silence to help other people avoid damnation."

"How can I bear this?" said Muriel, turning away.

"I will bear it with you, Muriel," said Jesus. "Truly, I have not ceased to pray since that day your father's pain began. And I *will not* cease until I hear My name fall from his lips with reverence. That day is coming soon. Mark My words. In time, your father will be a happy evangelist again. Then, neither snow, nor rain, nor heat, nor gloom of night will stay him from spreading the gospel in Ellenbach."

"I believe You," said Muriel. "I only wish it weren't taking Homer so long with the mail."

"Be patient, Muriel," said Jesus. "Difficult assignments have been known to detain an angel. Chaney has been here, though."

"He has?" said Muriel.

"Yes. He was sent back early from Ellenbach. I saw him in the cafe just this morning."

"Is there trouble?" asked Muriel.

"It seems our team members are a bit confused about their specific roles. At any rate, François forgot to stay behind to receive the new letters, and Chaney volunteered to go back to look for Homer."

"So, he's gone then. I'd hoped to hear how Father was doing," said Muriel, despondently.

"No, no. Chaney's still here."

Muriel brightened.

"He is? Oh, do tell me where. I must talk with him," she blurted.

"Last I saw of him, he was having pie with Gladys Pickens in the Cloud Cafe. You can probably still catch him there if you run fast."

"Thank You," said Muriel, slipping off the rock upon which she sat, and nearly falling straight into Jesus' lap. "I'm sorry, Lord. Please excuse me. I had wanted to talk . . . *truly* . . . and I still do . . . but at the moment, well, You can see that I really must be off, and—"

"Be off then," laughed Jesus.

At a sprint, Muriel turned and started upstream, leaving Bent's letter with Jesus and her footprints along the mossy path.

At the Cloud Cafe, T. Chaney Goodwin had talked more than he intended, and now he was explaining to Gladys why he couldn't deliver her mail to Ellenbach.

"I don't see why you can't," said Gladys. "The arrangement seems to be working out well for the Connistons."

"Shhh," said Chaney. "I asked you n-n-not to s-say that name so loud."

But it was too late. Gladys was a very large woman with a very large voice. And when she said *Conniston*, every soul who ever lived in Ellenbach and happened to be eating an early lunch that morning in the Cloud Cafe turned to look in her direction.

"Conniston? I knew a Conniston once," said Foster Jenson II.

"Yes, and if you're anything like me, it makes you exceedingly glad to hear that Chaney has been delivering letters to Walt Conniston. He will probably do the same for us. Isn't that right, Chaney?"

"Gladys, p-p-please," said Chaney. "I-I've only delivered one."

Foster had his eyes closed. He mumbled *Conniston* over and over, trying to recall the elusive first name to which he could attach it.

"Conniston. Conniston. Willy? Nope. Weldon? Uh-uh. That's not it."

"*Walter*, Foster. The name was Walter," offered Leta Ray. "He became a letter carrier the year after you turned the bank over to your son and moved up here."

Foster's face brightened.

"Walt Conniston? You mean the deacon?"

"Uh-hm."

"Never kept much of a balance in his account. But he brought me my mail on time. And he sure could preach," said Foster.

"That's him. He would have made a good one in the pulpit if he wasn't needed so much out on the sidewalk."

Chaney put his head in his hands and tried not to think about where this conversation was headed. *Oh, this can't be happening to me*, he thought. But of course it was. And of course things were going to get worse.

"Muriel Conniston is getting to write to her father? That's terrific," chimed Clinton Sanger, looking straight at the pale country angel.

"Well, she isn't exactly wrrr-riting *him*," said Chaney.

"Then, what exactly *is* she doing?" asked Gladys.

"I, w-w-well, you s-see, it's like this . . ."

Then for the next hour, Chaney tried to wriggle himself out of the mess he'd gotten into. And all along, Gladys tried to wriggle him back into delivering a letter of her own into Walter's bag. She'd already planned on addressing it: To the Honorable Judge Roy Pickens from His Honor's Buttercup.

"O-k-k-kay! I'll deliver it," blurted Chaney, when he could stand no more of her pressure. But he saw absolutely no reason whatsoever why he should take some trivial stock tip for Foster Jenson II to his son, and even less reason to be an errand boy for Clinton Sanger. There were plenty of fathers in heaven who looked back upon life and wished they could have done one or two things differently with their kids. "No. A thousand t-times, no," said Chaney. "I will n-not take perfume to the Sanger woman."

But in the end, Chaney left for earth before Muriel had

reached the cafe. And in his possession was a small satchel of letters, the stock tip, a fruitcake, an eighth-ounce bottle of Chloe Narcisse, a book of matches, a pocket watch, a tie clip, a handcrafted ballpoint pen, and a general disdain for being a popular angel, and a loose-lipped one, as well.

On a grassy knoll that rises above the campanile by the Eastern Wall, Jesus sat and watched a grumbling Chaney disappear toward the blue-green planet. He plucked a clover leaf, put it in His mouth, and called to a robin flitting by. The bird came and perched on the sandals He had kicked off in the soft, green grass.

"Hello, Robin Twittertail," said Jesus to the bird.

Robin chirped and came closer.

"How are things with your family?"

This time, Robin answered with a happy string of notes.

"Good," said Jesus. "I think about them daily. Would you like a bit of bread," He asked, taking from His pocket a loaf from the cafe and extending it toward the bird.

Robin fluttered to the cuff of Jesus' robe. He flashed his little, black eyes at Jesus and pecked the bread.

"Here, take all you want. Take some for the others. There's never any shortage."

Robin pecked again, then flew away singing.

"That's what I enjoy about you," said Jesus as Robin Twittertail glided out onto the currents above the Eastern Wall. "You sing the song I placed in you, regardless of your circumstances."

Then He looked down toward the planet—past a network of shooting stars and astral debris, past moons and meteors and cloud cover of varying thicknesses, past a knot of air traffic and the clutter of the air waves, past coastlines, and state lines and county lines, and all kinds of lines—straight into the town of Ellenbach, where He saw a common mail carrier. And He said to Himself, "But Walter's circumstances must get harder before he sings again."

# ~ 14 ~

*There is only one real tragedy in a woman's life. The fact that the past is always her lover, and her future invariably her husband.*

—Oscar Wilde, *An Ideal Husband, III*

ON Cistern Street, Walter dug in the morning sun until he hit limestone and the Pickleman twins came padding by with two big channel cats strung out on a coat hanger. James wore jeans cut off at the knees. His pockets showed holes three fingers wide, and his shirt barely covered his navel. Johnny wore the same, with bigger holes. Both were barefoot. Walter had hoped they would walk on by. But they didn't.

"Morning, Mr. Conniston," the twins said in unison.

"Morning boys," said Walter, looking from one end of the street to the other, and wishing that somehow Eunice Honeycutt's gout would flare up and and make her walk take longer than usual today. "Looks like you've got dinner for tonight."

"No, sir. We don't eat whiskerfish," said James.

"These are for the Peets and Judge Pickens," said Johnny. "They eat anything. You ought to see Earl Peet put a whole gourd in his mouth."

"I'm sure that's something," said Walter. "Did you catch any crawdads?"

"Couple," said James.

"Caught them on an old piece of bacon, on the hook of this coat hanger," said Johnny.

"What did you do with them?" asked Walter.

"Crushed them with a rock," said the boys grinning.

Walter acknowledged their ingenuity with a smile, wishing for his own childhood.

"Sorry I can't talk just now, boys," he said quickly. "I've got this box to put in for your new neighbor."

"She's pretty," said James.

"Yes, she is. Anyway boys, then I've got the mail to deliver and other things to do. So I haven't got time to *chat*," said Walter. "But next time you're passing out catfish, remember me . . . all right?"

"All right," said the twins. They padded away, drawing a wet line down the center of the sidewalk with the tail of their fish.

The sun was directly overhead as Walter tamped the last bit of dirt around the metal pole and wandered toward the gate in the hedge that separated the front yard from the back. Quietly, he released the latch and entered Marla's private world. On the brick patio behind the house, he found her rigging two fishing rods with heavy test line. She had changed into a pair of shorts and a T-shirt. Around her golden hair she had tied a striped ribbon to keep it from falling into her work. By her side, a garden hose gurgled at the base of a tomato plant.

"Finished already?" said Marla, looking up at the sound of Walter's chukkas shuffling through the long grass.

"Yes ma'am," said Walter. He forced himself to appear interested in Marla's tackle box until she looked back at the knot she was tying. Again, he was mesmerized by her beauty. "Phew," he exclaimed as he wiped his brow, and sat down in a lawn chair.

"It's a hot one, isn't it?" said Marla. "Say, how about that Coke? Or water? Or is there something else that sounds better?"

"Water will do just fine," said Walter.

Marla set the rod down and reached for the hose behind her.

"Here you go," she said. "It's not polite of me, but it's the coldest on the block. I guess the man who built this place had his own well dug. Don't ask me how he got past code."

Walter took the hose and drank loudly. His throat was parched, and already his shoulders ached from the digging. He could imagine how they'd feel in the morning when he woke up next to Donna and . . . Quickly, Walter brushed the thought away. He swallowed one last time and set the hose down in the grass.

"What kind of knot are you using?" he asked.

"It doesn't matter for catfish," said Marla. "At least that's what my father used to tell me. I can still hear his voice on the Blue Fork at midnight."

Marla cleared her throat and looked out over the rooftops.

"Marlie-girl. That's what he called me whenever my mother wasn't around. He'd say, Marlie-girl, most fish that are prowlers aren't very discriminating. They just keep moving until they find something to fill the hole in their stomachs. So forget the knot, and just tie on the bait.

"I can tie all sorts of knots, though," Marla added quickly. "Let's see. Fisherman's bend. Angler's knot. Barrel knot. Some people call it the blood knot, but not my father. He'd say, Marlie-girl, the sport of catfishing is messy enough without using uncivilized terms."

Walter laughed stiffly at the impersonation.

"Anyway," said Marla. "That's sort of how he sounded back then. A husky man with a husky voice, sitting there in the moonlight on the big, lazy Blue. I never could imitate him."

"I bet you miss him," said Walter.

"Pretty nice tomato plants for this time of the season, wouldn't you say?" said Marla, dancing nimbly away from the topic, as if she'd practiced the move for years.

"As good as any I've seen," said Walter.

For a long time it was quiet except for the cicadas droning slowly. Marla acted absorbed with attaching a weight to one of the lines. Walter drummed his fingers against the armrest of the chair.

"Did I ever ask if you had kids of your own?" asked Walter after a while.

"Yes, you did," said Marla. "Yesterday. And I told you I've never been married."

Of course, had Walter known that this response was a carefully choreographed step in the dance that Marla used to protect herself, he might have asked the question in a different way. But he let it go.

"So what brought you here?" he asked.

"To Ellenbach?" said Marla.

Walter nodded.

"Oh, not much. A hunch about a job, I guess. A good feeling about a place and a people. Would you like some lunch?" asked Marla, waltzing away to even safer ground where she could banter and be herself again.

"No, thank you. I really have got to be going," said Walter.

"That's too bad, because it's already made. And there's no way in the world I can eat it all."

"That's kind of you," said Walter. "But—"

"Oh, come on," protested Marla. "Do you *have* to go? What's the hurry? Look, I've got two rods here, and I was thinking we could go fishing."

"I really shouldn't ma'am," said Walter. "Not with all that mail to deliver."

"There're some awful big channel cats in Coon Creek, I hear," said Marla.

"I don't know, ma'am. I—"

"I told you once to stop ma'aming me," said Marla, almost angrily. "And could you forget about the mail for a while?" Not wanting to appear too anxious, she directed Walter's attention to the picnic basket that sat in the shade of the steps. "I've got turkey sandwiches," she said. "Swiss on rye ring a bell?"

Walter swallowed and said nothing.

"What's the matter with you, Walter Dale Conniston?" blurted Marla.

The weight of his full name caught Walter off guard. He sat up stiff in his chair, not knowing whether to fear this woman who was young enough to be his daughter or to let himself fall farther into her charms. At any rate, it wasn't normal for a stranger to know a thing like this about him.

"How did you get my middle name?" said Walter abruptly. "And how do you know I like turkey and Swiss on rye?"

"The same legal way I learned everything else about you, Walter," said Marla. "I asked."

Walter leaned back, his eyes growing wide as Marla inched across the patio toward him. The hose still gurgled in the grass beneath his chair. On the telephone wire above, a mourning dove sang softly. And out across the neighborhood, Walter thought he heard the sound of a hundred mailboxes slammed shut by the hand of a hundred angry customers.

"People have plenty to say on the topic of Walter Conniston," said Marla. "I just mention your name, and they shake their heads like something awful has come about in your life."

She was three feet from him now. He could smell her perfume; he could almost detect the precise spots where she'd scented her neck. He swallowed hard.

"Are you going to tell me what it is that makes you sad, Walter? Or am I going to have to say the words for you?" said Marla as she closed the distance between them.

Walter looked at Marla kneeling now at his knees. He saw the image of a child again, the one he'd seen the day before when she was standing on the porch. He pushed the chair back and stood up.

"I don't want to talk now," he said. "I don't have to. You haven't got a right to know those things." He headed for the gate in the hedge, but Marla beat him to it.

"Wait a minute," she said. "If you have a right to ask me whether I have children, or if I miss the only man who ever took me fishing or not, then I have a few rights, too."

"Excuse me, Miss Coe," said Walter. "I can't stand here all day. I've got a job to do. Please," he pleaded as he reached for the gate latch.

Marla put her foot at the bottom of the gate, pinning it shut.

"And I have a job, too," she said. "I have to find out what it is about those two graves at the edge of town that makes you go back there week after week."

Walter's face turned red.

"Have you been following me, lady?" asked Walter angrily.

"Yes, I have," declared Marla. "And I've been close enough to see the names on those two stones, too."

"That isn't right," said Walter. "That isn't your place."

"*Muriel Joyce,* and *Bentley Allen.* They're beautiful names. They must have been beautiful children," said Marla. She kept her foot against the gate.

"Let me pass," bellowed Walter. "Let me pass, so I can—"

"So you can what? So you can keep on running? So you can pretend you have no need for love anymore?"

"I've got needs," shouted Walter, no longer caring whether Cistern Street slept on or woke to the sound of his voice. "I've got needs for love, but I'm just not right inside about it."

"Exactly," said Marla. "You don't have the guts to try again."

"That's not what I meant," said Walter.

"What did you mean?" asked Marla, her thin nose flaring in the afternoon sun.

Walter didn't answer her. Instead, he backtracked toward the patio and ran around to the other side of the yard to see if there was another exit. But there was a solid row of bushes on that side of the house. Behind him, Marla kept pace.

"You can't keep running, Walter," she said.

Walter bolted toward the back of the yard. He saw a shed and a woodbox where he could get a leg up on the fence and disappear into the alley that ran the length of Cistern.

"Running can't change the way you feel," came Marla's voice.

Walter was nearly to the shed.

"Walter!" shouted Marla. And Walter stopped.

A squirrel leaped in the tender, topmost branches of the oak that sheltered the shed. It skittered down to larger forks, then to the trunk, and finally down into the alley where it froze momentarily, looking back at the man and the woman. Then it dashed away.

"Running can't bring your children back," said Marla.

"Leave me alone!" shouted Walter, keeping his face toward the shed. He could not escape this woman's pull. He was trapped in her presence.

"It can't change the fact that your kids are gone," said Marla.

"I can't change that either!"

"You could try to love again," she added. "You could take a chance."

"Chance?" said Walter whirling around to face Marla. "You don't know what chance is! You've never taken a chance like I took! You've never tried to hang on to something with all your might and have it ripped away from you! You've never begged God to—"

Walter cut his sentence short. He knew right away he was wrong. There's a pain mourners recognize in one another's eyes. Marla's was different from his. It was much older, perhaps less jagged. Nevertheless, her pain was present. And there it was, framed with golden hair and accented with flashing eyes, yet no less painful than his own.

"How am *I* supposed to love again?" said Walter, beating his chest.

"I told you," said Marla. "You have to take a chance."

"I can't," said Walter turning away toward the shed again.

"Yes, you can! You can let somebody love you. You can let *me* love you," said Marla.

There was no turning back. She had thrown it down now, this proposition for Walter's ears, and for Cistern's if its residents happened to be listening. Risking rumor, she went to Walter by the shed and put her arms around him.

"You can love me back, if you want," said Marla, sounding more like a little girl than a woman. The nudge against Walter's side made him feel both fear and fire at the same time. Not knowing what to do with his hands, he let them settle roughly at the small of Marla's back.

"This isn't proper," said Walter.

"It's not proper to go on living without love, either," said Marla.

"But it wouldn't be right."

"It's always right when someone who's lost gets found."

In the old mimosa by the side of Marla's house sat Greedo, Spleen, and Pater Mordo, watching with glee.

"Oh, these humans are so pitifully mushy," yawned Spleen. "It's too bad Dice and his crew were called away. They could have made things interesting. I can't imagine why we've been posted in this town since yesterday. I'm ready to get on with my promotion. After all, what could one, miserable postman possibly have to do with—"

"Look out," came a familiar voice from the sky.

It was Citizen Pogromme, preceded by a laughing, speeding Homer, in whose hands were the most recent letters from Bent and Muriel.

"Get up," screamed Pogromme. "Draw your swords. Don't let him reach that mailbag!"

"What's he saying?" said Spleen, straining to read his commander's lips.

In the junipers across the street from 602 Cistern, Ace saw Homer first.

"We've got incoming. François, you and Albert fly tactical," said Ace, forgetting that he addressed waiters, rather than soldiers.

"Excuse me, monsieur?" said François, clearly confused.

"Move it troopers," said Ace. His zoe was pumping madly, and for an instant he saw himself in ancient frays gone by. "Get up there and control the air. Interdict that moan."

François and Albert sat clueless.

"Don't let Pogromme reach the ground," shouted Ace, shoving the two angels out of the bushes. "Where is Chaney? He ought to be back by now."

Behind Ace, Doc cowered against the side of the house.

"Come on, Doc," said Ace, shaking his friend. "Snap out of it. I need you now."

"Too fast," cried Doc. "This is happening much too fast. I might have been ready tomorrow. I'll fight tomorrow. Can't we put this off until tomorrow?"

"We can't put it off. There's a soul at stake in Ellenbach."

"But I'm not up to this. I need time. Just a little more time."

Ace lifted the angel by his armpits and stood him on his feet. "The fight is today. Here. Now."

The abruptness of Ace's actions startled Doc. Nevertheless, something in the captain's voice changed him, too. Over Ace's shoulder the veteran surgeon saw Greedo, Spleen, and Pater Mordo scrambling over the ridge of Marla's roof. Greedo took to the air immediately, while Spleen spied the mailbag below and swung down on the gutter toward it. Doc blinked his eyes. He shook his head. He heard the clash of long ago battles.

"They're messing with our bag," said Doc.

"That's it," said Ace, seeing the old fire in Doc's eyes.

"But they can't do that," said Doc.

"You're right," said Ace. "And for Walter's sake, *we* have to stop them. Now, I'm going to need close support by that garage over there. Can you give it to me?"

"You got it," said Doc.

"Come on, let's go," said Ace.

High in the air, Homer rode the wind currents like a succession of waves, up and down and across the face of them, driving Citizen Pogromme crazy. Homer had lost the other moans way back by the gates of hell and had long since flung his postal uniform over a Kansas wheat field. Now, it was just a matter of getting to the bag. He saw a small swell rising. He flew just ahead of it until he felt himself lifting and Citizen Pogromme's hot breath on his feet. Then he swept his wings back and rocketed down into the trough at Mach speed.

"Awesome," shouted Homer, with his bright locks flying.

"Wait 'til I get my claws on you," roared Pogromme.

Homer laughed and shot back toward the current's crest. There he spotted François, far to the left of him, doing battle in the clouds with Greedo. Below, Albert was trying to draw Citizen Pogromme off his target.

"Hey, pokey," yelled Albert.

Pogromme turned his head.

"I've seen centuries go by faster than you," said Albert. "What do you say? Think you can catch me?"

Citizen Pogromme gnashed his teeth and veered toward Albert.

"I'll get you later, long hair," he spat at Homer.

Back on the ground, Ace caught Spleen just as he reached the mailbag. He drove the moan hard into the garage door. Letters and packages spilled out onto the driveway. Then, he whirled to face the charge of Pater

Mordo. But just as Ace turned, he caught sight of Walter rushing around the corner of the house, heading straight for his overturned mailbag. Behind him followed Marla waving her arms, and saying something about being sorry for her forwardness.

"It's the wind again," said Walter. "Look at this mess. I'll be lucky if I still have a job come tomorrow."

"I'll help you pick up," offered Marla, dropping to her knees only inches from Spleen and having no idea how close she was to the spirit world.

"Here," Ace shouted, flinging his sword to Doc. "These chumps are soft. I won't be needing this."

"I can't use a sword, Captain," said Doc hesitantly. "I'm sworn to healing by the Soteric oath."

"Not when it comes to moans," shouted Ace, as Pater Mordo came at him with his eyes blazing.

Pater Mordo, who had taken a good deal longer than Spleen to get down from the roof, came at Ace with his eyes blazing. Straight through the postman the brutish demon charged. And all Walter ever knew of it was that he lost his footing for a moment, and caught a sudden foul whiff, which he guessed was Ellenbach's aging sewer system.

"Are you all right?" asked Marla when she saw Walter stumble. "You did work awful hard today. Sun may have gotten to you. You can stay if you want—and rest, that is. I won't bother you. Here, you can just sit here on the porch for a while."

"No, I'm fine. I'd best be on my way," said Walter.

Behind him rumbled Pater Mordo like a freight train full of fat. Ace held his ground until the last second. Then he dove low at the moan's ankles, chopping the legs from under the beast. Pater Mordo's chin hit the concrete with an awful *crack!* And he bounced into the begonias.

Spleen jumped to his feet, cursing. He leaped over Marla and rushed at Doc with a vengeance, having no idea how proficient a surgeon can be with a blade. The two spirits' swords clanged together once in the summer sun. Then Spleen thrust steel at his foe's stomach, missing the mark horribly, and exposing his profile in the process. In a flash, Doc amputated the demon's nose. Spleen gave a surprised little squeal and stumbled forward, colorless blood sputtering from the middle of his face. Doc recoiled and surveyed the first wound he had ever inflicted. Spleen didn't wait for a second blow. He snatched his nose from the driveway and sped down the street, howling in pain.

From the begonias, Pater Mordo saw his partner fleeing. In spite of his incompetence, he knew right away that it was to his advantage to do the same. Pater Mordo struggled up and waddled after his partner.

"Nice work," said Ace. "But we're not finished, yet. Look."

At the end of the driveway, Walter stood with his bag and stared at Marla.

"I'm a married man, ma'am," he began. "I *won't* be coming back."

Marla sat silently by the garage.

Above them, while Citizen Pogromme chased Albert, and François grappled with Greedo, Homer saw his chance to make a dive at the mailbag. Like a bolt of lightning, he streaked toward Walter. Instantly, Greedo saw the angel's plan. And Pogromme saw it, too.

"After him," shrieked Pogromme, too distracted with Albert to give chase himself.

Greedo sank his fangs one last time into François's wing for the pleasure of it before he darted after Homer. Below him, he saw his comrades retreating to hell. *"Cowards,"* he hissed. Then he dipped swiftly into Homer's back draft and cut the distance between them.

"Greedo thinks he'd like to chew the freaky bird," he growled, when he was just a yard or so behind Homer.

Below loomed Walter and his bag, growing bigger by the second. Homer grasped the letters tightly and stretched his arms toward his destination. "Steady," said Homer to himself. "Be cool! Just a few more feet."

Ace saw Greedo draw up close behind Homer with his mouth opening wide.

"Pull out! Pull out!" Ace shouted. But his orders were ignored.

Homer was nearly to the ground when Greedo bit his heel. Homer tried to spread his wings to slow his descent, but he lost control. He somersaulted once in the air and slammed into Eunice Honeycutt's pyracantha bush. Greedo's fate was worse. He hit the grille of an Oldsmobile and got stuck there, kicking and twitching until he finally ceased to move. As for Bent's and Muriel's letters, they landed face up in the grass next to the sidewalk, catching Walter's eye and stopping him in his tracks.

"What's wrong?" chided Marla, when she saw Walter hesitate over the letters. "If you're going to go, go. But don't hang around here any longer, making things worse."

Walter bent to look at the addresses. When he saw his children's names, he shook his head and took a step backward.

"This isn't real," mumbled Walter. "It can't be happening again." He looked around him, as if to verify whether other things were real or not, also. He stumbled into the Oldsmobile, felt its windows and ran his hand along the hood. He glanced back at the letters in the grass. Then, he zeroed in on Marla.

"You," Walter shouted. "You're the one who is bringing this on me." He was unaware that by then half the neighborhood's residents were standing on their porches or peering through windows, listening.

"Bringing what on you? I don't know what you're talking about," said Marla, going toward him on the driveway, while Cistern stared and an unseen angel struggled to free himself from a thorn bush.

"Get away from me, you witch woman!"

"Did you hear *that*?" gasped Lydia Peet to her husband. "He called her a witch woman."

"I heard it," said Otis Peet. "Walter said she's a witch woman." And the rumor threaded its way fast through the neighborhood.

"Walter said she's a witch woman."

"A what?"

"A witch woman."

"A rich woman? She doesn't look to me like she's got money."

"No, not rich. *Witch.* Walter said she's a *witch* woman."

"A witch woman?"

"That's what I've been saying, a witch woman."

"Oh, my. She seemed so normal. What's he doing with someone like her?"

"Beats me. Must be sparking her."

"Doesn't make sense. He's got a fine woman of his own at home."

"Tsk, tsk. All that pain of the past. It was just a matter of time before he did something crazy."

With a *smack* Albert's limp body landed on top of the Oldsmobile, just as Citizen Pogromme buzzed over the trees and landed on the roof of Judge Roy Pickens's house.

"Old friend," Pogromme shouted at Ace. "I see you've chased my squadron away temporarily. *And* you've managed to get your letters into the hands of that pitiful human. So, I thought I'd even up the score a little, Captain Evermore," he said, with a snarl. At that, Pogromme leaped on top of the car and hurled Albert across Marla's lawn, where he skidded to a halt. The neighbors all wondered why in the world Icky Shackleford's dog was barking at that empty patch of grass.

"You monster," yelled Ace at his foe on the roof.

"I take it you and your friend were close?" asked Pogromme, cruelly.

"Quick, Doc! Take Albert back to Jesus. Hurry!"

"It'll never work," said Pogromme, laughing. "Even Jesus can't fix everything. You saw what happened to Him at His own execution. And don't give me that watery tripe about His coming to life again. I certainly haven't seen Him lately. Besides, if I ever do, I'll give His nose a good thump."

"Go on, Doc. Just ignore him," whispered Ace.

Meanwhile, Homer had an awful scare. Each moment he had to endure the sight of Albert's wounded body, Homer's desire to silence the creep on the roof increased. He had just managed to get one of his arms unstuck from the pyracantha when he heard a voice behind him. His heart raced.

"Pssst," said the voice.

"Who's there?" said Homer.

"Wh-wh-what's going on here?"

"Chaney," exclaimed Homer. "Where have you been? Forget that. Just help me get loose. We can talk later."

"I c-can't," said Chaney. "I've g-g-got something to do first."

Chaney looked around until he spied the mailbag. It was on the sidewalk next to Walter, but it was close enough to the bush that Citizen Pogromme wouldn't be able to see him if he crawled to it. Chaney wriggled on his belly until he was next to the bag. From underneath one of his wings, he took his satchel.

"Wh-wh-why does this stuff always happen to m-me?" he muttered, as he placed the various items from former Ellenbachians into Walter's bag.

When the task was through, the entire neighborhood roared with the sound of Pogromme taking off for hell. He shook his fist at Homer. He cursed fluently. He beat the air so furiously with his huge, black wings that Wilbur Finch, who was a weather forecaster, said there was going to be a storm. Everyone believed him and shivered in the wind. But no one understood how a clear, blue sky could turn on them so quickly.

When Pogromme was gone, Chaney walked from behind the bush, acting as matter-of-fact as he could.

"I w-w-won't miss *him* too soon," said Chaney.

"Where have you been?" asked Ace, still breathing heavily. "We could have used you."

Behind him, François came down from the sky, rubbing the wounds on his wings where Greedo had bitten him. Now, all the angels, except for Doc and Albert who were winging fast for heaven, waited for Chaney's answer.

"I j-just, well, you see, there was this woman in the cafe. And—"

"Did you stop for a piece of pie, Chaney?" asked Ace.

Cistern was quiet, except for Walter's mumbling on the sidewalk. He kept saying "Get away" to Marla everytime she went near him to offer comfort, and the letters still lay where they had fallen. The neighbors wondered if Walter had finally cracked under the weight of his sorrow.

"Did you have a piece of pie, Chaney Goodwin?" repeated Ace.

"Y-y-yes, sir," said Chaney.

*Here it comes*, thought Homer.

Captain Alistair Conrad Evermore looked at Chaney and grinned. "What kind was it?" he asked.

"Excuse me, sir?" asked Chaney.

"What kind of pie did you have?"

"G-g-gooseberry, sir."

"It figures you'd pick my favorite. Come on. I can smell the Cloud Cafe clear down here. Circle up for prayer."

François helped Homer from the bush, and the four sweating angels formed a ring around Walter. Behind them, the neighbors disappeared into their houses— some to their ballgames and other TV shows, some to their telephones to spread the rumor about "the witch woman." Over his shoulder, Ace saw Marla watching sadly from her porch. He bowed his head and prayed.

"Jesus," he began. "You are high and lifted up. You are First. You are Last. You are all things In-between. Thank You for this victory. Our wings will not rest—neither will our swords sleep in our hands until Albert is restored, the tongue of Walter is loosed, and the one soul in Ellenbach—whoever it may be—is brought safely into Your kingdom. Amen."

"Amen," said the others.

"Now," said Ace, gazing down at Walter. "Let's leave our man alone with his letters. We can only pray he'll take them to heart."

"Wait a moment, monsieur," said François, sniffing at the mailbag.

Chaney ducked his head and froze.

"I don't remember any perfume in that bag," continued François. Being a connoisseur of French accoutrements, he was always aware when he detected one.

"There's no time for that," said Ace, pointedly, "we must hurry home. Jesus is sure to have new orders for us. Besides, I'm starved. Chaney Goodwin?"

"Yes, C-Captain?"

"I've just got to know one more thing," said Ace, as the angels shot heavenward.

*Oh no*, thought Chaney, holding his breath. *He knows I put those things in the mailbag.*

"Did you have a scoop of ice cream, too, with your pie?" asked Ace.

"Y-y-yes, sir," said Chaney. And he exhaled, thankfully.

"That's what I thought," said Ace, licking his lips. "Well, now, all the more reason for haste." The clouds parted as Ace and his company passed through them and then beyond.

Cistern was still again. But over on Mulberry Court, Donna had found the boot box in the attic, and on Troost . . . something had driven Fern the Airedale mad.

# ~ 15 ~

*Oh, what a tangled web we weave,*
*When first we practice to deceive!*

—*Sir Walter Scott, Marmion, VI*

WITHOUT saying good-bye, Walter left Marla's house in the thinning light of day, pulled his coat collar tight around his neck, and ran off into the evening. May was brisk, and Walter's bag was heavy on his shoulder. He backtracked quickly along his route until he reached the Spradling's house on Springdale Avenue. Then he ran as fast as his bag would permit him—scrambling over fences, through gardens, and straight into spiderwebs a time or two on account of the approaching darkness, and all the while muttering as he delivered the mail, "It isn't real. This can't be real."

At Hampton Way, Walter paused beneath a streetlamp and forced himself to take the two new mysterious letters from his bag. In the bluish light, he shook the fear from his fingertips and worked the seal of Bent's letter until the flap came open neatly. The streets were empty. Most people were home for supper. Walter pulled the letter from its envelope and sat down on the curb to read.

Dear Muriel,

Thanks for writing back. It's okay that you don't know what to say yet. But it's also okay to tell me about heaven. I swear I won't get depressed or suicidal or anything. I mean, what am I going to do anyway, kill myself? Besides, you know me. I always pretty much make the best of things. Hey, our system works good enough, I think. It took a while for Stan to get the letter, though. I mean, it was about a week and a half. (And I always thought the postal service was bad at home!) See, Muriel—I can still laugh at things. I've got a feeling life is going to turn out okay for me down here. Oh yeah, I promised to send you the article that got me the promotion. Remember? I've stapled it below, so why don't you go ahead and read it now. Okay? Then, you can pick up in the next paragraph and finish the rest of this.

### Chili Supper in Sanctum 909

The men and women in sanctum 909 enjoyed some of hell's finest fare at noon today when Master Chef Moan DeCortez, always alert to his patrons' particular tastes, whipped up a batch of mouthwatering chili . . . enough to set one's tongue ablaze and one's heart yearning for home. Though only a relatively small circle of people were brave enough to sample the meal, those who did unanimously declared it sensational. Those who didn't thanked Chef DeCortez and agreed, "It's the thought that counts."

Muriel, I get sick every time I read this article, because I know it was written at the expense of all those people who are in that lousy sanctum because of their thoughts. But I just wanted to show you what kind of stuff Satan expects from me and what I have to keep doing unless I want to end up like all those other souls in 909—and it'll be a cold day in hell before I let that happen. I'm sorry if that sounds selfish.

Anyway, Satan thought the article was a real

laugh. And he sent me a telegram that talked about
my promotion right away. I haven't seen any action
yet on his promise, but hopefully soon . . . right?

I know the article doesn't really sound like me.
That's probably because I used a thesaurus on
every other word. But I'm really getting pretty
good, Sis. Mrs. Pope always said I had a sort of
flare for writing. I always regretted dropping out of
school—mostly because I missed her class—but I
didn't miss much else. I especially didn't miss seeing Tom Caudell's ugly face walking my girlfriend
down the hall. So I never bothered to go back.

Back to the article. Satan says I can have a fea-
tured column every day now. Actually, he ordered
me to do it. He wants it to be humorous, something
to give the moans a laugh. Satan is weird, Muriel.
He really is. There are five million pictures of him
around this place, but no one ever sees him. The
pictures—posters, actually—are all really handsome
of him. His hair is perfect, too. And he's always got
a tan.

Anyway, I'm rambling again. Why don't I just
answer your questions. (By the way, it's okay to
mother me if you want.) Here goes: My scar is fine.
The food stinks. My bed is hard. And if I could, I
would sleep all the time. At least then I wouldn't
have to think of all the times you told me about
Jesus, and I told you to stick it in your ear.

Do you see Him much? Jesus, I mean. Or, is He
just as mysterious as Satan? If He's half as good as
you used to brag about Him, then I think He sounds
pretty cool. I just wish I had thought so back then.

Anyway, give my love to anyone else up there
that I might know. And when you write back, I
really do want you to tell me about heaven. And
Jesus, too. Say some stuff about Him. Okay?

> Your brother,
> Bentley

P.S. Tomorrow I go to sanctum 73. That's where the baby killers are. I'm surprised Caudell wasn't in that group.

When he finished reading Bent's letter, Walter dropped it into the gutter, and its pages settled against the curb. Then he opened the one from Muriel, hoping it might soothe his nerves.

Dear Bentley,

Your letter made me feel much better. I'd love to tell you about heaven and about Jesus, too. It's hard to know where to begin. I think it's best to digress for a moment and write of earth. That's a common reference point for both of us, and at least you knew some good men up there to whom you can compare Jesus when I eventually begin speaking of Him.

Jack is probably the closest thing to Jesus I can think of, next to Mom and Dad, that is. But the three of you fought so much that it's probably better for you not to try to compare Jesus to our parents. Nevertheless, I always sensed that you respected Jack and was pleased when I married him. By the way, I shed no tears as I write of my husband, because I am not sad, Bentley. And I'm confident we will be together again someday.

Now, where was I? Oh, yes, Jack. If the sun shone brighter for every time Jack Robbins smiled, the universe would be an impossibly dazzling place to live. You recall his smile. I know you do. The two of you sat up all night that one Thanksgiving and told jokes until your cheeks hurt from laughing. I remember your telling me the next day at breakfast that you wished you could be as happy as Jack. But you didn't think you ever could be. Well, in comparison to Jack, Bentley, Jesus is the sun!

When I was ill, Jack was wonderful. He drove me
to all my treatments. He held me when I was nau-
seated, and he stroked my back ever so lightly.
Once, I almost got sick at the table in Luigi's, one of
our favorite restaurants. Even though I made a fool
of myself jumping up and bolting for the parking
lot, Jack never made a single apology for me to the
patrons who sat gaping at the spectacle. In fact, I
now believe that he was not the slightest bit embarrassed over the situation. He simply got up from
his chair, followed me outside to where I stood
slumped against the hood of our car, and wiped my
mouth with a damp napkin. He hugged me gently
and helped me into the front seat. Then, he went
back in, paid the check, left a generous tip, and
made sure he pocketed a matchbook to remember
the evening. He told me later that it was a good
opportunity to demonstrate his marriage vows and
that he didn't think he'd ever get that many people
together again in one room to watch him live out
the part about in sickness and in health.

Jack kept those matches until the day the doctors
said I would die. When it looked like I was really
slipping, Jack ordered everyone out of my presence
and he lit two dozen candles all around my hospital
room. We sat there in the dark on my bed—just
Jack and I. He held up that empty book of matches
in front of me and said, "Someday, Muriel, we will
hold hands across a table in heaven. We will eat a
wonderful meal, gaze into each other's eyes, and
laugh about that evening at Luigi's." Somehow,
Bentley, Jack's smile, and those candles, the feel of
his strong arms around my waist, and his warm
tears down the back of my neck made it all right to
go. And the brightness of that room became the
brightness of my Lord in the twinkling of an eye.

Now magnify the beauty of my Jack, sweet
Bentley, and you have a clearer picture of Jesus.
He has healed me in every way. My skin is no

longer yellow with chemotherapy. It glows with
such a healthy color to it that I'm sure it would
shame the tan of your handsome "boss."
Furthermore, Jesus has <u>been</u> my Jack to me in
every way, except, of course, in the physical ways
of matrimony.

Jack laughed, and the whole world laughed with
him. Jesus laughs, and the universe forgets its curse
for one brief moment. Do you see the comparison?

Now, to heaven.

No. I will save that for later. It would not be right
for me to overwhelm you with so much good. The
weight of its glory might suffocate you in that little
room of yours. Read these thoughts ever so slowly,
Bentley. Read them and know that I am thinking of
you. Read them and feel my love. And if you can,
try to cry.

> Your loving sister,
> Muriel

*I'm going wacko,* thought Walter. *There's not a soul in
town who wouldn't be laughing right now to see me sitting
here, pretending these letters are real. I've got work to do.
I've got bills to pay.* He got up from the curb, stuffed the letters back into his bag, and hurried off to finish the route.

With the delivery of each home's mail, Walter's bag
lightened. He began to tell himself it would all turn out
okay. Marla Coe didn't mean that much to him. She was
just a passing interest. Someone to fill the ditch that death
and a distant wife had gouged in his heart. He would make
it home in time to catch the sportscast. Donna would be
working on her novel. The boy would be doing homework.
He would eat a sandwich. Have some popcorn. Ignore the
letters. Forget about heaven and hell. Maybe even oil his
bag. No one would ever know how close he'd come to
stumbling. In the morning, he would still have his job.

Nevertheless, Walter's heart grew heavier and heavier as he went. At 517 Bedford, Foster Jenson III heard his mailbox creaking in the ivy below, and he flung open an upstairs window to give Walter a piece of his mind.

"You lazy—" shouted Foster Jenson, his gray head wagging in the shadows. "What's the meaning sneaking around at night delivering folks's mail? There's no telling how much money you cost me today while you were schmoozing with that witch woman. I depend upon you. I depend upon that *Wall Street Journal* for my investments! Why, I've a mind to call the post office first thing in the morning. Better still, I think I'll call your wife."

Walter opened his mouth to give some futile explanation. But Foster kept on going.

"And another thing," said Foster. "What do you think you're doing delivering all those strange letters and things to folks?"

Walter was truly confused.

"Don't look at me like you don't know what I'm talking about," said Foster. "I just got a call from William Ray on Birch. Says he saw you doing your job out there in the dark. And when he went to check his mailbox, do you know what he found, Walter?"

"Well, no, I—"

"He found a note from his dead wife, Leta, who has been gone for years. *That's* what he found! Nearly gave him a heart attack. Said *you* put it in there, too. Said he saw you with his own two eyes. What do you think of that, Walter?"

"That can't be," said Walter. "Why, I trayed the mail myself this morning. There was nothing but catalogs in there for Bill Ray. Nothing but a batch of late seed catalogs and a Sears invoice. Surely you don't think—"

"That's a pretty sick prank," said Foster. "Of all people, you're the last I thought would do that, knowing what you've been through."

"But I—"

"And that's not all, either," continued Foster. "Of course I don't need to tell *you* this, seeing as you're the one behind it all. But it seems William Ray took a call from Teeny Pittencheese down on Dill. She claims her daughter got a bottle of perfume from an uncle who passed last September."

"Mr. Jenson, if you just let me have a say, I reckon I can—"

"And a fruitcake for the Widow Spradling? Really, Walter. Of all people," repeated Foster, slamming down the window. In a minute, the widower was down the stairs and standing on the front porch in his robe and slippers.

"I'll take my mail straight from your hand, if that's all right with you," said Foster. "That way, there won't be any monkey business."

Walter handed over the mail and started down the sidewalk. But he wasn't even to the street before he heard Foster's voice again.

"What do you take me for?" said Foster.

"Excuse me, sir?" said Walter, turning around.

"You think I'm some kind of fool?" said Foster, waving the envelope Chaney had slipped into Walter's bag. "I know mail fraud when I see it. And I'm not about to believe for a second that my dear, dead father, God rest his soul, could be sending me a tip on the Dow Jones! You're after something, aren't you?"

"But, Mr. Jenson—"

"I don't know what you've got planned here. But you're not getting a cent of my money, Walter Conniston! Not a cent! Do you hear? And I can guarantee a visit from the authorities just as soon as I talk to my attorney. Good night, Walter," said Foster, disappearing through his front door and slamming it for dramatic effect.

Walter's heart not only grew heavier, it beat out a rhythm he felt sure would break his chest. In record time, he delivered Cistern, Pine Bluff, Montclair, and the rest of his route. By the time he got to Troost again, the sky was dark, with just a splinter of reddish light gouging the horizon.

"Dear God," Walter cried out loud, as he rounded the hedge where Fern usually waited in ambush. "I'm not even sure anymore if You're real. But if You are, just get me home. Just get me in my bed. Just let me sleep. Let me see this is nothing but a dream, a bad, bad dream. Dear God, I'm scared." Under the western sky, the ground looked blood-red. Walter doubled his pace.

"GRRR!" went the bushes to his left. Walter's knees buckled.

He saw Fern's teeth first, yellow points stringing saliva. She came at him with such a sound of satisfaction that one might have thought she had an enormous sweet tooth and that Walter's ankles were made of candy.

"Get back," said Walter, beginning to run. But the yellow points sank into his mailbag and held on.

"Get back, I said. Hey! That's my bag. Let go of my bag," shouted Walter, pulling with all his might. Fern had always been a nuisance, but she'd never acted quite like this.

Fern tugged harder and circled to her left. The sliver of red sky thinned and slid from the edge of the world. The moon began its ascent. Crickets sawed their song of the night. A rabbit trembled in the privet. All shadows drained into a single black pool. And there in the darkness, Walter danced with death at the other end of his mailbag.

"I'm not playing with you," said Walter. "See these boots? I'll throttle you. I swear I will. I'll kick you if you don't let go."

But Fern kept her grip. She looked at Walter, her glare burning the shoulder strap straight up the length of his arm and into his face and his eyes. Her red orbs locked with his fearful ones, and Walter could tell she wanted nothing more than to release the bag and tear him to pieces.

"I'm a grown man," said Walter. "I'm not afraid of you! You hear me?" he shouted. I'm not afraid of anybody. Now give me my bag."

Suddenly Fern let go, and Walter fell backward into the privet hedge. The crickets stopped abruptly. The trembling rabbit let out a squeal and bounded across Walter's chest into the night. And Fern was upon him.

"Help!" cried Walter, striking Fern in the face with his mailbag. The yellow points, with saliva flinging in all directions, flashed down toward Walter's neck. He shielded his jugular with the thick leather. He kicked. He screamed. "Oh, Jesus, please. Help me!"

Walter gave one last thrust of his bag at Fern's jaws and rolled out from under the hedge. At that moment a truck came speeding along the far lane of Washington Avenue with its headlights piercing the night. Instinctively, Fern jumped back into the shadows. Walter scrambled down toward the gutter. He tore his right palm on the curb and was nearly struck by another vehicle that came from the opposite direction. But he was up in a flash running. His legs plowed the pavement, both arms pumping freely without the weight of the mail on his shoulder. Behind him in the privet, Fern bit and tore at Walter's bag until it was mush.

At Mulberry Court, the glow of lights from his house calmed Walter. He walked slowly toward it, trying to catch his breath and all the while trying to fabricate an alibi for his missing mailbag. He saw Donna sitting on the top step of the porch, and he stopped in the street.

"Where've you been?" called Donna, quietly. In her hand she turned something slender and white.

"Finishing business," said Walter, feeling naked before his wife with that one part of his uniform so conspicuously absent.

"Where's your bag?" asked Donna.

"At the post office," said Walter, quickly. "I didn't think it needed oiling tonight. I dropped it off after work."

"And that's why you're late, I suppose."

"I'm not *that* late," said Walter, starting across the grass. When he reached the porch, he looked as if he might walk up the stairs and past his wife without a word, but Donna held up her hand to stop him.

She had been sitting on the porch since late afternoon with the letter in her lap. Twice, she had thought of going back up to the attic, returning the letter, and pretending she had never seen a thing. However, each time she'd been afraid that Walter might return from work and catch her snooping. So she clung to this one incontestable sign of her husband's infidelity.

"What's this?" Donna said flatly, when Walter arrived at the stair just below her. She had unfolded the letter and was dangling it in the breeze for Walter to read. She held only the last page of Muriel's first letter, which contained the words *I love you* written over and over. The page was signed MC, not Muriel Conniston Robbins, which would have put an end to Donna's suspicions and may well have drawn the grieving spouses together for the first time since they shoveled dirt on their daughter's grave.

"Looks like a letter," said Walter. He stared hard without his glasses. Then he saw the typescript more clearly, swallowed, and changed the subject. "I haven't had supper yet," he said, trying to go around his wife on the stairs. The last thing in all the world he wanted to do was discuss the awful grief he felt inside for his daughter and his son.

"Who's it from?" asked Donna. "Who's MC?"

"I don't know any MC," said Walter.

"That's a lie," said Donna, suddenly.

Walter froze against the railing. Through the screen door he saw Dallas pretending to work on something at the dining room table.

"Do you think I'm blind, Walter?" said Donna. "Did you think I'd find this and keep my mouth shut?"

Walter's tongue went dry. He whitened at the possibility of spilling out his sorrow, never once imagining that Donna was turning red because she thought he'd been unfaithful.

"I checked it out, you know," said Donna. "The people at the post office were more than glad to help me. There's an MC on your route, isn't there?"

Walter sighed inwardly. He was relieved by the opportunity to ignore the topic of his depression for one more day. But there was still the problem of covering the steps he had taken that morning. It didn't matter that he had gone to the woman's house innocently, and on top of that had done nothing. The fact that he was drawn there meant he was still the accused. It would hurt Donna to the core to know he had taken his pain to a stranger's doorstep. And Donna's pain would sentence the two of them to a greater silence.

"Well?" said Donna.

"Maybe there is, maybe there isn't," said Walter.

"And maybe a certain Marla Coe lives at 602 Cistern," said Donna, coldly.

"Can I get by?" said Walter.

"Can I have an explanation?" said Donna. She rose from the stair and stood in front of Walter.

"It's a free country. It isn't a crime for a lady to write a man if she wants to," said Walter, only vaguely aware that he was moving toward a lie.

"A *lady*?" shouted Donna. "Is that what you call that, that *tramp*?"

"You haven't met her, Donna, so you can't judge her," replied Walter.

"Oh, but I *can* judge," said Donna, feeling the anger of lost time boiling up inside her. "I can judge that she wasn't around for thirty years when I did your laundry and sewed your socks and cleaned your house and made your turkey sandwiches and sent you off to work grumbling, with hardly a kiss or a hug or a good-bye for the last twelve. I can judge!" said Donna. "I can read, too! And it doesn't take much to figure out what a man has in mind when he saves a woman's love letters, either."

"It's a free country," repeated Walter.

"Then you're free to make your own supper in this free country, as far as I'm concerned," shouted Donna.

"Suits me fine," said Walter.

"All right. Fine," said Donna.

The two of them stomped into the house, where Walter went straight to the attic to better conceal his boot box and Donna went straight to her word processor to take out her anger on the keys. Through it all, Dallas tried to appear as if he was working diligently at the table. But it's hard enough for a shy teenager to write a love letter, and harder still when his parents are at war.

"I'll be going next door to talk to Coach Ravelle," said Dallas. When no one answered him, he took his pencil and his stationery and walked out of the house, down the stairs, and across the lawn toward the one home on Mulberry Court that always seemed happy.

For the next three weeks, Walter left for work earlier than usual. The fight with Donna was the worst they'd ever been through, which may seem odd to those couples who scratch and claw like cats and yet somehow remain happier than the Connistons. Nevertheless, something about the incident made Walter feel alive. Not that he enjoyed conflict, but it made him see his wife as real, as if she were a three-dimensional character whom he might be able to love again. But loving someone, anyone, was the difficult part for Walter. So he purposed once again to forget love, and he spent the rest of June forgetting in the company of Marla Coe. And June was good for catfish on the Coon.

For a month of mornings, Walter doubled his deliveries so that he could have the afternoons free to be with Marla. Meanwhile, Satan's minions doubled their efforts to tempt and harass the troubled mail carrier. They had failed where their client's sexual nature was concerned. But there were other ways, even more effective ones for ruining an evangelist's credibility in Ellenbach. Immediately, they stoked the coals of bitterness in Walter's heart. Dice and crew flew endless circles around his head, whispering, sometimes shouting, "The Great Shepherd has failed you. He has led you by foul waters. He has made a mutton meal of you and served you to your enemies."

Soon, Walter's appetite disappeared. Instead of eating his lunch at noon, he quickly changed his clothes at the post office, stuffed them into the new mailbag he'd been issued upon reporting Fern, and sneaked directly to Marla's backyard, where the two of them baited their lines and headed down the alley to the creek.

Once, someone had spotted them, and the rumors had flown around town on dirty wings.

"Walter and the witch woman are at it again," said some people.

"Imagine a man that old sparking somebody her age."

"She could be his daughter."

"Sure could."

"It's a shame that Donna doesn't know. Seems like someone ought to tell her."

"I told her."

"And?"

"Didn't make any difference. She already knew. Besides, what's the woman going to do? Chain him up?"

"Guess you're right. It's still a shame."

So Walter went unfettered toward Cistern and Donna did nothing to stop him. In truth, though she didn't know it, Donna had no pressing *need* to stop him. After only one other round of seduction and rebuff, Walter and Marla settled into a curious relationship wherein one party made vicarious contact with a long-lost daughter, and the other found a dad. However, Satan made sure neither of them found what they really needed, which was release from their bonds of bitterness. All the while Donna's *Hearts on Fire* grew increasingly ugly in tone.

One afternoon, when the sky was high and blue and the catch of fish much slower than usual, Walter and Marla sat by the creek, sipping Cokes and saying repeatedly how they should be checking their lines to make sure the bait was still there. The day was so delightful that even Dice, who had been sent alone to maintain Walter's hedge of harassment, had reclined momentarily on the bank to warm himself in the sun. His break was short-lived. When he heard Marla ask Walter what he thought of God, he was at his client's side in a flash.

"Tell her there's not much to think about," whispered Dice. "And if there was, it wouldn't be good."

Walter shook his head at the buzzing in his ear.

"Something wrong?" asked Marla.

"Must have been a gnat," replied Walter with his head tilted.

"So what do you think of God?" Marla repeated.

"Tell her you don't know," ordered Dice.

"I don't know," said Walter.

"Uh-hm. I could've pegged you as an agnostic," said Marla.

"Well, there's no need for name-calling."

"No, Walter. An *agnostic* is someone who thinks there might be a god out there, but isn't sure of the phone number."

"I used to think I knew it," said Walter, sullenly.

"That's it, Walter," said Dice. "Just listen to me. Remember, yesterday's knowledge is today's foolishness."

"What do you mean, used to?" said Marla.

"Hm?"

"You said used to."

"What I meant was back before—"

"Before that so-called Lord of yours let you down," supplied Dice.

"I'd rather not talk about it," said Walter. He shook his head again and changed the subject.

"Say, I don't mean to pry, but I saw those pictures on your mantelpiece the other day. Who are they?"

"Nephew. Niece. The other girl is just a young friend," said Marla.

"Hmm. I would have bet they were yours," said Walter. "They look so much like you. I know you've never been married, but did you ever want to be?"

"Lots of times," said Marla. "It just never worked out. How about you, Walter? Did you ever wish you *weren't* married?"

Walter set his Coke on the bank to think. If he said yes, he would be lying. He had never really loved anyone but Donna, and a million trips to 602 Cistern could not change that. On the other hand, if he said no, he feared losing the only other thing besides delivering the mail that seemed to make him happy. Walter didn't know *why* Marla Coe made him happy. It was just that way. And he didn't want to jeopardize it.

"I've never thought about it, I guess," said Walter, finally. And, for the time being, his answer seemed good enough for Marla.

That evening, when Walter ran back to Mulberry Court, he found the neighborhood awash in red and blue. In front of his house sat a squad car with its CB squawking irregularly. As he came nearer, Walter saw Donna talking with an officer on the front porch. He recognized Deputy Turner Tubbs's profile, his three chins flashing on and off to the cadence of his emergency lights. Deputy Tubbs was fond of those lights. And since the crime rate in Ellenbach afforded him such slim chance of using them, Tubbs jumped at the opportunity whenever it came along. Right away, Walter had a hunch Foster Jenson III had finally spoken with his attorney.

"Evening deputy," said Walter, coming across the lawn. Donna jumped at Walter's voice. She took a step backward, as if she feared something. But when Tubbs touched her arm and steadied her, she managed a frail smile and the two of them greeted the wayward mail carrier.

"You seem out of breath, Walt," said Tubbs.

"I'm all right, I guess," said Walter.

"Awful late to be making rounds, isn't it?" asked Tubbs.

"I had an extra lot of mail today. Nothing special," said Walter.

"I see," said Tubbs, rubbing his chins. "An extra lot as in more than usual? Or an extra lot as in things one wouldn't normally deliver to the average mailbox, if one were a law-abiding government worker such as you?"

"Excuse me, sir?"

"Come on, Walt," said Tubbs. "Are you going to act like you don't know a thing I'm talking about and make this hard on everybody? Well, Walter Dale Conniston, you're under arrest. Sheriff Sweeney said you put a bunch of strange objects in folks's boxes a few weeks back. Anyway, you've got the right to keep quiet, the right to an attorney—"

"And the right to go to bed," said Walter, as he shoved past Deputy Tubbs. When he went by Donna, she seemed embarrassed to make eye contact with him. Instead, she glanced away.

"Hold it, Walter," said Tubbs.

"No, sir! You hold it, Deputy," shouted Walter, spinning and pointing a finger in Tubbs's direction. "You've got no cause coming here, arresting me—"

"I've got no bone with you, Walt," said Tubbs.

"Well, I've got one with you," said Walter. "And I'll have a bigger one if you don't let me go to bed."

"I know what you've been through, Walter," said Tubbs, stepping forward into the rectangle of light coming from the front door. "I knew you when you were a fine man, too. It isn't your fault. You know I'm not out to get you."

"So I *was* a fine man, huh, Deputy? *Was*? I *was* a fine man? Well, don't trouble yourself with the past anymore, especially mine. Do you understand? Goodnight, Deputy. Donna? Are you coming?" asked Walter, addressing his wife without looking at her.

Donna shot a pleading glance at Deputy Tubbs, who shrugged his shoulders and flung his final words at Walter's back.

"I hoped it wouldn't come to this," said Tubbs.

The first thing Walter saw when he stepped inside was a menacing black briefcase with an official-looking insignia on front. It was leaning against the stairs as if its owner had the authority to leave it wherever he wanted.

Simultaneously, Walter saw Dallas at the dining room table, and two men sitting on the sofa. Behind him in the doorway, Donna and Tubbs watched nervously.

"Hey, son. What are you doing?" said Walter, doing his best to ignore the men and appear lighthearted.

"Nothing much. Just writing a letter," said Dallas.

"Same one you've been working on for a month," said Walter. "I don't understand it, son. You haven't written a lick since you took up football. This isn't part of summer school is it? You aren't part of the slow class now, are you?" said Walter, suspiciously.

"Nah, Dad," said Dallas, with his hand placed intentionally over the spot on the page where he'd dreamily traced and retraced Eddy Lundy's name. "I ain't, I mean, I'm not taking summer school. It's for Coach Ravelle."

"Oh," said Walter. And when he said it, he was aware that one of the men on the couch had gotten up and was walking toward him. "Well, anyway," said Walter. "I guess that's okay, so long as it isn't any of Ravelle's Bible stuff. I never did trust him on account of the Sunset Grille shenanigans. He may be a coach now, but you know what they say, son, once a preacher always a preacher. And I believe it, too. Like I always said—"

"Pardon me, Mr. Conniston," said the man who was now standing next to Walter. "I'm Inspector Blackmon of the United States Postal Service. This is my partner, Inspector Davis."

The man on the couch nodded.

"Do you mind if we have a word with you?" asked Blackmon.

"Word? What for?" said Walter. "Wait a minute. Donna, what's an inspector doing in our house? What's going on here? I haven't done anything. And I'm not saying anything either."

Donna stood silent in the doorway. She looked hard at Dallas until he saw her looking at him. Then she motioned with her head for him to go to his room, and he gathered up his things and left.

"Would you like to have a seat, Mr. Conniston?" said Blackmon.

"I'd like to be in bed, if you don't mind," said Walter.

"We're here to talk about some serious charges," said Inspector Davis from the couch.

"I'll just stand," said Walter.

"Suit yourself," replied Davis. "We're just trying to accommodate you." Judging by what Walter could see of him sitting down, he was the taller of the two men. His teeth and hair were perfect, airbrushed, perhaps, onto this manikin of the state. Walter took note of Davis's government chukkas and the big, brown lip of a pipe that peeked over the top of his shirt pocket.

"That's nice of you," said Walter. "Now, may I—"

"Not so fast, Walter," said Inspector Davis, obviously the one in charge, though Blackmon had been the first to stand. From the inside of his coat, Davis pulled a photograph, glanced at it once, shook his head, and turned it around so Walter could see it.

"Got any idea who this is?" asked Davis.

"This is foolishness," said Walter, bending low without his glasses to look at the picture. Then, when he recognized Marla's face, he nearly gagged.

"I've seen her before. She's on my route," said Walter, trying to act casual. "Why would that matter? Why would you come here asking me those things, asking me in front of my family?"

"How would you feel if you knew she had committed a crime, Walter?" said Davis.

"Like what?" said Walter.

"Like leaving three little kids to fend for themselves while she took off," said Blackmon.

Walter's mind raced back to Marla's mantelpiece. "I'm responsible for her mail, sir, not her life," shot Walter.

"It's not the first time she's done this," said Davis. "You ought to have seen her children when we found them. Poor kids. Skinny as sticks."

"Is that what you came to arrest me for tonight?" said Walter.

"No," said Davis. "That's just to say we know the woman's in town. This time, we're going to watch her for a while to see what she's about. Her kids are with an aunt. So, we've got all the time in the world. By the way, her name is Coe, Marla Coe."

Donna bit her lip and strained to see the picture.

"Is that all?" said Walter.

"Not quite, Conniston," said Inspector Blackmon. Behind him, Tubbs and Donna stood nervously in the doorway. "I couldn't help noticing you were out of breath when you came in tonight," Blackmon continued.

"You and everybody else," said Walter.

"And it didn't make sense to me, because a man who gets as much exercise as you ought to be able to run a mile and hardly break a sweat. Have you been running tonight, Mr. Conniston?" asked Blackmon.

"Maybe," said Walter. "Maybe not. I don't know. Some days I go faster than others just to get the mail delivered. Is it a crime now to run, too?"

"No. Just wondering," said Blackmon.

"By the way, Walter," said Davis, "we got a call this

evening over in Topeka from an attorney. We were close enough, and this was important enough, that Inspector Blackmon and I decided to come to Ellenbach and check out some things tonight. Now, will you talk with us or not?"

"Depends on what you want to talk about," said Walter.

"How's this for starters," said Blackmon, holding up a fragrance bottle. "One of your clients said she found this in her mailbox."

"Folks get all kinds of things in the mail. I've got nothing to do with that."

"Hold it," interrupted Davis, rising from the couch and walking toward Walter. He had dropped his cordial tone. "You've got everything to do with that, Mr. Conniston. Part of your job is to double-check for return addresses! Let's suppose I come into the office some morning while you're traying mail. And let's suppose I buy some stamps from you, and then leave a letter there on the counter while I walk off."

Walter knew what was coming.

"Now, let's suppose I've put some wisecrack return on the envelope like Triple Zero Nowheresville. Do you know what I'd do to you if you failed to stop me before I drove off in my car?"

Walter looked tired in the pale living room light.

"You sorry sap," said Inspector Davis. Then he looked down at a sheet of paper in his hand and laughed. "You'd have to be a fool to deliver perfume from a dead man whose return address is 33 Cherry Lane, The City of God."

"That's not all, though," said Blackmon. "And this is the part you might do time for. Do you understand the meaning of mail fraud?"

Walter nodded.

"Apparently not. Because if you did, you wouldn't have tried to trick a certain Foster Jenson III into making investments on some alleged stock tip from his own dead father."

"What you're accused of is a felony," said Inspector Davis. "It's the attempted acquisition or deprivation of money or property through the mail. If you talk with us tonight, you might be able to make it easier for yourself."

"I told you I haven't done anything," said Walter.

"Mail fraud is against the law of the land, sir," said Blackmon. "Unless you call this thing with Jenson a practical joke."

"Who made that call to Topeka?" said Walter. "I'd like to tell them a thing or two."

"You can tell it to the judge," said Blackmon.

"I'm not saying anything more," said Walter.

"Do as you like, Mr. Conniston," said Davis. "But if you're not going to cooperate, then the only thing I can guarantee you when this thing goes to trial is a lot of pain. Do you understand me, sir?"

"Plain as day," said Walter. And he started down the hallway toward the bedroom.

"One more thing, Mr. Conniston," said Davis.

Walter stopped to listen.

"You'll have to go with us tonight to Topeka."

"Topeka?" said Walter.

"That's right. You can post bond there," said Davis.

Walter was too numb to resist. Inspector Blackmon followed him to his room, where he got a change of clothes from the closet, a toothbrush, and a comb. With his head bowed he walked past Donna, who was crying softly on the front porch, and allowed himself to be cuffed without a struggle. From his bedroom window, Dallas watched as the squad car bore his father into the night.

"He's still a fine man, Mrs. Conniston," said Deputy Tubbs, doing that part of his job he was least proficient in.

"I know he is. It's just that sometimes it seems hell itself has come into this house."

"There, now. Easy, now. That kind of talk won't help matters."

"No, you don't understand," said Donna, pulling away. "Hell has come to stay and torment my husband and bring bad things on us all. Times aren't ever going to be like they used to be."

"Come on now, Mrs. Conniston. No use stirring yourself up," said Tubbs. "Anyway, if there is nothing more I can do, I'd best be on my way. Goodnight, ma'am. I guess I'll be seeing you at the, uh, trial. And that's not to say there's going to be a trial, you understand. What I was saying was—"

"Goodnight, Deputy," said Donna. "Thanks for your help."

Donna went inside and waited for Deputy Tubbs to drive away before she turned out the porch lights. Then she sank to her knees on the living room carpet and did something she hadn't done since Muriel's death.

"Oh, God," she sobbed. "Please do something good for my family."

## ~ *16* ~

*No light, but rather darkness visible.*

—John Milton, *Paradise Lost, I*

SOMETHING good *was* being done for the Connistons. And it was being done in such a way, and with such an unwilling participant, that doubt could not be shed on who the author of that good thing really was.

It is bad enough to be a citizen in hell. But to be a forgotten citizen, set aside in some dark hole and left to rot or go insane from the darkness, one might almost wish for torment, purely for the validation it affords. Such was Ripskin's sentence for the rest of eternity.

Sitting in the gun-barrel blackness of C-storage, Ripskin wished for many things. He wished for his home at 121 Styx Bald Ridge. He wished for light and sound and regular meals rather than the rats he'd stooped to catching in order to survive. He wished for freedom and revenge. He wished for a companion. But most of all, Ripskin wished for a blanket. For unlike the rest of hell, storage is always bitter cold.

C-storage is the size of a small convention center—rectangular, high-ceilinged, unadorned. Its floor is wooden, which made it possible for Ripskin to hear the rats when they scurried through, over, and under the mountains of belongings brought by souls to hell. Indeed, a month without food had made him long for the clickety-clack of nails and a fat tail dragging. Still, Ripskin was not so starved yet as to become undiscerning. He was well aware when the sound in question was large enough to be predator instead of prey. In those cases, he hurried in the opposite direction.

Ripskin had just been running from one of the largest-sounding rats he'd encountered since his induction into C-storage when he took the fortunate turn into some coatracks. He could hear the rodent floundering behind him in a heap of sleeves and lapels.

"That was close," gasped Ripskin, feeling inside his pockets for the book of matches given to him at his sentencing. He remembered the words of the old judge who'd been appointed by Satan to preside over his case.

"Postal negligence is a high crime, Mr. Ripskin," the judge had said. "I don't look favorably upon it. Therefore, I hereby sentence you to eternity in C-storage. You shall be given food sporadically, clothing occasionally, and a thorough investigation regularly. After all, we *ex*pect only what we *in*spect. And we *expect* you to keep the premises tidy. The last fellow in C frittered away his time, and we're still not sure where he's gotten to. You may come across him in your work. In the meantime, however, I suggest you strive to become as dissimilar to your predecessor as possible. So, Mr. Ripskin, spick-and-span is the ticket. Do your job. Bide your time. Things could go well for you. And since I'm a compassionate moan who wouldn't dream of sending someone into utter darkness without at least a ray of hope, I give you these," said the judge, extending a book of matches toward Ripskin. "I trust you'll use them sparingly. Oh, and one more thing. Watch out for the rats."

"Postal negligence, my hind foot," hissed Ripskin at the memory of the judge's words. "Some compassion! I'd hate to catch him on a *bad* day."

His fingers found what they were looking for in the bottom of his pocket, and they curled around its grimy cover. He drew the book of matches out and hesitated, for until now he had done his best to conserve.

"I could light just one," he whispered to himself in the darkness. "One won't hurt. I'll have a look around, see if that nasty rat is nearby, maybe even light a fire."

The thought of warmth lit a smile on Ripskin's face. Nevertheless, he'd be punished if caught. For he had been sent to organize and categorize the junk, not to burn it. But he was so unbearably cold! And there was the matter of the rat who was stalking him.

"Blast the vermin," shouted Ripskin. His voice was like a single drop in an ocean of ink. "How do they grow so large?"

Behind him, the ruffling in the coatracks had turned to rage. Ripskin considered his options. He fingered the matchbook. He felt about the tangle of worldly possessions that mocked the cliché, "You can't take it with you." In groping braille, he read a history of humanity's passions—a wallet, a watch, the rotting remnants of a fine fur coat. The truth is, as far as Satan is concerned, if it'll fit inside the casket, a person *can* take it—but can't ever play with it.

Ripskin's hand brushed across some papers, and he made his decision. Quickly he snatched them up and rolled them into the shape of a small torch. Then, while holding the papers between his knees, Ripskin struck a match, and his pupils closed down to pinholes. He could hear the rat thrashing about in the piles of people things.

"He'll eat me if he catches me," squealed Ripskin. His eyes came into focus, and he could see the roll of papers before him. They were pages from a politician's diary, the binding of which had long since been chewed away. Ripskin lit the pages, and a pale yellow circle grew around him. To his right, he saw a stack of picture frames. The photographs they once held had returned to dust, except for a solitary corner of paper that clung to the wood. There, a boy and his dog smiled a faded smile.

Behind the frames Ripskin saw a camera, a rusted tripod, a scarf, a coin box, a broken umbrella, books piled high into the blackness, books bound tight with leather straps, more books with bindings missing, dusty books scattered here and there as far as the yellow circle permitted him to see.

And then he saw something shiny in the center of a clearing.

The sovereignty of Jesus is a curious thing, and it is doubly curious when one stumbles across it in a place like hell. Nevertheless, one finds it even there. And that is the singularly most distressing thing to Satan in all of creation, that his own kingdom is really not his own but is yet another annex of Jesus' rule. His will is done regardless of location or temperature.

And so the hand of Jesus allowed the eye of Ripskin to fall upon the shiny thing, and Ripskin waded through the pile until he was standing over it. The light from his torch was nearly gone now. He could feel the fire flickering against the flesh of his thumb and forefinger. Yet there was enough of the flame left for Ripskin to see that, wrapped around the base of a reading lamp, was a set of dog tags with the inscription:

**Bentley Allen Conniston, PFC**
**17634**

Ripskin's torch sputtered. He stared hard at the tags, wondering why he was drawn to them. Then, he grabbed them and stuffed them in his pocket, just as he heard a *snap*.

The brown rat squealed as it sprang from the shadows. Ripskin thrust the hot remains of the diary into its face, and the rat squeaked wild with pain. Again and again, Ripskin stabbed with his glowing torch until the rat caught fire and went running around the clearing like a dying comet. It smashed into an antique cuckoo clock. Eventually the rat burned out, and it was dark again.

But the rat's cries had summoned others. Great ones. Small ones. Fast ones. Over the rubbish they poured.

Ripskin's heart was a timepiece ticking. Behind him was a large opening, a tunnel of sorts, leading away beneath the debris. He'd seen it when the torch was burning. He'd have to make the best of it, even though he knew that running from creatures whose eyes were made for night was a losing cause. In the blackness before him, the rat he'd killed lay smoldering. Ripskin kicked it once to make sure it was really dead. And when he did, little sparks went circling up toward the ceiling of C-storage.

"Hooves and ol' Harry! This thing must be half my size!" groaned Ripskin as he dragged the smoking rat to the tunnel and ducked inside. With the brown host drawing nearer, Ripskin wedged the last inch of the rat's corpse into the opening. "There! That should hold them for a while!" He ran off panting—never once questioning the existence of a tunnel in that shrine to materialism, nor imagining that something far bigger than he had dug it.

As he ran, Ripskin felt the dog tags jangling in his pocket. Suddenly, he knew why he'd taken the time to pick them up. It was that name, *Conniston*. Where had he seen it before? In Classified Files? No. On a tombstone? No. No. Where was it, then?

"Aha!" said Ripskin, coming to a halt in the gloom of the tunnel. I saw it on that very last letter I delivered in the golden mail slot."

And truly he had, though he'd have been a lot better off at this moment had he noticed the relationship between the sender and the addressee. If he had, he'd have never delivered the thing. He'd still have his job and be enjoying the relative affluence of 121 Styx Bald Ridge instead of this warehouse of horrors.

Ahead in the darkness, Ripskin thought he heard the sound of breathing—little, halting snatches of breath—and the sound of scratching, too. But when he held his own breath to listen, he heard nothing. So he set off again with the name of Conniston on his lips. And all the while, Ripskin was forming a theory.

*If* he was being punished for some postal treason, and *if* the crime in question somehow involved a letter from Bentley Allen Conniston to someone in heaven, and *if* Satan was so foaming mad about the affair that he took the time to file the charges himself rather than having one of his aides do it for him, *then maybe* there was more to the letter than meets the eye.

*After all, letters from souls in hell have made it to heaven before, with far less outrage than this. What was one letter going to matter when there is nothing the quick can do about the dead? Unless—* Then Ripskin hit upon it. Like a wall it stopped him in his tracks.

"That's it!" said Ripskin to the darkness. "What Satan really fears is that letter reaching earth. So I'll make sure it does, along with these dog tags, as well."

So confident of his theory was he that Ripskin began to do a little jig right there in the tunnel. And he accompanied his dance with a devilish song.

> *Fat rat, the devil's cat!*
> *Who'd have thought it would come to that?*
> *Burn your eye with a politician's lies,*
> *And fly away with the speed of a bat!*

It was a wonderful moment for Ripskin. In his pocket he held the key to his revenge—and perhaps his freedom, too—if he could get out and fly far enough away. Nevertheless, he should have kept his thoughts to himself. For while Ripskin was singing and dancing and carrying on, there was a great deal of noise up ahead in the tunnel that would have troubled him had he heard it.

A hundred yards behind him, the rats had managed to push their way past their fallen comrade. They clicked ahead on razor nails with sharp teeth shining, whiskers twitching, noses sniffing into side tunnels, and then on again.

The average brown rat measures from eight to ten inches long, not including the tail. And that was the only size of rat with whom—until his recent harrowing escape—Ripskin had firmly believed he shared his dark detention.

But he was wrong.

The ones he had trapped were mere babes with small ears, blunt snouts, and coarse fur. They weighed a pound at most. But it was their angered parents, who were thirty times the size of their offspring, that poured beneath the pile of people-things like a river of scalding coffee. They would find the little demon who had the gall to torch their brother. And when they did, they'd kill him quickly and devour him slowly.

At that precise moment, Ripskin rounded the last curve in the tunnel and stood looking at a wall, though by now his eyes had only partially adjusted to the gloom of his surroundings.

"Who's there?" Ripskin cried when he heard the sound of breathing again.

The sound was thick and wide. The breather sat with its back against the wall, where the rubbish met the sides of the warehouse. It licked its lips and gathered its haunches beneath its ninety-five pound bulk and went at Ripskin with the deftness of a word in the dark.

"Aaa!" screamed Ripskin when the rats hit him squarely in the chest and knocked him to the floor of the tunnel. Instinctively, Ripskin reached into his pocket where he usually kept his knife. He found the dog tags and yanked them out in time to catch a set of teeth coming down toward his face. He felt the incisors sink deep into his forearm as great hind claws scratched upward toward his belly.

With his left hand, Ripskin grabbed the metal chain of the dog tags and looped them once around a head that was now just inches from his chin. He pulled the chain tight against the fur and twisted. The teeth along his forearm loosened. The claws quit digging higher. The rat hissed and squeaked. It pulled against the chain. It reeled backward, driving Ripskin into the tunnel wall. Still, Ripskin hung on. He rode the rat like a rodeo bronc, twisting hard upon the metal reins, spurring fat and fur in the impossible dark.

All the while, the squealing river drew nearer in the tunnel. Tighter and tighter Ripskin twisted the chain until the creature beneath him went limp and quiet. Then he unwrapped the chain, stuffed it in his pocket, and dove into a jumble of souls' possessions, just as the first of the rats came clicking into the dead end.

Back and back Ripskin shoved, until he felt the frigid wall of C-storage against his shoulders. He could hear the rats' mad cries—could almost see their red eyes glowing, as they gathered round their patriarch's body. Then one of them smelled Ripskin, and they all tore into the pile.

"Stop! Get away! You can't do this to me! I was an angel once in heaven!"

Suddenly, Ripskin felt an impression in the wall behind him. He turned over on his side and reached a little farther in. The impression became a hollow. And when he stretched his hand as far as it could go, the hollow became a definite hole. And the farther he reached into the hole, the warmer the hard floor of hell began to feel and the faster Ripskin's heart began to beat.

He had found a way of escape.

He kicked and dug and finally wriggled his body halfway into the hole. But now something had his cloven foot.

"Not now!" screamed Ripskin, at the pain of the rat's incisors. "Not when I'm so close." With his last shred of strength, Ripskin lurched forward and hit his head on something hard. It was a woman's makeup case, small enough to have been placed in her casket for some sentimental reason, but large enough to bar his path. Ripskin cursed the obstruction. "I will *not* be ravaged by a rat!" He shook his foot furiously and the rat lost its hold. Heedless of the pain, Ripskin squeezed past the makeup case, shot through the opening, and pulled the case behind him, just as the rats beat hard against the other side.

As Ripskin hurried away, he could hear the rats lamenting his luck. But just as soon as he had reached the main path, Ripskin heard the beat of booted hooves coming toward him, and he ducked into a doorway.

"Alpha Order," gasped Ripskin, as he watched a troop of thirty moans march past. That troop gave way to another troop and another and another and another, until hundreds of the warring demons had gone by and Ripskin was faint with the counting of them. He was a fugitive. His palms began to sweat. He wiped his brow with the back of his hand, realizing his stint in C-storage had made him forget how hot the rest of hell could be.

*What now?* thought Ripskin. *Where do I go? The front gates? The portals on the west side? Oh, triple sixes! They'll be creeping now with moans, particularly if they know of my escape. Then where? The service entrance? The chimney?*

Ripskin hit upon a possibility, and the possibility became a plan. Before he knew it, the plan had turned into a pell-mell, serpentine rush between boulders and behind stalactites, down and down and down into the gut of hell, where there is a little metal door with two red words scrawled dismally upon it—LAUNDRY CHUTE.

Ripskin trembled as he stood surrounded by mounds of filthy rags before the door.

*Dare I go in there?* thought Ripskin, for he had long heard the warnings about this chute. Nevertheless, he knew it was his only way of escape. Ripskin opened the door and peered upward. Right away, something nimble ran down his back. Ripskin brushed wildly with his hands, and he shook his arms and legs until he believed the thing was gone. He remembered.

There are things so vile in there, even a moan would be offended, the stories went. Offended? That's an understatement. The chute is full of vicious things. Corrupt and ruinous. A moan would be lucky to spend a minute in there and escape with his sanity.

Ripskin shivered at the thoughts. Still, he questioned. *What could possibly be so bad about a laundry chute?* he said to himself.

But this was not just *any* laundry chute. In fact, it had nothing to do with the conventional concept of clothing and its maintenance, and certainly not for clothes that belong to the inhabitants of hell. This particular laundry chute had a far "nobler" function than the average one. In fact, if the one who painted those sprawling, red letters had taken the time to consider just exactly what duty that chute performs, he might have used the words GARBAGE BIN.

Since the coming of Christ, men and women earthside have been lifting its lid and sending foul garments down into the darkness. They have been—as the Holy Scriptures mention—putting off their old selves, casting aside all manner of dirty underclothes, outerclothes, and other things that weigh a person down. Anger. Wrath. Malice. Immorality. Many a sinner has thrown one or two of these down the chute before.

Ripskin heard the sound of boots again—and this time they were running. "Dickens!" hissed Ripskin. "They know I'm out. There must have been a silent alarm. I need more time." He took a deep breath, stepped into the chute, and closed the door behind him. When he heard muffled voices on the other side, Ripskin crawled ten feet up into the cobwebs and sat motionless.

"Look! Here's more blood. And his footprints end right here," said one voice.

"Give me that torch, you idiot," said a second.

The door to the chute cracked open, as if the one opening it was every bit as reluctant as Ripskin had been. When nothing nightmarish assaulted him, the moan flung the door wide and shone the torch into the dark.

Below him, Ripskin saw the Alpha moan's thick frontal lobe and then his eyes when he tilted his head upward. Ripskin held his breath and cursed his circumstances.

"Nothing," growled the moan. "I might have known. There's not a demon alive dumb enough to shinny up there. Come on, we've got work to do. We've got to find the little creep."

With that he slammed the door and turned the latch tight.

Now Ripskin was *really* alone. If he thought that C-storage was a somber place, he was about to enter a world so black that coal stands out like starlight, the wind becomes a mournful mongrel, and the fig leaves of Eden drift downward in the dark. Snatching a deep breath, Ripskin clutched Bent's dog tags . . .

. . . and started climbing.

## ~ 17 ~

*God Almighty hates a quitter.*

—Gen. Samuel Fessenden,
at the Republican Convention, 1896

I CAN'T believe he did it," Ace said to Jesus. They were at a table in the quietest corner of the Cloud Cafe.

"Let it go, Captain," said Jesus, smiling. "A bottle of Chloe and a fruitcake won't hurt the campaign. By the way, have you seen Chaney lately?"

"No, I haven't," said Ace. And then he rushed back into his old train of thought. "But a stock tip, my Lord? Our man is in the Topeka jail."

"Nothing I haven't planned for," said Jesus. "Remember, Alistair, every good thing bestowed and every perfect gift is from above. Change of subject, now. Let's talk battle casualties."

"How's Albert? asked Ace.

"Doc will have him good as new in no time. What I meant was, how are *you?*"

"Me, Sir?" said Ace, fidgeting at the suggestion.

"Yes, *you,* Alistair. How are *you* holding up?"

"Famously, Sir. I handled Citizen Pogromme with no trouble at all. Why, I've—"

"You've begun just as you did before," said Jesus.

Ace sank back in his chair, closed his eyes, and listened

to the bustle of the cafe. Inside, he felt the same old fears bubbling inside him, for he knew that Pogromme had not even begun to show his worst colors yet.

"Listen to me now, Captain, for what I'm about to say is for your good," said Jesus. "The battle for Walter's tongue will be difficult. At this very moment the moans are oiling their wings and filing their teeth. Satan will do anything to keep one more soul from hearing the gospel."

"Then we'll call in more troops."

"They're all deployed elsewhere, Alistair," said Jesus. "In fact, we have even fewer for Ellenbach now. Albert's out. So is Doc. That leaves François and Homer and Chaney."

Ace stood looking down at the table for a moment.

"You've always been a strategist," said Jesus. "And a good one at that."

"Thank you, Sir," said Ace quietly.

"This time, be a *wise* one," said Jesus. "Call on Me, my friend. I give grace to the humble."

"I'm trying, Sir. I really am. I'm doing the best I can."

"Rest in Me, Alistair, and your best will be better."

There was courage in his Master's words, enough to pick Ace up again and send him back into the fray. That afternoon, the diminished company of angels began working around the clock.

There still had been no sign of Chaney, and Ace wondered if he'd been too hard on him when he found out about the extras in Walter's bag. Nevertheless, the mission continued. Homer flew daily to hell under all types of disguises: a photographer for the *Chronicle,* a janitor, a driver, a sorter. Once he disguised himself as a moan looking for the spa who took the wrong turn and found himself in the mail room without the slightest idea of how to get back to where he started. Because Satan already knew the players in Jesus' plan, he made absolutely sure that the envelopes Stan passed on contained nothing more than blank pieces of paper. And he told the moans to leave the angel alone. So Homer continued to waltz in and out of hell with empty letters, while Bent was sent to Sanctum 909. All the while, Satan watched his monitors closely. He deluded himself by thinking Jesus knew nothing of the blank letters, and he waited for the perfect opportunity to ambush the squad of waiters.

Up on earth, Walter languished in Topeka. His boot box began to bulge with pseudo correspondence, and his bag was shouldered by various interim carriers during his absence. But it wasn't long before Ellenbach realized just how much it missed its veteran mailman. Packages began arriving late, and those that came on time were either dirty or damaged. Aldo Cobb got Junior Withers's social security check. And Junior got Aldo's insulin. Foster Jenson got a prom dress. And Suzie Parsons got a *Wall Street Journal.* And those who were the most angry with Walter for what he'd done, stayed angry. For they were also the ones who were the most angry with God about the way life had gone for them. But the rest of the town's citizens began to talk amongst themselves. They talked of the "old days" and the "old Walter" and the time when God seemed closer to them all. And pretty soon, a sort of line was drawn down the center of Ellenbach's Main Street, from either side of which one camp lobbed logic at the other.

"There's no *way* the letters are real!"

"That's what Walter told the reporters in Topeka. I read it in the paper."

"They're still not real."

"They are too! Because God is real. And if He wants to fit Himself inside a mailbox, then I reckon that's His business."

"That's the most foolish talk I've ever heard. It doesn't take but a look to see what God—if there is one—has done to folks's lives around here. Take Bill Ray, for

190 ~ *Will Cunningham*

instance. The man used to be as God fearing as the best of them, until God took his crops three summers running. Now, look at him. He's drunker than a one-legged duck."

"That isn't God's fault. He didn't buy the booze."

"I figured talking to you would be like talking to a stump. So, what about the Widow Spradling?"

"What about her?"

"She hasn't been waving Jesus since her Terrence died."

"What do you expect her to do? A dance? Folks are always somber when their people die."

"Ten years somber? Nah, she's got smart like the rest of us and gave up on Jesus. Walter's done it, too, while we're on it. He's found himself another rabbit foot to rub."

And day after day the debate in Ellenbach raged over whether God had caused Widow Spradling's widowhood, Emma Sanger's divorce, Aldo Cobb's diabetes, Judge Pickens's glaucoma, Fern the Airedale's rabies, and Bill Ray's drunkenness. Of course, God never got much credit for the days Bill Ray stayed sober.

In Topeka, Walter waited for Donna to wire him the money for bail. But July came and went, and the money never came. The district attorney, Mr. Combs, was a loophole lover with the congeniality of a snail. Whenever the topic of settling out of court was brought up by the defense, Combs kept himself and Foster Jenson III inside a shell of legal doublespeak. And so the trial drew swiftly nearer.

The defense consisted solely of Jack Robbins, who had returned from the halls of Harvard where he'd studied and taught law after Muriel's death. He had come to defend his father-in-law and to give Donna emotional support. He had come to put flowers on a grave, to remember, to cry, to steel himself for further solitary living. He had also come to throw the ball in the front yard with Dallas and to get his wife's little brother ready for two-a-days.

Sometime in late August, Dallas took his finished love letter and started to look for Larry Ravelle.

"Where are you headed?" said Jack, as he saw Dallas wheel his bike out of the driveway and across the cul-de-sac.

"Looking for Coach Ravelle. He isn't at home. I've already tried there."

"Try the church, Dallas," said Jack. "If I remember correctly, he's just as likely to be there as anyplace. Talking to God about the Laird game, listening, reading, that sort of thing. Go on, Dallas. Your mom will have dinner by the time you get back. Don't be late. And tell Coach hi for me."

"Okay, Jack. See you."

Sure enough, Coach Ravelle was at the front of the sanctuary in Ellenbach Community Church. He was slumped forward, with the crown of his ball cap just visible over the top of the pew when Dallas spotted him. Larry heard his friend's footsteps and turned around.

"Hello, son," said Larry.

"Sorry to bother you, Coach. I'm done," said Dallas, holding out his letter.

"Ah, yes. All those Sunday nights paid off, didn't they?" He took the letter, unfolded it, and began to scan the text.

"Hmm, let's see . . . eyes like shining pools of oil . . . not bad, not bad . . . flowing locks . . . skin as smooth as silk . . . good . . . and not a single *ain't* in the whole letter. It's a little mushy, but I think it'll do. If I were Eddy Lundy, I'd be pleased to hear this stuff! You've done all right, Dallas. I'm proud of you. How's your arm coming along, son?"

"Looser than it's ever been, Coach," said Dallas. "Me and Jack, I mean, Jack and I have been throwing the ball some. I put ten in a row the other day through that old tire swing in the Cottonwood behind Henry Commons's place."

"You don't say," said Larry. Then more solemnly he added, "How is Jack?"

"He's fine," said Dallas.

"I hear he's in town to defend your father," said Larry.

Dallas looked at his feet, and Larry continued, hesitantly.

"How's your dad, son?" he asked.

"He ain't doing well, Coach," said Dallas. This time Larry didn't correct the boy's English.

"That's what I've been praying about this afternoon, Dallas," said Larry. "Believe me, I know what it's like to have the whole town looking down its nose at you."

"You mean you aren't here asking God to help us beat Laird?" asked Dallas.

Larry laughed at the question.

"Okay. Just a little, maybe," he admitted. "But I'm asking more for Him to help us in the bigger game, the bigger battle."

"Bigger than the Laird game, Coach?"

"Oh, son," said Larry, breathing deeply, then exhaling long and slow. "Lots of things are bigger than the Laird game. But there's nothing bigger than what goes on around us in the air."

Dallas followed Larry's finger up into the dusty, stained-glass light of the sanctuary, where reds, greens, purples, and golds slashed at the dark.

"Up there?" asked Dallas.

"Uh-huh," said Larry. "I preached for years about them from that pulpit, back when I was a pastor. And I believed what I preached, too. But I never *really* believed until . . . until I felt them at the Sunset Grille."

As most people in Ellenbach were accustomed to doing, Dallas looked away when he heard those two words. Still, he was curious.

"Who's *them*, Coach?" he asked.

"The rulers of the unseen world, the princes of darkness. Angels and demons, son. You've heard of them before. Haven't you?"

Dallas stared into the shadowy space above. He had

heard, but he wasn't sure he believed. He wasn't sure of anything spiritual ever since his father stopped believing. But in the rafters above sat good reason for belief.

A thousand pairs of yellow eyes peered down from those heights. A thousand others filled the balcony. Where the tops of the organ pipes ended in shadows, Citizen Pogromme perched with his thick brows twitching.

"Hisss," he called to the others. "The Enemy is a dog. And a dumb one, at that. Can you believe He'd leave this town unoccupied?"

The rafters buzzed with laughter.

"Our great lord Dickens . . ." said Citizen Pogromme, using one of Satan's more formal titles.

And the others sang out the obligatory, "Dickens be praised!"

". . . has, in his infinite wisdom, deemed it necessary to withdraw us from our ranks in Chicago, Calcutta, Rio, and other cities to place us here. And the Enemy has done nothing to stop us."

"The Twit! The Everlasting Fool!" rang the rafters.

"We are here to keep the mail from going through."

"Stop the mail! Stop the mail!"

"We are here to crush the mail carrier and his family."

"Crush them! Beat them! Bash them!"

"More than anything, we are here to make sure Ellenbach is not reintroduced to that hideous gospel on account of a handful of waiters."

"Waiters? Ho-ho."

"Let's not keep them waiting," cried Pogromme.

At that, the demons streamed from the church, fluttering out across the town like an army of bats. Indeed, they *were* an army, the very army that Ripskin had witnessed marching along the pathways outside of C-storage. And had Larry and Dallas seen them too, they would have screamed and covered their heads, so horrible are the faces of the Alpha Order.

* * *

"Mail that letter as soon as you can, son," ordered Larry. "Better still, deliver it in person."

"Yes, sir, I will, Coach. As soon as I get up the nerve, I'll put it right in Eddy's hand." Dallas almost skipped down the red-carpeted aisle to where his bike waited on the front porch of the church.

Sitting on the chimney of the Connistons' house, Chaney Goodwin felt just awful. It hadn't taken Ace to tell him what a mess he'd made of things. Because of him, poor Walter was in jail and the family was crumbling fast. Worst of all, Chaney had let Jesus down—at least he thought he had—which made him fairly certain he'd never be asked to serve in battle again.

*But,* thought Chaney, *I've got to repair the damage I've caused.*

The weather had been bad when Chaney left the East Wall of heaven, and was likely to get worse. Consequently, it had taken him days to get to earth. Now, not wanting to be cut off from his own kind, Chaney went about his business in a hurry. He shinnied down the chimney to a spot where the flue slanted inward. There, he heard the sound of crying. It was coming from the attic. He stepped through the wall of cinder blocks and paused to let his eyes adjust.

In a patch of horizontal light that came from the gable vent, Donna Conniston knelt weeping. At her knees was Walter's boot box, which she'd found again on the evening he was taken away. In it were a dozen letters, letters that had come in Walter's absence. She'd discovered them on her doorstep, under her pillow, in her marigolds, weighted down by the wipers on her windshield. They'd arrived almost daily. And every day Donna cut them open with a knife and read them for herself. The ones from Muriel were all of happiness and heaven. The ones from Bent were strangely blank.

*Dear Lord, she must be broken,* thought Chaney, as he watched the woman cry.

And broken she was, for Donna had seen the error of her way. There was no secret lover, no clandestine affair, no reason for jealousy after all. She had learned from the letters that MC was none other than her own sweet daughter.

"My Muriel," sobbed Donna. "And Bentley, oh, Bentley."

In Donna's hand, Chaney saw what probably was the last letter Bent had written on the day he was discovered. He repositioned himself behind the woman so he could read the words. And immediately, he saw that the letter was really just a note, typed hastily and full of misspellings, as if the one who'd written it had little time to use his dictionary. Most alarming were the smudges of blood at the bottom of the page.

Dear Muriel,

Thanks for doing this as long as we did, Sis. Well, today I got cuaght for writing you. I'm going to sanctum 909. I love you Muriel. I love Mom and Dad too. I wished I'd told them more. I wished I'd told Dallas too. Hell is a bad place to be. I would have made friends with Jesus if I could do it all over. I'll try to get this to Stan. Maybe they havent cuaght him yet. The moans are coming now. I hear thier boots. gotta go

Love Bent

By Donna's side, Chaney saw a plate of cookies with a sealed envelope placed on top. He strained his eyes to read the words SWEET MURIEL typed on its front. Right away he knew what Donna was doing.

*The poor, dear woman,* thought Chaney. *There is hardly a soul on earth who doesn't think of us at least a little bit like elves doing Jesus' good bidding, and of Jesus Himself like Santa. But I can't take something from earth back with me. I've messed things up enough for a while.*

While Chaney sat there thinking, Donna's tears flowed like rain against a roof.

"Please," cried Donna, up into the trusses. "Please, if there's anyone out there listening, please take this letter to my daughter."

*You don't know what you're asking ma'am,* said Chaney to himself.

"Oh, please, pleeeaaase," wailed Donna. She put the lid back on the boot box, rearranged the cookies, and left the attic, which still rang with her sobs.

"I c-can't let the woman go on weeping," said Chaney as he swept up the letter with a decisive motion. He was turning to step back through the cinder blocks when he thought of the cookies. His smile brightened the attic.

"Oh, well," Chaney said, taking the biggest cookie on the plate. He had never tasted anything from the blue planet, so he studied the cookie cautiously. When he'd determined it was safe, Chaney closed his eyes and bit down slowly. "Why, it's good," he exclaimed.

Chaney returned the uneaten portion to the plate. He looked around the attic. Though he saw no moans, it had the distinct odor of hell. He offered a benediction over the place, asking God to sow His blessings through the ceiling, down into the house, down onto the head of Donna Conniston who wept softly in the kitchen. When he was finished, he stepped into the chimney and crawled out into the open air.

From the rooftop Chaney saw the cloud heading his way. It moved faster than a cloud should move, and it sounded "uncloudly," too. It squawked and cursed and lurched ahead on leathery membranes. He could smell it as it came.

"Imp-p-possible, it c-c-can't be," he whispered. "They're all supposed to be in the cities."

Chaney slid down the back side of the roof and landed in the grass. All of Mulberry Court was darkened. Dogs barked. Birds fluttered. Emma Sanger went out on her front porch and swore at the sky. Chaney crouched behind a garbage can as the first of the mighty Alpha Order touched down on the shingles. Soon the Conniston home was covered with the black and sinewed bodies from hell. They cussed loudly. They beat against the roof. They tossed their heads from side to side.

Fifty feet of lawn lay between Chaney and the woods behind the house. Ten feet farther from its edge, trunks of elms dissolved into gray cover. Grass grew high as a dog's head there. Twigs and sticks broke the background of deeper, solid colors. There an angel might be taken for a stump and thus be spared a painful torture. Trembling by the can, Chaney eyed the woods. He tucked Donna's letter to Muriel underneath the thin rope belt he wore around his middle and folded his feathers down over it. He took note of several objects in the yard. A birdbath. A stack of logs unburned from last season. A hammock. A toolshed.

*Run as fast as you can, Chaney. Then fly into those woods,* he thought.

T. Chaney Goodwin was a brave angel, even if he had, in his mind, botched the mission single-handedly. It was his courage that caused him to return alone to earth. It was his courage that made him eat the cookie. It was his courage that motivated his legs across the Connistons' backyard that night. Nevertheless, courage alone has never been a match for angry demons. Before he reached the birdbath, Pogromme was upon him.

"The gig is up, cowboy," said Citizen Pogromme. "We're going to have some fun with you!"

"H-help," shouted Chaney.

"Why waste your breath? You're all alone, little angel. And so very far from home."

The roof load of moans shrieked with laughter.

"Have you ever wished that jibbering tongue of yours didn't stutter so much?" asked Pogromme, as he produced a pair of iron pincers from underneath his wing. "I could grant that wish, you know. With just a snip or two, I could help you with your problem immensely. Here, you won't feel a thing."

Pogromme aimed the pincers toward the soft skin beneath Chaney's chin, and his eyes became hot slits. With a burst of adrenaline, Chaney wiggled loose. He scrambled toward the woods, tripping on the hammock, to the delight of the Alpha Order. In seconds, Pogromme had him pinned again. He was breathing heavily now, and was in no mood for further exercise.

"All right. I'll put it to you quite simply, so you can get it all. I will serve you as hors d'oeuvres to my friends unless you tell me everything I want to know. Now, for starters you can tell me where that worthless captain of yours is."

Chaney lay motionless and kept his mouth shut. Pogromme slapped him hard across the face. This produced less than a whimper.

"Nothing?" said Pogromme. "Very well. But I must tell you, I've spent an eternity studying the fine points of pain."

Chaney was silent.

"So be it," hissed Pogromme.

# ~ 18 ~

*Judges ought to be more learned than witty,*
*more reverend than plausible, and more*
*advised than confident. Above all things,*
*integrity is their portion and proper virtue.*

—Francis Bacon, *Essays: Of Judicature*

COMPARED to its counterpart in Topeka, the Johnson County Courthouse—with its stone columns half the width, and its shutters covered with half the paint—was a rather poor imitation. Nevertheless, far less injustice went on there as well, which was a good thing for Walter, who was being brought to trial in Laird, rather than in Topeka.

Inside were the smells of old plaster and even older briefs yellowing in cubbyholes. Around the halls solicitors moved, fingering the dust on window ledges and rehearsing pending cases. Through a crack in his chamber doors, Judge Pickens sometimes eyed them. He watched them browbeat unseen witnesses. He watched their tongues working madly at bits of egg salad stuck between teeth. And as he watched, District Judge Roy Pickens thanked the stars he'd been spared his colleagues' existence. For on the same day he was elevated to his present position of prominence, Judge Pickens was stricken with glaucoma. Consequently, he spent far less time reading cases and a great deal more time outside in the square, sitting beneath a crabapple tree and listening to Beethoven. The partial loss of sight had saved him from the grind of his four-year appointment. Nevertheless, he missed the comforts of driving, sifting through his mail, and doing all the other things that most people take for granted.

And, he missed Gladys.

Most days, at the stroke of nine, Judge Pickens arrived in Laird via Eunice Honeycutt and her Oldsmobile, which had been giving the old woman fits ever since Greedo graced its grille. After closing the car door, the judge thanked his neighbor, strode up the stairs, and passed through the gloomy building's doors into the world of torts.

"Top of the morning," he'd say to the tax assessor and the tax collector, whose cubicles he had to pass en route to his own chamber in the side of the gray stone wall. Then to the county clerk he'd give a courteous nod, and to the county solicitor a wink, which said "good morning" but really meant, "While you're studying law, I'll be listening to *Pastorale* beside my favorite tree." And to the circuit clerk and the judge of probate and the paralegals and the secretaries and the occasional visiting justice, Judge Pickens never failed to say "Hello, hello, hello," all the way down the hall. In his chamber, he found solace.

Today, however, he found Jack Robbins, Mr. Combs, and an oatmeal-colored court reporter waiting to meet with him. He stood in the doorway sizing up the three people responsible for disturbing his morning, just as they'd disturbed every other morning for the last three weeks. Indeed, the recent indictment process and the preliminary hearing had been too long for Judge Pickens's liking.

"I suppose you're here to whine your way into my good graces concerning Conniston," Judge Pickens said morosely. He held this case in contempt—largely because of the defendant's steadfast claim that the postal items in question must have come from heaven. It was common knowledge that Judge Pickens didn't believe in the supernatural.

"Your honor," began Combs, "I'm still concerned with your interpretation of *Carpenter* v. *United States* when it comes to intangible property."

"Oh, put an end to it, Combs," said Judge Pickens, crossing to his desk where a stack of unanswered correspondence teetered precariously on its edge. "For the forty-seventh time, you may not present a fruitcake from heaven in my court! Neither sob nor sigh will change my mind on that topic. Anyway, I have a terrible headache this morning, which is not unrelated to the presence of you three gentlemen."

"But the weight of evidence, sir—"

"The weight of evidence, Mr. Combs, shows only that there is probable cause to bind over this insignificant postal worker for trial," said Judge Pickens, holding his head where it ached the most. "He is accused of fraud, not of terrorizing the elderly with poisoned goodies. Good heavens, Combs, leave the man some shred of decency."

"Your honor, if I might interject—" said Jack.

"Go right ahead," said Judge Pickens. "You're going to whether I permit it or not."

Jack Robbins ran a hand through his thick black hair and considered his most recent discussion with Walter in Topeka.

"For the sake of progress, I make a motion *in limine* that the fruitcake, as evidence, not be permitted and that we could just stop talking about it."

Combs rolled his eyes.

"I wholeheartedly agree," said Judge Pickens. "Besides, I've never liked the things. Why people give them as tokens of Christmas cheer is beyond me. The fruitcake is out. End of discussion."

202 ～ Will Cunningham

"Well, your honor," said Combs, irritably. "I *do* still have a peremptory challenge or two."

"You have nothing of the sort," said Judge Pickens. "You've used them all in your attempt to populate the jury with every widow in Johnson County who ever had a gripe with the post office."

"I have not," argued Combs.

"Oh, yes you have! And it's going to stop!"

"Then I have a challenge for *cause*, Your honor," blurted Combs.

"Oh, shut up," said Judge Pickens.

Combs bit his lip and looked at the bookshelves.

Jack saw his chance.

"Your honor, clearly, there was no *tangible* gain to my client by delivering Mr. Jenson's mail," he began. He looked at Combs when he emphasized the word *tangible*. "Perhaps we could settle this whole thing out of court, and you could get back to more important matters," said Jack, nodding at Pickens's collection of Beethoven and his prescription eyedrops for intraocular pressure, which sat on top of his stereo.

"Don't press your luck, counselor," said Judge Pickens. "I don't like you any more than I like Combs, here."

Over in the corner, the court reporter looked up from his work, wondering if he should include that last remark.

"Put it down," said the judge, having noticed the reporter's pause. "It's no secret I detest lawyers. I detest everything about law except the law itself. I detest you, too, Woodberry, with your incessant pecking. Now, have we sullied my chambers enough today with all this nonsense?"

Neither lawyer said a word.

"Very well," said Judge Pickens. "This meeting is adjourned, and I will be indisposed until the trial tomorrow. Good day, gentlemen."

The three men exited the room posthaste, with Combs and Woodberry hurrying ahead of Jack who was stopping to close the door behind him. Just before the latch clicked shut, he caught a glimpse of the old judge reaching toward his stereo.

In the dimness of his chamber, Judge Pickens leaned far back in his chair and forced his right eye wide with thumb and forefinger. With his other hand, he poised the bottle and squeezed. Three precious drops fell into his eye. He was glad to be finished with the evidential ruling. The sixty-eight-year-old man switched on the stereo and relaxed in the arms of *Missa solemnis*.

"Letters from dead people," he muttered. "What a ridiculous way to end one's career. Perhaps in later years, I'll hand down decisions on the roundness of the earth or the existence of witches in Johnson County."

A light flickered suddenly in the fuzzy air above him. Judge Pickens turned his head to focus on the disturbance. Around the ceiling lamp, a rainbowlike ring hovered. He closed his eyes, touched his lids, and pressed hard against the spheres beneath them. He expected severe pain, but he felt nothing.

*They said there'd be a stab when this finally happened*, thought Judge Pickens, in reference to the acute congestive condition that the doctors had told him might occur suddenly at any time. His eyes felt fine, though.

There was movement to the side of him. He turned his head again.

"Woodberry? Is that you?" said Judge Pickens. His voice fell onto the rich, red carpet.

"Lousy glaucoma," growled the judge.

Above him the room was lit with the polychromatic tracers of Alpha Order moans rocketing around the judge's chambers.

"Hail, fellow," they cried to one another, as their paths crisscrossed. "Fie on the one who damns us to the underworld."

Still rubbing his eyes, Judge Pickens got up from his chair and took his robe from a hook on the wall. As always, he donned the vestment of his occupation before he studied. He opened the file cabinet adjacent to his desk and removed the Conniston folder.

"Let's see," he said, flipping through the papers inside. "What in all creation would a mail carrier stand to gain from delivering a stock tip?" Then, he muttered again, "A stock tip from a dead man, no less."

"There's no such thing as a dead man," shrieked the leader of the Order overhead. "Humans live forever and ever, amen."

Again, Judge Pickens glanced toward the ceiling where the demons of his damaged optic nerve danced around the light fixture.

"There are no dividends beyond the grave," said the judge to himself, looking back down at his desk. "Okay, old man. You know Walt Conniston. He's a decent enough citizen. A bit reclusive, but decent. Is he guilty, though? Come on, Roy. Think. Think. Title 18 lays out two schemes in regard to fraud."

"Fraud," screamed another moan. "The whole world's a fraud."

Then Judge Pickens rummaged about in the folder and produced a sheet of paper that was marked with his own handwriting. He cradled his brow in his hands as he read the words.

"Let's see . . ." he mumbled, scanning the paper. "There is nothing on the face of the statute or anywhere in the legislative history of either the original 1872 . . . or the 1909 amendment to suggest that Congress contemplated the criminalization of schemes that were not aimed at either money or property. Which means that there is no basis for the assumption that the specific reference to . . . clause two was meant to expand the concept of *defraud* in clause one to include nonproperty interests . . . oh bother," said Judge Pickens, crumpling the paper and throwing it in the trash. "This is the craziest thing I've ever been a part of."

"Crazy. He thinks we're crazy," said the leader moan.

"Just the type of thinking we appreciate," said another.

"Yes," cried the leader again. "Keep right on with those thoughts, Judge Roy Arthur Pickens, and soon enough you and others like you will be in hell with us. And you'll bow before the craziest judge of all!"

Judge Pickens bowed his head to his desk, massaging his temples and speaking into the folds of his robe.

"Forgive us, Gladys," he said, dryly. "Forgive us for denying you the right to privacy of the grave. I, for one, am certain you've gone no farther than your own pine box. Someday, we'll lie together again in the ground. Until then, Buttercup," he concluded, dabbing at his eye with a moist sleeve.

But when it came to Gladys and her postmortem whereabouts, Judge Pickens was both far from the truth and quite near it at the same time. For scarcely a foot and a half away from his elbow, balancing at the top of his unanswered pile of mail, was evidence beyond reasonable doubt that the judge's dear, sweet Buttercup was very, very much alive and well.

And similar pieces of evidence were soon to be introduced.

# ~ 19 ~

*And throughout all eternity*
*I forgive you, you forgive me.*

—William Blake, "My Specter"

THE morning before the trial, the winds were higher than they'd ever been around the East Wall of heaven. Gales went wolfishly about the pearl doorstep. Cosmic trash whirled past. And through the golden mail slot, Ace surveyed the weather, deep in thought.

"It's soup out there," he said in a low voice. "I haven't seen it this bad since the Beginning. It's no use making plans today."

"Might we have a better view through the gate, monsieur?" asked François.

"Believe me, I'd love to, François," said Ace. "But I'm afraid if we opened it, it would blow right off its hinges. See for yourself," he added, relinquishing the slot. Ace shook his head, and for the hundredth time lamented Chaney's absence.

"He'll be coming home soon. You'll see," said Homer.

"I wish I believed that, Homer," said Ace. "But I've got a feeling he's probably trapped on the battlefield."

Suddenly, François gave a little cry.

*"Celui! Celui!"* said the French angel, babbling in his favored language—something he resorted to whenever

he was under pressure. "Hurry. All angels to the gates. Chaney's being followed."

When Ace looked through the slot he saw a black speck flapping upward through the tempest. And behind the speck, there came a host of others flapping even faster.

"Fly, Chaney. Fly," shouted Ace as he and the others sprang toward the pearl portal.

The three angels strained against the gate's thickness, and slowly it began to open. Cold wind licked against the crack. The angels stepped out on the ledge. They jumped up and down, beating their arms about themselves and calling to their friend to hurry.

The speck came wobbling on its course, as if it had flown a long way. When it drew closer, its face came into view and François gasped.

"It is not Monsieur Chaney," he cried. "It is a demon! Quick. Back inside. Close the gate."

"No, François," shouted Ace. "Listen. He's saying something now."

Ace cupped his ear, and heard Ripskin's voice wailing above the wind.

"HEEELLLP," cried Ripskin. "Don't close the gates."

"We have to help him," said Homer.

"I don't know, monsieur," said François. All the while, the wind was whipping up around their ankles, threatening to blow them into space. It would be impossible for the visitor to land without spattering himself against the side of the city.

"Come on, François," said Homer, grinning. "I've been visiting their city the better part of a summer. It's time they came to our place. What do you say, Captain?"

Ace shrugged.

At that, Homer swung down on the ledge, and hung by one arm. In the face of the powerful wind, his wings flogged him mercilessly, and his hair was a gold flag. The moans saw him reaching out toward Ripskin, and they doubled their speed.

"What are you doing, Monsieur Homer?" shouted François. Homer held tenuously to the side of heaven.

"He needs a hand," said Homer.

"He is a demon," said François.

"And a former brother," said Homer.

"Whatever he is, we should not invite him in for lunch," said François.

Ripskin was almost to them now. He was reaching for something shiny around his neck.

"Forget that," shouted Homer above the wind. "Your hands. Give me your hands."

Ace flopped to his belly and reached an arm toward the ragged Ripskin. François followed suit. He could see the Alpha Order moans plainly now. Their teeth shone like needles in the bright light of God's great city.

"Don't let them take me back," squealed Ripskin as he flew. He stretched his black fingertips toward Homer's hand, touched it for just a moment, and then the wind sheered their grip.

"Nooo," screamed Ripskin. He was a scant five feet below the edge now. Despite his mad flapping, he could make no further progress. It was as if the wind held him there, granting him a glimpse of his previous home and nothing more.

Then Homer saw that it was not the wind at all that held him, but an enormous, wretched Alpha moan. He had overtaken Ripskin ahead of the others. With his jaws he clamped down hard on that same part of Ripskin's foot where the rat had bitten, and with his wings he backflapped.

"Hold me by my ankles, Captain," yelled Homer.

"I don't advise it," said Ace.

"Please, sir," said Homer, uncertain as to why he cared so much for the grotesque figure before him. "Look at him. He needs us."

"We can't wrench him free from that brute," said François, beseeching Ace. "Besides, monsieur, the others . . ." François's voice trailed away as he saw the cloud of Alphas drawing nearer.

"Captain, please," begged Homer.

"All right," said Ace. "But if he starts to pull away from you, don't try and hang on."

"Excuse me for saying so, but I think you are both *mad*," said François, wagging his head. "But, *cela va sans dire.* I am just as mad for helping you."

Taking hold of one ankle each, Ace and François lowered Homer in the howling wind.

"Almost there," shouted Homer, when he was only a foot from Ripskin's outstretched hands. He could see down deep into the demon's mouth, where a scream had got stuck. The pain in Ripskin's foot was so terrible that it froze him.

"Don't worry," said Homer, as their fingers met. "We're going to get you out of this mess."

Feeling Ripskin's black nails cut into his wrist, Homer tightened his grip and pulled with all his strength. Above him, Ace and François were straining, too.

"Pull, brothers, pull," shouted Homer.

"Pull, brothers, pull," mocked the Alpha moan. His own dead weight pulled Ripskin in the opposite direction.

A little squeak came from Ripskin's gullet, and then a wrenching scream that might be expected from one being drawn and quartered.

Suddenly, when the rest of the moans had nearly closed the distance between them, a blast of wind hit Ripskin's captor in the face and sent him spinning down the wall. The angels would have fallen themselves had it not been for Ripskin's scrambling so quickly upward and bracing Homer just long enough for Ace and François to pull them both up. And then all four were on the ledge and through the doorway. They slammed shut the East Gate of heaven.

Outside, a moan howled and pounded on the door. He was soon joined by others, and the pounding made a thunderous noise.

"You're lucky you came in with us," said Ace to Ripskin. "No fallen angel makes it through those doors without an escort."

Homer was looking hard at Ripskin, trying to make sense of that face and its familiarity. Ripskin sat with his hand over his eyes, shielding them from heaven's awesome light. He had squatted on his haunches due to fatigue.

"Well, monsieurs, now we have him here. What shall we do with him?" asked François.

Ace eyed Ripskin carefully. Like Homer, he thought he remembered this demon, too. He recognized the filth that covered Ripskin's long, black wings as the remnants of discarded sins and temptations. He looked in disbelief at Ripskin's face, for he had never met anyone who'd traveled through the legendary laundry chute.

"We'll have to take him to Jesus," said Ace.

"I won't be staying long," croaked Ripskin. "I just wanted to deliver these," he said, holding up the dog tags, but not handing them over just yet.

Ace looked closer at the demon's features, then took a chance.

"Hello, Pax," said Ace.

Ripskin cocked his ear toward the sound of his former name, and Homer's eyes brightened when he heard it.

"How are you?" asked Ace.

"What do you care?" muttered Ripskin. Having accomplished his task of arriving safely in heaven, he was neither amiable nor interested in his rescuers. "Now, if we can cut the formalities, I'll just tell you about these—"

"Pax?" whispered Homer, gaping at the shell of his former buddy. "Pax!?" Is that you?"

"The name's Ripskin, pal. Now, can we get on with it?" asked Ripskin.

Homer shook his head sadly.

"He's not our brother, anymore," said Ace. "He has a new home, and a new name, too. Besides, he won't be staying long."

"Here," said Ripskin, removing the dog tags from his neck and forcing them into Homer's hand. Already, the bitterness of comparing heaven to his own frightening hole in C-storage was rising in his throat. "These tags have something to do with a man named Conniston in Ellenbach, Kansas. I believe he's a client of yours. See that they get to him," he snapped.

"Those are Bent Conniston's," gasped François, when he caught a glimpse of the name.

"Exactly. And our good friend Bentley is about to become barbecue when he gets caught for smuggling letters, if it hasn't happened already."

"But monsieur, Pax, or whoever you are, I don't understand," said François.

"And what don't you understand?" said Ripskin.

"Why would you bother to come all this way to deliver these tags? Surely, you know you have committed high treason against your boss."

"Boss," snorted Ripskin. "Let's just say I'm doing a little freelance work." Ripskin glared at Ace. "I have no home and no name, either. I'm a rogue who's about to inflict himself upon the forces of this universe. The more damage I can do to either side, the better."

Then, in spite of the mob that still pounded on the door for his release, Ripskin turned to leave.

"But Pax, it's me," pleaded Homer.

"Shut your face, angel. I don't know anybody by the name of Pax," said Ripskin.

For a moment, Ripskin stood drinking in the sights of heaven that he hadn't seen for centuries. There were the trees he used to climb. There were the woods to his right. There was a corner of the Crystal Sea that could be seen from where he stood.

Someone began shouting on the other side of the gates.

"Evermore!" came the voice of Citizen Pogromme. Ace's features stiffened. What a strange turn of events had occurred when Pogromme, having beaten the information from Chaney that his captain was in heaven, had happened to come across Ripskin on his way here. And knowing that the demon should have been in C-storage, he immediately gave chase.

"Seems you have one of our boys inside. Well, we have one of yours, too," shouted Pogromme.

"Chaney," said François, moving toward the sound. "They have Monsieur Chaney!"

"Don't!" said Ace, grabbing François by the wrist. "Don't open that door." He called through the thick gates. "Chaney? Chaney Goodwin, are you out there?"

"Y-y-yes, sir, C-captain," came the reply.

"What's your first initial?" asked Ace skeptically.

"T-tee, sir. Tee for t-truly, truly s-s-sorry. I shouldn't have left, Captain."

Ace leaned his head against the gate, and a bright line of sweat ran down his cheek.

"Open it," he said. Slowly, François and Homer pushed the great gate open.

On the doorstep of heaven, Ace and Ripskin stood facing the battalion of Alpha Order, which stretched as far as the eye could see. In front of them all hovered Pogromme. By his side, held by two moans, was Chaney. His eyes were swollen shut, his wings in tatters.

"How nice to see you again, Captain," said Pogromme, spitting into the wind. Neither he nor his horde of minions had any idea that Ripskin had brought the dog tags with him, much less that he had turned them over to the Enemy. They merely knew he had escaped from his incarceration.

"Give me Chaney first," shouted Ace.

"Oh, no," said Pogromme. "You hand me the fugitive, and then you'll have your precious buddy."

"I don't trust you," said Ace.

"I don't blame you," Pogromme replied. "With so many of us and so few of you, I'm surprised you opened the door in the first place. But you always were a risk-taker, weren't you?" growled Pogromme. "I've longed to get back here, Captain Evermore. What I wouldn't give to fight you on a great, wide battlefield again. Let me step inside for a rematch. Eh? What do you say? We'll give Jesus a ringside seat."

All at once, Ripskin wriggled free from Ace's grip. Aiming for a gap in the mob, he bolted from the ledge. But the gap closed around Ripskin with such fury that Homer had to look away.

"Jump, Chaney," shouted Ace. But the moans held Chaney tighter.

"Take the city," roared Pogromme, leaping toward the ledge. "Plunder! Pillage! Storm the throne!"

As the Alpha Order pressed in on them, Ace fell back against Homer, who fell against François, and all three landed in a heap just inside the East Gate, with Ace kicking wildly at the onslaught of teeth and claws. Then, as if a ghostly uppercut had stood them straight, the charging moans staggered backward. On their cheeks and foreheads were deep, glowing burns from where those parts had crossed the threshhold into heaven uninvited. Pogromme started at the gate again. But once more, he was driven back the moment he reached the opening. He shook his fist and cursed the invisible force that separated him from his rival. Behind him, the moans who'd been burned howled in pain. Others flapped about nervously.

"You think you've won, Evermore," shouted Pogromme, shaking his finger just inches from Ace's face, all the while careful not to get too close. "Well, I've still got your angel friend, remember. Sooner or later, you'll have to come out and get him. And when you do—"

As Pogromme was shouting, a wide and whistling downdraft came over the top edge of the wall, picked up the pompous demon, and dropped him and his lackeys like stones to the base of the city. Ace inched forward in the wind to the edge of the doorstep and looked down. Fifteen hundred miles below, he saw a thousand antlike bodies moving about on the jeweled foundation. And somewhere in their midst, he hoped that Chaney was okay.

Ace crawled back inside and shut the gate behind him. He sat slumped against it with his chest heaving.

"Monsieur Pogromme is right, sir," said François. "We'll have to help Chaney. Somehow we'll have to get down that wall."

"Captain?" said Homer cautiously. For though he knew Ace would never waver from Jesus' orders, he could almost see the weight of responsibility tugging at his shoulders.

"What is it?" mumbled Ace.

"Walter's trial starts soon. Whatever we do, we better get down to earth to help the man."

Ace put his head in his hands. "I'm just a waiter," he said. "Oh, God, where do You go when a waiter needs You?"

"Monsieur Captain?" said François, kneeling at the foot of the gate by Ace. "You have always been one of my heroes."

Ace heaved a long, tired sigh.

"It's true," François continued. "I have known for centuries that you would fly again in service of our Lord. You are far above the rest of us in leadership."

Ace covered his ears.

"I was a coward," shouted Ace. Then, as if the very word had released an eternity of pain, Ace raised his voice to the top of the celestial city, and cried, "Whyyy?! Why was I afraid?!" Far off, to the south of the East Gate, the outlets of the Crystal Sea gurgled their reply, and Ace began to say the things he'd kept secret since the Battle of Ascension at the beginning of time.

"I trusted Colonel Sky," Ace said mournfully. The very sound of Pogromme's former name brought instant pain to Ace's eyes. "I would have flown anywhere for him. He was my friend, my commander. I couldn't bring myself to hurt him, so I let that wicked angel take a slew of good ones with him when he fell," Ace wailed.

"Impossible," said François. "Only bad ones fell."

"Don't you see?" said Ace. "Don't you remember? I could have stopped him. I had the power to cut Sky into little pieces and dish him through that hole in heaven's floor. But—"

Ace paused.

"But what, Captain?" asked Homer.

"I looked into his eyes," shouted Ace. "I saw hatred there for the first time. I gazed around and saw it in another angel's eyes, too. And another and another and another. The more I saw of hate, the more I was afraid that love had fled forever. In my moment of hesitation, Sky whipped a dozen other good angels into a frenzy, and they all went falling through that hole together."

"But you did your best, monsieur," said François.

"My best got in the way," cried Ace. "Don't you understand? There are angels in hell, because of me!"

"Wrong," said Homer. "They're in hell because they defied God. Trying to stop Pogromme wouldn't have changed a thing."

"Homer speaks the truth, monsieur," said François. "Hate in little pieces is still hate."

"But I failed," said Ace.

"And therein lies your fear," said François. "But that is not a noble fear. Jesus has chosen *you* to do His bidding! I suggest Monsieur Pogromme's tumble into the netherworld, and that of his colleagues as well, was not at all surprising to our Lord. But if you still feel guilt, monsieur, then I forgive you, and so does Homer, and we want to hear nothing more of the incident again. *Comprends-tu?*" said François, as he adjusted his beret. Homer nodded in agreement. "Now, monsieur, will you lead us into battle?"

As is often the case with confession, the sweet release of pardon washed over Ace. It bathed him in love, and brought him to his feet.

"I'm willing," said Ace. "But I'm not sure how to go about it."

"Excellent, monsieur," said François, drawing paper and pen from beneath his wing. "I thought you would never ask. After all, we are here to help each other, *n'est-ce pas*? Come closer. Both of you. I have a plan."

# ~ 20 ~

*It hain't no use to grumble and complain,*
*It's jest as easy to rejoice;*
*When God sorts out the weather and sends rain,*
*Why rain's my choice.*

—James Whitcomb Riley, *Wet-Weather Talk*

Aᴿᴱ you absolutely sure this idea is safe, François?" asked Ace as he pulled the nylon webbing tightly around his waist and fastened the carabiner into it.

"Only as safe as you are, monsieur," said François, kneeling in front of the captain to rotate the safety lock that Ace had overlooked.

"François," said Ace, "after centuries in His service, I am still making sense of the Lord's wisdom. It is times like this, when He lets us fend for ourselves, that I am most perplexed. He could stop the wind, I'm sure."

"Of course He could, monsieur," replied François. "But He knows what's best for us. Besides, I've done this a thousand times, in worse weather, and with fat, Swiss farmers hanging on my back, as well. This will be, as you say, a piece of cake. Besides, if we do not try, we will never reach the foundation where the winds are weaker. If we do not reach the foundation, we will never be able to take off. If we do not take off soon, monsieurs, then

Walter will go to trial alone. And of course there is the one soul."

François's expertise as a mountaineer was something he rarely talked about. Few, therefore, knew of the years he'd spent in service to the Eiger, Mönch, and Jungfrau.

"When I wore less experienced wings," said François, turning to check Homer's gear, "I worked the winters in the Lake Constance region, on the Swiss side of the water. I tell you, monsieurs, in those days even the toughest angels went weak-kneed at the thought of traveling into Germany, it was so full of devils then. The villagers had no idea how real their superstitions were."

"Ow! Watch it," said Homer, when François yanked the harness.

"I am sorry, Monsieur Homer," said François. "If it is not snug, it will not help you. There you are, Monsieur Homer. You are safe now.

"Here," said François to Ace. "Take this eyebolt and screw it into the wall to the left of the ledge."

Ace's biceps bulged as he screwed the iron bolt with the ring on the end of it into the side of heaven. Homer ran his hand along the hundred-mile pitch of rope, feeling for cuts and frayed places, just as François had instructed.

"Find the middle of the rope, Monsieur Homer. I have marked it with a bit of cloth," said François, digging through a gigantic canvas rucksack that leaned against the East Gate. "And Captain, here is another eyebolt. Put it three feet to the right of the other one, and tie this webbing between them."

Ace took the webbing and the bolt and turned back toward the wall. He gazed over the edge at the encampment of moans far below.

"I suggest you are no longer afraid of failure, monsieur. Now, you are afraid of heights," said François, almost chuckling.

"But I fly all the time. I'm not afraid of heights," said Ace.

"Oh, my captain. I assure you, flying is quite different from what we are about to do. Especially with the wind so strong and fierce."

Ace closed his eyes and felt his stomach doing somersaults.

"But remember," said François. "Jesus has felt fear, too. He cried out in Gethsemane, and with far more pain to face than one rappel can inflict. Your fear makes you no less worthy than the rest of us. Oh, monsieur, the stories I could tell you of my own fear. But we have no time for stories. Quickly, now. Tend to your anchor point. And turn to the One who makes brave those who quake."

"Here's the middle point of the rope," said Homer. "What do you want me to do now?"

"As soon as Monsieur Ace secures both eyebolts and the webbing, you can hang that line over it," said François, pointing to the wall where Ace was working. "Then we will have to make the most of one fifty-mile pitch at a time."

"But that's thirty pitches to the bottom," said Homer. "What if they see us coming?"

"That's another reason for our haste, monsieur. We've waited until most of them are sleeping, and only two or three are standing guard. The brightness of the wall will blind the sentries and veil our descent. Oh, I am certain they will see us, eventually," said François, "but too late for them. We will be at the foundation by then. And even if they all wake up, they will leave us alone, for we will stay close to the wall. Jasper burns them worse than brimstone from their own home, remember? They'll keep their distance until Pogromme orders them to charge us. That is when our real problems will begin. We will have to take off quickly and fly all the way to the blue planet without a rest. But it is our only chance, monsieurs. It is *Walter's* only chance. Jesus will be with us. I am also certain of that."

"There," said Ace. "The bolts are set and the webbing in place."

"*Très bien,*" said François, inspecting the anchor point. "Homer, have you tied a hayhook in each end of the rope?"

"Was I supposed to?"

"That is my fault! I am just as nervous as anyone, perhaps. Thank goodness, we discovered it! We would have had a fast trip down. Tie it for him, please, Captain. Now, Homer, stand up so I can fit you with a sling-rope seat, as I have done for Monsieur Ace."

Homer stood while François placed the middle of a short piece of webbing on his hip and brought it around to the front where he tied it with an overhand knot. Then François ran the rope around Homer's legs to the short side and fastened it with a square knot and half hitches.

"Take this carabiner and put it through the single rope around your waist and through the two ropes that form the knot in front," said François. "Do it with the gate down, and the opening toward your body."

As Homer followed François's instructions, Ace checked his own sling for good measure.

"Now both of you, rotate your carabiner one half-turn so that the gate is up and opened away from your body. Check that gate, monsieurs. Is it working correctly? Here is a second carabiner for you to snap to the first one. But leave the gate open. We are almost ready to go on rappel."

François checked Ace's anchor point to make sure the rope moved freely. Then he motioned for Ace and Homer to watch him, since he would be going first to set the next anchor point fifty miles down the wall.

"Tuck your wings back, monsieurs. And tie them with a piece of webbing, as I have. That goes for your swords, too. You will not like it if they get tangled in the ropes, I promise you that. When it is your turn to go—and by the way, Captain, you should follow me with Monsieur Homer bringing up the rear—when it is your turn to go, face the anchor point and make sure the rope runs behind you on your left side."

"Like you said, a piece of cake," said Homer.

"Monsieur Homer, you are a model student," said François.

"How do I hook onto the line, François?" asked Ace.

"I was just coming to that, monsieur," said François, stepping closer to the rope, but not too close to the edge yet. "Snap the rappel line into the carabiner twice, so it makes one smooth loop around the left side. See? I am now, as they say in Germany, *abseilen,* or going down a rope. I am on rappel."

"But you're not going *now*, are you?" asked Ace anxiously.

"Of course not. There is more," said François.

"I was afraid of that," said Ace.

"Captain, you will be just fine," said François. "I am honored to be rappeling with you. But you must not forget to do the thing I am about to tell you. Always lock and reverse the carabiner so that the rope doesn't touch the gate. We should take no chances with cutting our ropes. *Comprenez-vous,* monsieurs?"

"Understood," said Ace.

"Monsieur Homer?" said François when he saw that Homer was more interested in all his glittering gear.

"It's all right, François. I'll remember it all," said Ace.

"One last thing before I go, my friends," said François. "When I reach the end of this first pitch, I will use a prusik sling to hang out while I set our next anchor point. Then you will feel me tug three times on the rope. That is your signal that I am off rappel. I would yell to you if I could, but you would never hear me in these strong winds. So three tugs. Any questions?"

"No. I think we have it," said Ace.

"Have I forgotten anything?" asked François.

"A prayer perhaps?" said Ace.

"Ah, *bien*, Monsieur Ace. That is why you are the captain and I am a mountain patroller. Shall we bow, monsieurs? I will offer the prayer of St. Gotthard's Tunnel, where I once spent the night in the belly of the earth comforting a fräu and six children."

So with François leaning out over the universe and Ace and Homer hanging onto the rappel line to avoid being blown from the ledge, the prayer was offered.

"O God of wind and ice, holy are You in Your purposes. Let Your servants see the light of another day. Amen."

"That was beautiful, François. Whatever happened to the fräu and the kids?"

"A large dog came at dawn, and dug them out," said François. "Watch closely so you will know what to do."

François passed the rope around his left hip and grasped it behind him with his right hand. Then, with his left hand above the carabiner for balance, he lowered himself slowly from the diamond ledge until just the top of his head was showing.

"Courage, monsieurs," he said, as he disappeared altogether.

It seemed an eternity until Ace felt three strong tugs on the rope and it was his turn to go. Meticulously, he followed François's instructions for going on rappel, and soon he was on his way down the side of heaven. For the first ten pitches, *in fact,* Ace was careful not to become over-confident. Homer, on the other hand, slid down shouting every other time he kicked off from the wall.

At the end of the twenty-ninth pitch, Homer met Ace and François at the final anchor point, and the three angels rejoiced over the cloud bank that had rolled up from under the great city.

"They don't even know we're upon them," said Ace, who by now was enjoying the experience.

"Yes," exclaimed Homer. "We'll have Chaney in a heartbeat."

"Shhh!" insisted François. "We are lucky to have come this far without their hearing us." François lowered himself through the thick veil in order to survey the camp below. Suddenly, he poked his head back up through the clouds.

"They are all gone, monsieurs. Every last one of them.

"No moans?" asked Ace.

"No Chaney either, monsieur," said François. "And the winds are absent, too. The call is yours, Captain. I defer to you for further orders."

Ace scratched the bridge of his nose.

"Homer?" he said after a moment.

"Yes, Captain," said Homer.

"Do you want to do this last pitch before we take off?"

"No. I'm ready to go."

"All right then, does everyone have his sword?"

"Got it," chimed Homer and François.

"Do you have the dog tags, Homer?" asked Ace.

"Right here in my fist," he said.

"Good. I think I know where we'll find Pogromme. Let's finish what we started."

"May Jesus go with us, monsieurs, for I fear the time for helping Walter is running out."

"Then, may *we* go with Jesus," said Ace, as the three angels swan dived toward the planet.

# ~ 21 ~

Of Course—I prayed—
And did God care?
He cared as much as on the Air
A Bird—had stamped her foot—
And cried "Give me"—

—Emily Dickinson,
*The Complete Poems of Emily Dickinson, No. 376*

BENEATH the Foster Jenson II Memorial Stadium, Pogromme and his legion waited in ambush. Within the ranks were Spleen and Pater Mordo, though Greedo had been much too affected by the Oldsmobile incident to see action for a very long time. Spleen sported a splint in the middle of his face. And though the splint was suspect as to whether it would actually remedy Spleen's condition, the consensus was that it improved his looks. Pater Mordo was the same as always: slow of mind and foot and twice as ugly.

From his vantage point under the bleachers, Pogromme ground his teeth and watched the sky. He was glad to have abandoned the wind-whipped foundation of that city. Now he hoped to lure Ace onto the stadium's freshly mown turf by placing Chaney and a few moans at midfield. When Ace came to rescue his friend, ohhh! The idea of being rid of his nemesis was almost too much for Pogromme to imagine.

"Where are they?" he worried aloud. "They should be here by now. Surely when they arrived at the bottom of the East Wall and found us gone they'd be worried for their brother, wouldn't they? They'd have to come to Ellenbach, wouldn't they? Their client is in Ellenbach, and his trial is soon. Where else could they go?"

Behind Pogromme and surrounded by a half-dozen burly Alpha moans, Chaney sang at the top of his lungs, partly to alert Ace, if by chance he should hear him, and partly to annoy Citizen Pogromme.

"Shut him up," hissed Pogromme to the moans who guarded Chaney. He had listened for an hour straight to the country angel's version of "Home on the Range," and Pogromme was more than glad to provide a discouraging word if it would put an end to the misery.

"What's the problem, boss?" jeered one of the enormous guards. "A little worried that our army can't lick a handful of the good guys?"

The moan stood, whirled, and delivered a roundhouse kick to Chaney's right cheek, leaving a cloven footprint and a thin line of zoe oozing beneath his eye. Chaney, whose face was already melon-sized from swelling, fell back against the concrete. Pogromme grinned, wondering why he hadn't chosen tougher troops than Greedo, Spleen, and Pater Mordo in the first place.

"One more word out of you, Mr. Country and Western, and I'll have Jacques remove your lips. Everybody listen," said Pogromme to the huge rally of demons around him. "They ought to be coming into view soon. I want absolute silence from here on out. No laughing. No talking. Nothing. Have I made myself perfectly clear?"

A sea of hands went up in silent salute.

"Good. Now, I'll need twelve of you," he added, looking around. The sea went dry. Even Jacques with the karate moves averted his eyes. "What? You mean to tell me there's not one of you who'll volunteer to make angel pâté out of these do-gooders? You sniveling cowards!"

"But sir," said one moan. "What about their swords?"

"Their swords?" shrieked Pogromme. "Do you still believe that legendary hogwash about the magic blades of heaven?"

"Not magic, sir," said the moan. "Just . . . er . . . just better than ours."

"Better than ours?" said Pogromme.

"Well, they do have better smelts, sir," offered another. "They're able to forge much harder weapons. We did not have the foresight to . . . uh . . . grab the smelting manuals on that morning when we fell out of heaven. And, uh . . . well . . . we've never quite been up to par in manufacturing."

"Never quite been up to par in manufacturing," repeated Pogromme. "I'll tell you what's not going to be up to par!" he roared. But his tirade was cut short suddenly when he became aware of the immense light coming up over the north rim of the stadium. He spun around and froze at what he saw. At the center of the field was Captain Alistair Conrad Evermore. Behind him stood François and Homer. They were surrounded by a billion drops of dew on fresh-cut grass, reflecting the glory of the angels. And farther past them was groundskeeper Icky Shackleford, who was just finishing the final touches to the end zone on his riding lawn mower.

"I love the smell of competition in the morning," said Ace. "Hello, Pogromme. I had a feeling you'd choose a place like this. Here's your great, wide battlefield. So, where's the battle?"

From their hiding places, Pogromme and his army looked out into the stadium.

"He's nervous," whispered Pogromme to the nearest officer who could hear him. "Look at him. Look at his eyes. Look at the way his hands rub up and down the hilt of his sword. I've seen that look before. I remember that look from long ago."

"I'm here to take my friend back," said Ace. "And to make sure that Walter Conniston gets a fair trial. I suggest you hand Chaney over and go on home."

"Hah! Is that so?" laughed Pogromme. He motioned to his troops to circle beneath the bleachers and wait for his signal. "Why don't you call it quits, Captain? We smelled your little plan a long time ago. Bent's been shooting blanks since the day we caught him. That's right! All that trouble for a few sheets of empty paper."

"Give me Chaney," Ace demanded.

"You talk a mighty big game, considering there's only three of you!"

"Tsk, tsk, Pogromme. You forget a very large Fourth Factor who is on our side," said Ace. "But math was never your strong suit, was it?"

"What if I was to tell you that at this very moment, you are being surrounded by a thousand demons of the highest order?" said Pogromme. "And that in a few moments more, you three angels are going to be ground cover for the upcoming football season? What would you say to that?"

"Bring it on," said Ace, smiling.

Pogromme ran his tongue along the sharp edges of his teeth and smiled. With a wave of his hand, he shrieked, "Now!" And the legion of moans poured onto the field.

The three angels drew their swords and raised them toward the sky.

The first moans to reach the midfield never even felt Ace's blade. On their captain's command, Homer and François ducked, as Ace flashed around with his massive sword, severing his enemies with a single blow.

"Stay tight. Back to back. Fight the zone in front of you. And don't forget the air above," shouted Ace, just in time to parry the blow of an oncoming Alpha.

A cross-eyed giant, with rusted blade raised overhead, came rushing at Homer. The long-haired angel skipped nimbly to the right, and the moan brought his sword down on the wrong image.

"Swing, and a miss," teased Homer, hopping back to the left. The moan swung errantly again, and Homer cleft him head to toe.

"Get your eyes checked," said Homer to the vanishing halves in the grass.

"Stay tight," repeated Ace, panting hard. "We can't be loose in combat. There's too many of—Hey! Where are you going? Come back here, Homer!"

It was too late. Homer had spied the moans responsible for harming Pax outside the East Gate, and he was off in their direction.

"Aaagh!" screamed François. Ace glanced left and saw zoe flowing fast from François's shoulder. Whirling back, Ace thrust his blade through the moan who'd wounded his brother and bent to retrieve the sword François had dropped.

"Can you still fight, François?" cried Ace as he fended off another blow.

"I think so, monsieur."

"All right. Fight with your other hand," cried Ace, handing the sword to his partner.

"I'm losing zoe, monsieur," cried François.

"Stop the flow with some feathers from your wings. Oh, dear Jesus, help us now!"

The moans came in reluctant waves, shrinking back at first, then charging on with confidence as they saw their foe was wounded. But nowhere in their midst was Citizen Pogromme.

"Where is that fiend?" shouted Ace. "He's here somewhere. I can feel him."

By the concession stand, Homer cornered the moans he was chasing. They had made the mistake of jumping over the counter and hiding behind the newly stocked inventory of condiments.

"This is for Pax," shouted Homer, slicing down through wood, awning, and boxes of ketchup. Red exploded everywhere.

Even above the roar of his mower, Icky Shackleford heard the sound of splintering and wheeled his machine around in the end zone to see what was going on.

"What?!" he exclaimed, when he saw the concession stand's torn green awning and shattered counter at the opposite end of the field. Jamming the mower in gear he headed to investigate, quite unaware of the demon that now accompanied him.

"Roll this hunk of junk," screamed Citizen Pogromme, perched behind Icky on the mower. Pogromme had witnessed the commotion caused by Homer and saw it as his chance to seize the battle. His comrades saw it, too. Straightaway they strong-armed Ace and François, who had been momentarily distracted by the explosion, and pinned them to the ground. Then, for whatever reason— whether as groundskeeper he felt responsible for the incident or whether at that moment he truly heard Pogromme's command—Icky Shackleford gave the mower every last ounce of throttle it had, and the mortal with his evil jockey went racing toward Ace.

"Faster boy! Faster!" Citizen Pogromme screamed at Icky as they bore down on the helpless captain. "Steer a little to the right. There you go. That's it. That's the ticket. We'll take care of the others later. But this one is all mine."

In vain Ace struggled against his captors. Several strapping Alpha moans held him splayed on the fifty-yard line, with the intentions of letting him go just as Pogromme reached him. In his chest Ace felt his old fear rising. It wasn't the fear of pain, but the fear of failing Jesus once again that gripped him.

"How does it feel, Captain Evermore?" shouted Pogromme. "You're about to become one with this God-forsaken ball of dust!"

*My God? Have You forsaken me?* thought Ace.

Pogromme and his driver were at the forty-yard line when at once the words came back to Ace. "If you ever get into trouble, just say my name, and I'll be there."

"JESUS!" shouted Ace, and immediately the moans let go of him, staggering back amongst their brothers. Wide-eyed, they all looked heavenward and their knees began to quake, for they had heard the sound that had been with them since the first tick of time.

It began as just the tiniest click. Then the click became a crrraaack! that stretched until it tore the sky and came crashing down as fire so awesome that it licked up half the legion of moans and sent the remainder of them flying from the stadium.

"Electrical storm," shouted Icky, to whom, he wasn't sure. For he certainly had no idea that before him stood the Chief Cornerstone of the universe, with the broadest smile in all creation and His foot on the neck of Citizen Pogromme, who'd been thrown for a five-yard gain when Icky hit the brakes. At any rate, the boy leaped from the machine and fled, running straight for the newspaper to report what he had seen.

"What's the matter, Captain? Is this riffraff giving you some trouble?" asked Jesus.

"I knew You'd be here, my Lord," said Ace.

"And I knew you'd do a bang-up job of things, Captain. Hello, François," said Jesus.

"Monsieur," said François, doffing his beret with his good arm.

"Would you like to send this one packing, Alistair? Or should I do the honors," asked Jesus, eyeing Pogromme and then the goalpost at the end of the field.

"That's a long kick," replied Ace, smiling.

"For the sake of My children, I slew king Sihon of the Amorites. I crushed Og of Bashan, and all those other despots of Canaan. In comparison, surely this fifty-yarder is quite simple."

"I'll be good. I promise," whimpered Citizen Pogromme.

"Be quiet, rebel," ordered Jesus. "Goodness escapes you."

Then Jesus—who while on earth was called a "man of sorrows"—took great joy in booting Satan's highest ranking officer through the uprights and far out over Ellenbach. Throughout the stadium the remaining moans went pell-mell in all directions.

"Nice kick, Jesus," said Ace. Behind him, by the concession stand, the sound of Homer's singing wafted over the field.

"Turn out the lights. The party's over."

"Not quite yet, my friends. This battle is *far* from over. In fact, you still have a long way to the goal," said Jesus, motioning for François. Jesus touched François's shoulder and then hugged the angel tightly. "There, good as new," He said.

"Thank You, Monsieur. You are a physician extraordinaire," said François.

"And you, François, are all the more equipped to help an ailing mail carrier. Now go, My friends. Rescue Walter. The victory is nearly ours."

# ~ 22 ~

*Stone walls do not a prison make,*
  *Nor iron bars a cage;*
*Minds innocent and quiet take*
  *That for an hermitage;*
*If I have freedom in my love,*
  *And in my soul am free,*
*Angels alone that soar above*
  *Enjoy such liberty.*

—Richard Lovelace,
*To Althea: From Prison*

STRANGER things have taken place within the four walls of cells before. Joseph dreamed in jail and got his freedom back. Daniel, in a cell of sorts, slept peacefully with beasts. In fact, to say whole societies have been changed because of one man's imprisonment would not be far awry. Certainly, Philippi was shaken by its shackled Paul. And Rome across the sea could not have helped but notice. Witness, also, contemporary politicians who, finding themselves on the unpleasant side of bars that they legislated, come eye to eye with the one, true Lawgiver and are born again.

Yes, stranger things have happened.

But who are we to say to Walter, in the Topeka County Jail, that the strangest sight this world has ever known was *not* the sight of Coach Larry Ravelle standing stalwartly at the door of cell 9, waiting for the guard to let him in so he could rekindle the flame in a former evangelist's heart?

"There you go," said the wide expanse of blue-uniformed jailer as the tumblers clicked and the door swung open. "Mind yourself, though. He's crazy. Word is, this one gets his mail from God. Can you believe it? What a joke!" the guard guffawed. The door clanged shut, and Larry listened to the man's heavy footsteps scuffling away down the cold corridor until he could hear them no longer. Unable to believe his eyes, Walter rubbed them hard with a wad of dirty fingers and sat up on his cot. He was wearing a bright orange jumpsuit.

"Morning, Walt," said Larry.

"Uh, morning," said Walter, shocked that this neighbor of his, who'd traversed the lawn between their houses only once to borrow a cup of sugar, had come so far to visit him now. The moment of silence that begs for someone to break it settled over the cell, and Larry helped himself to the only other piece of furniture available, a metal stool.

"I don't blame you for being surprised to see me," said Larry, after a while. "Can't say that I've been the best of neighbors. Truth is, I never thought you liked me."

"Truth is, I don't," mumbled Walter. But in his heart, Walter felt a spark of gladness for a visitor, any visitor, even if it *was* the man who by his former deeds had pushed him farther from God than anyone or anything else, save the deaths of his children.

"I understand," said Larry. "I let a lot of people down when my private life went public. I lost every good elder and deacon I ever had, but none was as good as you, Walt."

Walter scowled at the compliment, as those with charges pending often do when people call them good.

"Thank God I didn't lose my family," added Larry. "That would have been too much for me, I believe."

At the mention of such loss, Walter turned his head toward the wall.

"Well, I won't keep you long. I just brought these things for you," said Larry. He placed a Bible and what appeared to be a small, felt jewelry box on the cot, then turned to leave.

"Wait," said Walter, turning suddenly toward Larry and clasping his arm. "You don't have to go, do you? I mean, you can stay. I'm not bothered much by your being here."

"All right," said Larry. "I'll stay. But I've got some things to say, some questions to ask. I hope you don't mind."

"Go ahead. Ask," said Walter, who had questions of his own—questions about heaven, hell, whether a man who gets letters from God is really crazy. *Who better to ask but a preacher?* thought Walter. Or, at least, a former preacher.

"Okay, here goes," said Larry. "But don't get offended. I'm not trying to cause you any more trouble. There're just some things that make me curious."

"I said you could ask," said Walter.

Larry leaned as far forward on the metal stool as possible, so close to Walter's face that he could have counted the pores in his skin if he'd wanted. And as he spoke, there was a melancholy note to his voice.

"I had a wandering eye once, too," said Larry.

"What's that?" asked Walter, though he knew what was meant.

"It's the telltale sign of a starving heart."

"Are you saying my heart is starving?"

"Maybe. Maybe not," said Larry. "But I know you've been doing more than just delivering mail to 602 Cistern lately."

"Seems like a lot of people have been poking their noses into other peoples' business lately, too," said Walter.

"Come on, Walt," said Larry. "I know I disappointed you years ago. But you have to admit, we were friends, then. At least, we respected each other."

Walter gave a grunt.

"And I think you respected Donna a whole lot more than you do right now, too."

"How do *you* know who I respect and who I don't?" said Walter.

"Walt, it's not a secret anymore. Once the townsfolk got those strange things in their boxes, well, you know, they started watching you more closely. And what they saw was Walter Conniston with Marla Coe. See what I'm saying? Folks are none too happy about that."

"There's nothing to the rumors," muttered Walter.

"Then why don't you head on back to Donna, Walt? She's a beautiful woman. She needs you, you know. More than ever with your two eldest gone. For that matter, Dallas needs you, too."

"Well, you see, pastor, there's just one problem. I'm stuck here, in case you hadn't noticed."

"I'm talking about when this whole trial thing is over. *Then!* Won't you at least consider giving her your heart again then?"

"You've got an awful lot of answers for everybody else's life, don't you? Well, what if I told you I didn't have a heart for anybody anymore?"

"I wouldn't believe it," said Larry.

Walter lay back on his cot and became interested in the ceiling.

"Those letters . . ." said Larry, changing the subject.

Walter stiffened.

"Did you really have no idea how they got in your bag? I don't mean to doubt you, Walt. But talk around Ellenbach is that the only reason you told those inspectors they were messages from God was to get off the hook."

The joint of Walter's jaw worked slowly up and down. But he lay like a stone on his cot.

"Some folks say you're a cruel prankster. Others want to take the stand in your defense. The Lord knows I'm not trying to mock you, Walt. I talk as much to God as I ever did when I was Pastor Ravelle. Probably more.

I believe He talks to me, too. Not audibly, of course. I've been so close to heaven and to hell before, that I could almost hear the harps and feel the heat. I'm not here to mock you. I'm here to ask you plain and simple, did you invent those letters yourself?" Larry believed Walter, but a part of him had to hear Walter speak the truth.

Walter's face turned red and he sat up on the edge of the cot.

"Why you hypocrite!" shouted Walter. "If that isn't the pot calling the kettle black, then I don't know what is."

"Whoa now, Walt," said Larry.

"Don't whoa me," shouted Walter. "My so-called crimes aren't anything compared to what you did at the Sunset Grille back when you could still hold your head up high around town, preacher man!"

The words stung Larry, even though he knew he'd come again into the good graces of his fellow citizens. Most of them had forgiven him quite handily, a move that well-behooved many of them, since Larry had not been the first *or* last Ellenbachian to patronize the county's only strip joint. But he had been the only pastor to go there. Nevertheless, he concluded within himself as he sat just inches from red-faced Walter that *life is not about holding one's head up high.*

"I told you I didn't come here to offend you, Walt," said Larry, calmly. "How could someone who believes you offend you?"

"And I told *you* and the rest of that good-for-nothing town that I—" Walter stopped, and his stubbled, blotchy face softened in amazement. "You *what?*" he asked.

"I believe you," said Larry.

"You do?" said Walter.

"Yes, I do."

"You mean, you don't think I made all those stories up?"

"No, sir. Not a one of them," said Larry. "Here, I'll show you why."

Larry motioned toward the Bible and the felt box on the cot beside Walter.

"I had to sneak the box past the guard," said Larry, hurrying on. "I must admit, at first I had my doubts, Walt. I told myself there was no way possible that Walter Conniston could be telling the truth about those letters being from heaven and hell. After a while, I began to pity you."

Reluctantly, Walter picked up the box and stared at it.

"But then I thought about what happened to me back in my days at the Grille. I thought about all those times when God was trying so hard to get my attention that I promise you—and I've never told anyone this before—that I could almost hear His footsteps at times."

Walter shifted on his cot. Such talk of God chafed him and made him bristle. After all, was it not God who swallowed up two-thirds of the fruit of his loins? Had He not promised peace and given him pain?

"Who gives a rip about your religion," blurted Walter. "I know I said the letters were from heaven and hell, but that doesn't mean I believe in God."

"What does it mean, then?" asked Larry.

"It means I didn't write them. And I wasn't playing tricks on anybody. And I sure don't want to go to jail for fraud. I was just doing my job. That's what it means. But, if you asked me if they came from some other world, I'd say no."

"So you've stopped believing the way you used to believe when you were a deacon?"

"I never did believe," shouted Walter. "Not then and not now."

"Not in God? Not in His Son? Not in angels?" asked Larry.

"Angels?" said Walter.

"That's right," replied Larry, hurrying on to his next sentence before Walter had the chance to build another angry head of steam. "And demons, too. I think you've got a whole bunch of them hot on your tail. When I was stuck in that Grille thing, I—"

238 ～ *Will Cunningham*

"You're a crazy man," shouted Walter. But deep inside, he knew Larry was answering his questions before he'd even asked them.

"Oh, no. I'm not at all crazy," said Larry. "I studied it in seminary, in a class called, angelology. They said I couldn't graduate unless I took it. At first, I thought it was going to be boring. But when I learned there were more than three hundred references to angels in the Bible, I decided to give it a chance. For instance . . ." said Larry, pausing. At this point, he took Walter firmly by his shoulders and looked him in the eyes. "Did you know the Bible says there are millions of them? Not just Michael and Gabriel, Walt. But millions of them."

Walter squirmed, but Larry Ravelle's grip was a strong one.

"The Bible says they're spirits! Servants of God! Look at me, Walt! Don't look away! I'm trying to explain what's happening to you! I'm trying to help you!"

"I don't want your help," said Walter. The two men's voices were so loud by now that the guard heard the commotion and came running.

"Leave me alone," shouted Walter. But Larry held him tighter.

"Hey! What's going on down there?" came the guard's voice, still halfway down the hall.

"It's true, Walter," said Larry, rushing to have his say before the guard arrived. "All day long the angels worship God and do His bidding. At least, the good ones do. But that's not all. Angels are free willed. They are second only in wisdom to God. They never marry and they have feelings."

The guard came into view with his keys in hand.

"Hey, you," the guard bellowed at Walter. "You better not be causing any—" Then he saw that it was *Larry* who had the upper hand and that Walter's eyes were round with fear. The guard fumbled with the keys.

"Just a minute, sir," said Larry. "Now listen hard, Walt," he shouted into his face. "An angel can materialize."

"What is this?" shouted the guard, jamming the wrong key into the hole and cursing his misfortune. "Some sort of wacko prison ministry thing? I tell you, a man can't even lock himself up to get away from your type."

"You've got to believe me, Walt," said Larry, slapping the Bible on the cot. "It's all right here in Genesis. The part about Lot and the strangers who came to Sodom! Look in Luke, too. The first chapter. Read it for yourself, Walt. Angels can become whatever God needs them to become. Do you understand? They can be a man. They can be a woman. They can be anything. And if *they* can materialize—"

"All right wise guy," said the guard, swinging the door open, and bringing his gloved hand down firmly on Larry's shoulder. "If the prisoner says he doesn't want anything to do with you, then he doesn't want anything to do with you. You're coming with me!"

Larry jerked loose from the guard's grip, and backed toward the cell door.

"Walter, if an angel can materialize, then a letter can, too."

"That's enough, mister," said the guard.

"Your letters *are* from heaven and hell."

"I'm warning you."

"They're just as real as any angel ever was. Matter itself is no obstacle to God. Trust me, Walt."

"That's it," screamed the guard, shoving Larry out into the hall. "Letters from heaven. I've heard it all."

After being roughly escorted to the parking lot, Larry joined his wife, Rose, and Donna Conniston in his pickup. The look on Larry's face told Donna immediately that her husband was in no state of mind to meet with her.

"I'm sorry," said Larry, wrapping his arm around Donna, who sat in the middle of the bench seat, by the gearshift. "I did my best to test the waters. Your husband's hurt bad, Donna."

"I know," she said, trying hard to hold her tears. "I'm torn up, too, inside. It took me years to say that God was real again. I'm still not sure if He's good."

Rose looked across Donna's shoulders at her husband, and mouthed the question, *"Now?"*

Larry nodded a might-as-well kind of nod.

"Donna?" said Rose lightly, as she placed her hand at the base of the woman's neck. "Did you get a chance to talk with Marla Coe?"

"Yes," said Donna, her shoulders slumping forward.

"Did you go by yourself?"

Donna nodded.

"What does she do for a living?" asked Rose, glancing at Larry for help.

"She's a professional runaway."

"A what?"

"Oh, I don't know. She probably waits tables or sells perfume at malls or something. But every year or so, she leaves her kids and goes looking for a father," said Donna, abruptly.

"Marla told you that?" asked Larry.

"No, it was those men from Topeka, those officers, Blackmon and Davis. They said her father died when she was young. Said he was a postal worker. She's been married three times to government employees. All three of them abused her."

"I see," said Rose. "So Marla thinks she's found a dad in Walter."

"Um-hm," nodded Donna, the tears beginning to drop between her knees onto the floorboard. "What scares me is that she's found one who's looking for his kids. They're a perfect match, aren't they?"

"Were you able to tell her your true feelings? Were you able to find out what's been going on?" asked Larry.

Again, Donna nodded.

"Then, are they involved with each other?"

At that, Donna began to sob and laugh hysterically.

"Oh, yes, deeply involved. They drink Cokes and go fishing together. It's all quite harmless," she erupted. "I thought I knew the woman. Can you imagine that? I've written enough about her in my novel. The sleazy mistress in chapter seventeen. I had her painted as a loose woman, and I never even met her."

Larry leaned against the window and closed his eyes.

"The women in my writer's club love it," said Donna. "You should see how green with envy they are about the story. They say they wish *their* plots were half as steamy. Emma raves like it's got best-seller written all over it. She says the characters are round and the conflicts convincing."

"Donna?" whispered Rose, stroking the shattered woman's hair. But Donna went right on spilling her pain.

"Isn't it funny when life imitates art? Everybody laugh, now. Everybody rave. Isn't it all a scream? You know, I'd resolved the wench's character with a pewter candlestick to the back of the head and was just about to carve her up and mail the pieces to her married lover in chapter eighteen, when I . . ."

"When you found the letters," said Larry.

Donna stopped abruptly. The letters had brought the specters of her dear, dead children right into her home. They had put God in her face with all His love, boundless power, and unpredictable plans. And they had made her think of Muriel.

"Those letters," sobbed Donna. "They had to come, didn't they! They had to come at just the time when I could finally hate God for all those years of silence." She pushed Rose's hand away from her hair and drew her knees up to her chest.

The engine of the pickup chuffed as a background to the childlike sounds that came from Donna. Back and forth, she rocked herself. Larry was glad he hadn't shown her the contents of the jewelry box.

"There's nothing more we can do now except wait for the trial. We'll take you home, Donna," said Larry.

"I've got a pot of soup on the stove. Will you join us for supper?" asked Rose. "There's plenty for Dallas."

Donna answered with her rhythmic rocking. The August sun was scorching hot as Larry put his truck in reverse and backed it out of the parking lot onto the road leading south.

"Donna," he said, to the ball of knees and arms next to him. "I know I haven't seen what's in those letters. But I have a feeling they're forcing you to see that someone out there loves you. And from what I'm hearing here, I think you see your love for Walter, too. You still love him, don't you Donna?"

For a quarter of a mile the cab was silent, save for the weary eight-cylinder, and the whine of tread on pavement. Then Donna raised her head, and her hair fell in tired strands down her face.

"I'd like to have a Coke with the man I married," she said to the dashboard.

On his cot, Walter tossed and tugged at the blankets until the thin hours of the morning. From down the corridor, the monitors at the main desk cast a pale light on the floor outside his cell. He was being watched.

Truly, Walter had felt a sense of unwanted surveillance long before he set foot inside this institution. And though it irritated him, he knew that Larry had been right. There *was* something going on. What other explanation could there be for botched tray-outs, mysterious fruitcakes, messages from the dead? Unless, of course, he was finally going over the edge. Could he have imagined it all? No! This very cot was a reality. His upcoming trial was a veritable noose hanging over his head.

From the pocket of his jumpsuit, Walter drew the small, felt box.

Slowly, so as not to draw attention on the monitors, Walter turned on his side and faced the wall. Light from the corridor was reflected there, and it was easy for him to see what he was doing. He brought the box up to his chest and opened the lid. Inside was a tiny piece of paper with writing on it.

Walter . . . I don't pretend to understand it all, so I'll just begin by telling you I found this item on the fifty-yard line at Jenson Stadium. I was patching sod last Saturday getting ready for the Laird game—it looked like lightning tore up the field. Anyway, something shiny caught my eye. At first I thought it was a sprinkler head. But then I moved some grass aside. My heart skipped a beat when I read the wording on the metal.

Walter, I don't know what else to say except, I did the funeral. Remember? I saw this go into the casket, and the casket into the ground, and the dirt dumped on top. Whatever else you want to make out of this is your business. But please don't miss the possibility that God is trying to make contact with you. Your friend, Larry.

From under the piece of paper and a layer of cotton, Walter pulled a familiar chain with tags attached.

And he began to cry.

# ~ 23 ~

*And whether you're an honest man or whether*
  *you're a thief*
*Depends on whose solicitor has given me my*
  *brief.*

—Sir William Schwenck Gilbert,
*Utopia, Limited, I*

ON the hottest day in August Walter's trial began, and regardless of the heat, Ellenbachians came in droves along the highway. Old Ford Galaxies and pickups forged eastward, as did Pintos, Skylarks, Falcons, Valiants, Vista Cruisers, Country Squires, and other models indicative of a town that clung to the past. Each bore its load to Laird for different reasons. Some people came to support Walter, some to see him convicted, some to allay their fears. What they feared most was the possibility that Walter was telling the truth about the letters and that heaven really *had* come quite casually into their mailboxes.

On the roof of the gray stone courthouse, Ace spoke hurriedly to Homer.

"What do you mean you don't have the tags?" he asked. "Come on, Homer, think," said Ace. "You've got to recall where you had them last."

"They were in my pocket. They must have fallen out during the fight. I don't remember."

Ace couldn't believe they'd come this far for this to happen. "I'll tell you where I think they are," he said. "They're probably sitting this very minute on that football field, waiting to get trampled into the dirt by a Bulldog linebacker."

"We could go back for them," suggested Homer.

"It's too late for that," said Ace. "And without those tags, I have no idea how we're going to convince Walter— or the judge either, for that matter—of the letters' true nature. I suggest we put our heads together to see what we can salvage."

The angels drew together in a tight triangle, and bowed for prayer.

Forty feet below them, the people in the courtroom hunkered down in silence as the prosecuting attorney, Mr. Combs, took off his glasses and strolled toward the witness stand, where Foster Jenson III sat stiffly. Already, the trial had been under way for an hour. To Jenson's right, perched like a black-robed rooster behind the bench, Judge Pickens gazed out over his house with ailing eyes. To the left of Jenson was the jury. They were mostly cattle ranchers—eight to be exact—with a plumber, a businesswoman, and two wheat sharecroppers to round out the bunch. Above them was a wide, leaded window, through which the sun beat mercilessly. The men mopped their faces with their caps. The lone woman, less conspicuous in her attempts to escape the irresistible heat, dabbed at her temple with the folded tip of a handkerchief and steeled herself for duty.

Combs was a deliberate man who took his time in court. He had the patience of a person planning the perfect crime. In truth, some decisions he had won were outrageous crimes against defendants less guilty of their charges than Combs himself. He was feared in courtrooms, shunned by other circuit prosecutors, tolerated by judges, and held in disgust by his own wife, who many said remained in marriage only for the sake of money. And when it came to *money*, people like Foster Jenson III were the reason Combs had plenty of it. But far more obvious than any other fact about him was the fact that Jeremy Combs was a cigar-smoking Christian hater.

In front of the bench sat a long table with the articles of evidence placed across it. As he walked by, Mr. Combs ran his finger along its scarred edge, noting once again what was there: a bottle of perfume, a stock tip addressed to Mr. Jenson, a pocket watch, a fruitcake that Judge Pickens had surprisingly changed his mind to allow, a ballpoint pen, several other items allegedly from heaven, and most important, a boot box full of letters that Combs had submitted just minutes before the trial. From where she sat with Dallas, ten feet from the table, Donna Conniston eyed the box and wondered who had the audacity to trespass in her attic.

Combs came to a halt in front of the jury, turned toward Jenson, and smiled amiably.

"Mr. Jenson," said Combs. "I believe you were speaking about your earnings. Do you make a good living?"

"A fair one, yes," said Jenson, somewhat apologetically, for he knew that the majority present would have gladly agreed to live on a very small percentage of his "fair" salary.

"But that's not really the issue here, is it?" said Combs. "This really isn't about money at all. Am I correct?"

"Objection, your honor," said Jack Robbins. "Counsel's leading the witness."

"Overruled," said Judge Pickens. "Answer the question, Mr. Jenson."

"Well, no. It's not at all about money," said Jenson unconvincingly.

"Of course it isn't," said the sly Combs, who was trying to perform the miraculous feat of establishing

Jenson's credibility as a man who didn't care a wit about his wealth but who was very much concerned about being deprived of other holdings less tangible. "Where were we? Ah, yes, money. There are some who would say that money lies at the very heart of this case. They would say that 'the deprivation of the almighty dollar' is the essence of fraud, a point on which you disagree dearly, is that not right, Mr. Jenson?"

"Objection," said Jack.

"Overruled. Mr. Combs, from now on you will refrain from speaking for the witness," said Judge Pickens.

"Forgive me," said Combs. "But if it pleases the court, I must show beyond reasonable doubt that Mr. Jenson—and several others in Ellenbach—were both willfully and maliciously defrauded by the defendant of things that cannot be assigned a monetary value."

"It would please the court, counsel, for you to mount your case sometime before the turn of the century," said Judge Pickens, looking at his watch.

While Combs was pleasing the court, Ace, Homer, and François settled into the top row of the balcony, behind a woman and her two very active boys. One of them was picking bits of red fuzz from the seat cushions and placing them over the air-conditioning register, just to see them sail out across the courtroom onto unsuspecting persons. He nudged his brother every time one of the bits landed in Emma Sanger's hairdo. And the longer the afternoon drew on, the more proficient they became at targeting her head, and the more obvious their laughter became.

In the meantime, Combs attempted to show that on the night of June 3, Walter Conniston had indeed carried out a scheme to deprive his client of emotional stability, trust, peace, and the right to responsible government—in this case, the federally regulated delivery of the mail. Furthermore, he did it solely from the motive of angry jealousy. "In short," said Combs, "Walter Conniston envied souls who were perfectly content with the idea of themselves and their deceased loved ones simply living once and then going into the ground. Because of this envy, he acted with intent to make everyone around him as neurotically obsessed with the false hope of an after-life as he is."

"Incredible," said Jack Robbins, when he finally got the opportunity to cross-examine Foster Jenson. "My hat is truly off to you and your esteemed attorney for rewriting the definition of fraud. "I, rather, *we*," said Jack, sweeping his hand across the entire courtroom, "are to believe that Walter Conniston hates his neighbors enough to pull such a stunt. Is that right?"

"*Hate* is a harsh word, sir," said Jenson.

"Would *strongly dislike* more accurately describe it, Mr. Jenson?" asked Jack.

"Well—"

"Isn't it more accurate to say that up until the time of two very tragic occurrences in Walt Conniston's life, you and all of Ellenbach spoke quite openly of him as one of the finest men your town has ever known?"

"Yes, but—"

"And isn't it also true that my client thought of his fel-low man in much the same way?"

"I suppose that's true."

"Um-hm. You suppose. Does that mean that Walt Connis-ton *was* one of the finest men you ever knew?" asked Jack.

"I suppose he was," said Jenson.

"One last question, your honor. Then I'll let the wit-ness step down," said Jack, turning toward the jury but directing every word toward the heart of Foster Jenson.

"What did you do with the stock tip in question?" asked Jack.

"How's that?"

"The stock tip, you know, the one from heaven. What was done with it?"

At that, Jenson sat so long, staring into his lap, that Judge Pickens had to order him to give an answer. When he finally spoke, his voice was low enough that Judge Pickens gave the same command again.

"I heeded it," said Jenson, clearly.

"You heeded it," repeated Jack. "Meaning, you acted upon the tip's advice?"

"Yes."

"Yes what? Yes, you made an investment? Yes, you talked it over with your broker? What does *yes* mean, Mr. Jenson?"

"It means I put fifty thousand dollars into Wisdom Software. Does that satisfy your curiosity?" shouted Foster.

"Not quite," said Jack, wryly.

"Objection," yelled Combs. "The defense is bullying the witness. Besides, I fail to see where all this is leading, since the court has clearly established that fraud in the case of *Conniston* v. *Jenson* has nothing to do with money."

"I wasn't aware the court had established anything," said Judge Pickens. "Prosecution is overruled. And, while the defense is showing relevancy, would he please recall who is on trial here?"

In the balcony, Ace cupped his hands and cheered.

"Attaboy, Jack," he shouted, since he could not be readily seen or heard. By now, Homer had completely forgotten about the trial, and was thoroughly engrossed in the antics of the boys and their cushion fuzz. The air was filled with tiny, red helicopters.

"Things are finally going our way, monsieur," said François, nudging Ace.

"Uh-oh. I'm not so sure of that," said Ace, squinting his eyes at a greasy shadow that spilled from beneath the table where the evidence lay. "Looks like we have company again."

\* \* \*

"Certainly, Your honor," said Jack. "For the record, I agree with the prosecution, although I differ wholeheartedly with Mr. Combs on the interpretation of *fraud*. Otherwise, he's right. This case has nothing to do with money. In fact, it's neither linked to the deprivation of tangible *or* intangible property. This is not about fraud at all. This is about whether Mr. Jenson, and the town of Ellenbach, are comfortable with the idea of a supernatural *One* who cares enough to make contact with us through the items we refer to as Exhibits A, B, and so forth," said Jack, pointing to the table of evidence.

A collective titter sounded throughout the room, a titter that Combs deemed favorable. He eyed his opponent, smugly. Nevertheless, Jack produced a *Wall Street Journal* from his inside pocket, spun toward Jenson, and slapped the paper on the railing of the witness stand.

"Mr. Jenson, would you please educate the court as to the results of your recent investment."

"Objection," shouted Combs, leaping from his chair. "This is not an audit."

"Oh, be quiet," Judge Pickens replied, having become increasingly aware that for this trial to ever proceed past its first witness, it would take some judicial intervention. With each tick of the clock that stared from the wall at the rear of the room, Pickens's loathing of lawyers grew exponentially. He closed his eyes and tried to focus on retirement. How he wished that he and Gladys could be sailing somewhere south of Florida at this very moment. *But alas, Gladys is in the grave, while I am here to govern idiots*. To Judge Roy Pickens at that moment in time, being in the grave seemed the better of the two.

Combs sat back down again, rubbing the vein on the side of his neck. Jack leaned in closer to his quarry and asked the question again.

"I'm sorry, Mr. Jenson. In all that commotion, I didn't hear your answer. What *were* the results of your investment?"

"It split," said Mr. Jenson, quietly.

"I still couldn't hear that. Would you like me to read it myself?" asked Jack, beginning to unfold the paper in his hand.

"It split," repeated Mr. Jenson.

"Split?" said Jack. "Could you tell the court what that term means, for those of the jury who may not know?"

"It means I made a lot of money," said Jenson.

Combs held his brow in his hands and studied his notes. This was not going at all well for his client.

"A lot of money. Hmm. I see," said Jack. "Seems like a man with that kind of luck ought to be so elated about life that he's out playing golf or sailing in his yacht or something. Do you sail, Mr. Jenson?" he asked, knowing perfectly well that the man had bought an expensive boat not long after his investment skyrocketed in late June. In fact, he'd already been to the Gulf for its maiden voyage.

"Yes, I sail," said Jenson.

"Since when?" asked Jack.

"Since July."

"Ahhh. July. Wonderful time for being on the water. I've lived back East for years now, near some gorgeous harbors. Full of boats, just like yours. Of course, none of them is quite so big as yours—a schooner, I think. It's a large one isn't it, Mr. Jenson?"

"Objection."

"Overruled."

"I don't have to answer this," shouted Jenson, trying desperately to exempt himself with volume.

"But you already have," said Jack. "Your refusal to do so is answer enough for all of us. For the life of me, though, I can't understand how a man of your good fortune could bite the hand of the one who delivered it to him."

"He defrauded me, that's how," said Jenson, glaring at Walter. "That man robbed me of the right to remember my own dead father in the way I want to remember him, resting in peace. I don't want to remember him galavanting around the universe, keeping track of the exchange!"

"This case has a *lot* to do with your father, doesn't it?"

"Objection," said Combs.

"Proceed," replied Judge Pickens.

"He was a wonderful gentleman, God bless him," said Jack, sincerely, as he walked toward the evidence table. "Such a mind for numbers, too. Seems to me, he always kept a fairly tight rein on your business dealings as a younger man. Isn't that true?"

"What's that got to do with anything?" said Jenson.

"Not much," said Jack, "except that he was right again, I suppose."

Jenson looked away.

"He *was* right, wasn't he?" repeated Jack.

"Right about what?"

"Right about this," said Jack, lifting the stock tip from the table and opening the envelope marked Exhibit C. "It says here—and I quote—'Put your money on Wisdom Software, son. It's a blue-chipper if there ever was one, Love, Dad.'"

The gallery began to buzz. Combs objected and was once again denied.

"That bothers you, doesn't it, Mr. Jenson?" continued Jack. "It bothers you that even in death your father knows more about the market than you do. You can hardly stomach the reminder, though you profit from it nicely. Isn't *that* the real reason we're in this court today, sir? Isn't it true that you were so mad at Walter for delivering that reminder of your inadequacy that you went straight to your lawyer? But *not* before you made the investment, of course. Isn't it also true that you hold fully to the doctrine of heaven, though you're not so sure you want to live there for fear you'll suffer by comparison with your father? You can't stand being anything like him, can you?"

"Why, you disrespectful, little twerp," said Jenson, rising from his chair. "You'll never hold an account in a bank again. Mine, or anyone else's. I'll see to that!"

"Order!" shouted Judge Pickens, but the rich man from Ellenbach was too roiling mad to stop.

"Your financial reputation is so—"

"Order!"

"—tarnished that—"

"Bailiff. Remove this man from the courtroom," yelled Judge Pickens.

But the damage was done. Those in the gallery who sat on the side of a closed universe wherein a god—if one existed—could not possibly communicate with its inhabitants were so furious with Jack Robbins's presentation that they all began yammering at once.

"He defrauded me, too!" shouted Emma Sanger, even though she was wearing the Chloe Narcisse that her father had sent her.

"And me, as well," said the Widow Spradling, pointing to her fruitcake on the table.

On the other hand, those who thought it quite possible that God could call anytime He wanted were just as vocal with their opinions.

"There isn't a reason in the world why that note *didn't* come from my Leta," said Bill Ray, nodding toward the table. "Looks just like her writing. Walter never knew her well enough to copy her hand."

"And my Sarah got the same kind of perfume her Uncle Evan used to send her every Christmas before he passed away," sniffed Teeny Pittencheese. "I don't know how Walter could have guessed the brand."

"Order! Orderrrrrr!" shouted Judge Pickens, rapping his gavel so hard that it sailed from his hand and landed on the clerk's desk, at which Woodberry was busy pecking away, having the hardest day of his life.

"I will not have my court turned into a circus! Do you hear me, people? I don't care if some of you believe in God or not. I don't care if you go to church. I don't care if you think you're the reincarnation of St. Augustine himself. But you will not stage another outburst like that in this room. That I *do* care about. And for *that* I'll hold you in contempt if it happens again! Combs. Robbins. At the bench, now," said Judge Pickens.

The moment the two attorneys arrived at the front, Combs was pleading his case.

"Your honor," said Combs. "The defense is deliberately trying to steer the trial away from the expressed charges. On several occasions, he has alluded to his opinion that these procedures have nothing to do with fraud and has successfully caused pandemonium in this fine court. Now, if you will just let me—"

"I'll let you do nothing, Combs," seethed Judge Pickens. "I want to make it crystal clear to both of you that I have no interest in the spiritual nature of this trial. I simply want to be done with it all and go fishing. Is that too much to require of you?" asked the judge.

"No, your honor," said Jack. "And if it pleases the court, I will do my best to stay within the lines of the initial indictment. But I would also like to remind my colleague, in your presence, your honor, that there is nothing on the face of the mail fraud statute or anywhere in the legislative history of the original 1872 enactment or the 1909 amendment to suggest that Congress contemplated the criminalization of schemes that were not aimed at either money or property. Furthermore, I believe there's nothing wrong with introducing certain aspects of God as relevant material in this case."

"Bravo, Mr. Robbins. That was a nice speech," said Judge Pickens. "I can see we're going to be here until Jesus' second coming!"

"Just a minute," said Combs, looking straight at Judge Pickens. "Since my colleague is so glad to remind me of the law, perhaps I should remind him of a thing or two."

"Oh, pleeeaaase," sighed Judge Pickens. And he leaned back in his chair.

"What about *Haas* v. *Henkel*?" asked Combs.

"Apples and oranges," replied Jack. "*Haas* v. *Henkel* dealt with the protection and welfare of government. Here, we're talking about individual rights."

"Well, *your* client robbed *my* client of his individual rights to emotional stability, to trust, to peace, to—"

"You told us that before."

"Okay, so, what about *Carpenter* v. *United States*?" asked Combs. "Didn't that substantiate the necessity for considering property that is intangible?"

"Your honor," said Jack.

"And didn't Justice Stevens side with me in his dissent in *McNally* when he pointed out the unanimity of the courts of appeals in supporting the intangible rights theory? Well, didn't he?"

"Your honor," Jack repeated, "I think—"

"And didn't Stevens disagree with the majority's reading of the original purpose of Congress? Didn't he argue that, whatever the original purpose of Congress in 1872, the court should not be bound by it today, given that the terms of the statute supported the intangible rights approach? Well? Well?"

"This is ridiculous. Your honor, the prosecution is trying to turn this meeting into a law class."

"Seems to me you're both showing off," said Judge Pickens. "Now, either you call your next witness, Combs, or I'll find some obscure reason to label this thing a mistrial and we'll all be home for early supper. Understood?"

"Yes, sir," chimed Jack and Combs.

"I'd thought you'd never see it," said Judge Pickens. "Shall we give it a try then, Combs?"

"Yes, sir," said Combs.

After that, the prosecution called Emma Sanger, who came forward with a head full of fuzz to the amusement of the courtroom. Again Judge Pickens had to punish his desk with the gavel. This time when the room quieted down, he heard a distinct giggling in the balcony, and he squinted up toward the window. *There are those lights again*, he thought, *like the ones I saw in my office that day.* He rubbed his eyes with the heel of one hand, feeling around in the drawer for his eyedrops with the other. *How could I have forgotten my drops?* he moaned inwardly.

When questioned, Emma Sanger said it didn't matter if Walter's wife *was* her best friend. "The man ought to be cut off from society for foisting God on right-thinking Americans," she insisted.

Next, a weepy Widow Spradling testified that sending that fruitcake was just about the meanest thing anybody had ever done to her, considering that fruitcake was her sweet Terrence's favorite dessert up until the day he died, "God rest his soul." And even though the widow was not really a full-fledged member of the deity doubters, like Emma and Jenson, she still preferred her God as a kind, old man in the sky, who would never disturb the peace of a town in the manner Walter claimed.

One after another, witnesses from both sides came forward to say what they thought of Walter's alleged deeds. The Pittencheeses said it was the nicest thing that had ever happened to them. Bill Ray claimed he had become a man of faith overnight.

At a quarter of five, the defense called its final witness to the stand. And when he came forward, silence covered the court, and all mouths were deathly still.

# ~ 24 ~

*Justice is a machine that, when someone has once given it the starting push, rolls on of itself.*

—John Galsworthy, *Justice*

FROM the long, wooden bench that separated the gallery from the rest of the court, Walter rose and went slowly across the floor. His shirt was soaked with sweat, and when he turned to take the oath, everyone could see his cheeks were glistening, too.

"—so help me God," he exhaled, then sat down. The room was quiet as a grave, save for Woodberry's tapping in the corner.

"How long have you lived in Ellenbach, Walter?" asked Jack after a minute had lapsed.

"Twenty-seven, twenty-eight years. I'm not certain. It's been a long time," said Walter.

"During that time, what jobs have you held?"

"You know that, Jack. You were part of the family long enough to know."

Jack winced and held up his hand. It was no secret to the jury that he was defending his father-in-law. But it didn't help to direct their attention to it.

"What jobs, Walter?"

"Just the one."

"And where is that?"

"I've been at the post office the whole twenty-seven, -eight years."

Jack paused to let the jury digest that statistic.

"During that time, Walter, did you ever have any problems?"

"What do you mean, problems?"

"Disagreements with management, run-ins with disgruntled customers, that sort of thing."

"If you mean did I rub any folks raw, then no."

"During that time were you ever negligent of your duties?"

"Excuse me?" asked Walter.

"Did you ever not show up on time, put the wrong mail in someone's box, or, worse yet, put something in someone's box that was illegal?"

"I haven't tried to cause trouble for anybody. And no one said I was trouble, until—"

"Until you were accused of fraud for the routine execution of your job. Is that it?" said Jack.

Walter nodded.

"I have no further questions, your honor."

Judge Pickens watched Jack return to his seat and then said, "Any questions, Mr. Combs?"

"Yes," said Combs. His chair was cocked like a gun aimed at Walter, and he fired his first shots from a sitting position.

"Mr. Conniston, how many children do you have?"

"One," answered Walter, his hands tightening into fists on his lap. In the gallery, Donna squeezed Rose's wrist.

"Weren't there more at one time?"

"Objection, your honor," said Jack. "My client's children are irrelevant to the case."

"Overruled. Counsel, please show relevance," ordered Judge Pickens.

Walter bit down hard on his lip.

"I'm sure it must be hard for you," said Combs, pivoting toward the jury. "Perhaps it would be simpler if I just told the court that at one time Walter and Donna Conniston had three children, two boys and a girl. The girl, I believe her name was Muriel, was lost to melanoma. And the boy, named Bentley, was . . ."

"Put to death for something he didn't do," said Walter, flatly.

"Yes. Quite tragic," said Combs. "At any rate, it was a murder that he 'didn't do.'"

The people in the gallery shook their heads at the memory, and Combs proceeded. He stood to ask his questions and walked with deliberate slowness toward the front of the court.

"Mr. Conniston, was Bentley's execution before or after you resigned from your position as deacon at Ellenbach Community Church?"

"I think it was before. I'm not sure."

"Correct, sir. It was before. Three days before, to be exact. And what happened on that third day, Mr. Conniston?"

"I don't understand the question."

"Who did you talk to on that morning, Mr. Conniston?"

"I . . ."

"Let me put it differently," said Combs. "Did you or did you not, just seventy-two hours after your son was executed, storm into the office of Pastor Larry Ravelle and swear at him so loudly and profusely that his secretary could hear every word you said through the walls?"

"I was angry," said Walter.

"You were angry," echoed Combs. "That's absolutely true, Mr. Conniston. You were angry. Angry enough to promise your pastor that you would, quote, 'sweat in hell' before you ever trusted God again. And for the longest time you joined the mass of us logical citizens who don't have a problem with God when their loved ones die because they get along quite well believing God does not exist!"

With a flash, Homer drew his sword.
"Put that away!" commanded Ace. "What are you going to do? Stab a lawyer?"
"He could use a lesson," said Homer.
"The man is misinformed, monsieur," said François.
"All right. I'll put it away."

Combs circled around to Walter's side. He leaned against the railing, his breaths coming so heavily that they stirred the hair on Walter's head.
"I know exactly how it feels, Walter," said Combs. "I lost my youngest at the Tet offensive to a nest of North Vietnamese. When the machine guns finally stopped, my boy's buddies found seventy-eight holes in his mid section. Do you think I believe in God now? Life is a sad comedy. The best we can do is learn the joke, and laugh our way through it.
"So, there you have it, Mr. Conniston. I don't blame you for what you were feeling. But here's what I *do* blame you for, sir," said Combs. He struck a dramatic pose construed to plant the jury so firmly in his camp that no counterpoint could uproot them.
"Somewhere in those dark years after your second child died . . ."
"Objection."
"Overruled," said Judge Pickens. He leaned toward Combs and spoke in a tone that underscored his disapproval. "Counsel will proceed with whatever shred of compassion he possesses."
"Of course," said Combs. He pressed ahead, hardly pausing for a breath.
"Sometime when your newfound logic was at its most vulnerable hour and your mind's defenses were on hold,

there came a knock," crooned Combs, rapping sharply on the railing as he spoke. "Let me in. Let me in. It's God, and I need a heart to dwell in," he mimicked in a high-pitched, childish voice. "And then you reopened the door to all those infantile traditions that you held at one time, and that you longed so badly to believe in still. You'd found you had a need for heaven, hadn't you? A pretty place for your daughter and your son to lay their heads. You lost your objectivity, Walter. You grew obsessed with life outside of life and forgot the punch line to the joke. So I'll refresh your mind. There is no supernatural postman, Walter. There is no one else but *you* who could have put those things in your neighbors' boxes. Therefore, Mr. Conniston, I have come to a conclusion."

Suddenly, everything in the courtroom—the clock, the people, the chairs, the desks, the jury, the great overhanging balcony, the relentless stream of sun, and all the portraits of all the judges who had sat on the bench and who now passed judgment from their places on the wall— seemed to tilt with such a weight toward the witness stand that a child could have felled them with a shove.

"And my conclusion is this," said Combs. "That you, Walter Conniston, have committed something far worse than fraud."

The jury stirred. Jack Robbins looked up from his notes.

"In fact," said Combs. "*You* are a fraud! By your pranks, you stole your neighbors' laughter. You ruined the joke for Ellenbach by dangling heaven in front of them, when heaven is as near as a good cigar but not one iota farther. You invented that boot box full of letters yourself, didn't you, Walter?"

"I—"

"You bought the perfume, didn't you? And the fruitcake. And the watch. And all the other things we see before us on this table. And then you tried to pass them off as noble gifts from heaven."

"But I—"

"You robbed your town of its right to religious freedom by forcing your God upon them, Walter Conniston. And therein lies the essence of your crime."

"What a stupid individual," said François.
"I agree," said Homer.
"Shhh," said Ace. "Something's happening."

Trembling, Walter had risen from the chair on the witness stand, and was saying something to the crowd.

"I never meant it to come to this," he began. "But now that I'm sitting here and you're all staring at me, I might as well tell you the truth."

Those in the gallery who wished for a conviction smiled. Others shook their heads. Jack Robbins tossed his pencil on the table and leaned back in disbelief. Behind him, Donna slumped at Larry's side. *It all comes down to this*, thought Jack. *All the work. All the pain. All the years of tragedy. Walter is about to bring it to a halt by confessing to something he didn't do.*

But high in the balcony, Ace began to smile.

"I *am* a fraud," said Walter, wiping his eyes with his fist. "I *did* defraud you all, and I've been doing it for years."

Combs stepped quietly away from the stand, giving the appearance of reverence for the moment but all the while celebrating his victory. His joy, however, was premature.

"I didn't do it with the letters, though," Walter continued. "They're on the up and up. My fraud was of a worse kind. I took something far more precious than your money or your privacy. I stole your hope. And here's how I did it.

"When I was a younger man, I was full of life and sap, God's sap, I think it was because I believed in God then. In those days, I used to tell myself that God hadn't done anything wrong by me. He was a good enough God then. That made me think I ought to be good back to Him. So I became a deacon. You all saw how I did at that. You saw me helping with a happy heart and telling folks about God's goodness."

A few in the gallery smiled knowingly.

"Then, something came over God, I figured. Or maybe something came over me and God, I don't know. Anyhow, when Muriel had those awful lesions on her skin and the pain dragged her to bed, I used to pray so hard. But nothing happened. So I prayed some more. And nothing happened again. When we buried her and Pastor Ravelle said some fine words over her, I left a piece of my happy heart in that box with her, and I haven't seen it since," said Walter, his face so wet with tears he didn't bother drying them.

"Your honor," said a desperate Combs. "For the sake of Mr. Conniston's dignity, we should permit him to mourn in private. Perhaps a recess is in order."

"And perhaps you should let the man have his say," said Judge Pickens. This brought a welcomed humor to the moment, but then Walter was speaking again, as if he'd hardly noticed the interruption.

"My heart got halved with Muriel, and halved again when Bentley was killed," said Walter. "Pretty soon, I had such a thin heart I was walking around town delivering letters like an empty mailbox on legs. That's when I quit being a deacon. I quit a lot of things. My friends, my boy, my Donna. I've hardly talked to her in years."

Walter paused and looked toward his wife. But she didn't raise her head.

"I quit everybody and everything except my job. I kept at that until it was all that ever mattered. All the while, the townsfolk were bragging on me. They said they didn't know how I made it, losing so much of my family and still being on time with the mail.

"Well, I *wasn't* making it! I was a cold, hard stone inside. And here's where the fraud comes in. I figured it all out last night in my cell. I'll just finish my piece and then I'll sit down. And if you see fit to send me back to jail, then so be it. The Lord knows, I deserve worse."

264 ～ Will Cunningham

"But you haven't done anything," shouted Bill Ray from the gallery. "At least nothing that the rest of us wouldn't have done."

"Order," said Judge Pickens with a bang. "We'll let the jury be the judge of that."

"The judge is right," said Walter. "But you're right, too, in a way, Bill. I never did know what was in the letters and packages I delivered until I heard folks talking about them. If the inspectors hadn't have come to my house, I would have just gone on doing my job, sapping hope out of the lives of good folks."

"Sapping hope? How?" came another voice. Before Judge Pickens could give another warning, Walter replied.

"You didn't see me when Terrence Spradling died, did you?"

There was no response from the gallery.

"Of course not. I was too busy feeling sorry for myself to tend to other folks in time of need. How about Clinton Sanger? The man was a neighbor of mine in his sick years. I could have thrown a rock and hit his daughter's house, he was so close. But did I ever go to see him? No, I didn't, even though I'd been through exactly what that woman was going through and I could have brought her hope," said Walter, pointing straight at Emma. "Instead, I went on letting every man and woman in Ellenbach say 'there goes a fine man,' as I went walking on my way. And why didn't I stop and help folks through their own pain?"

The ticking of the clock on the wall fell like thunder.

"Because I wanted folks to be just as hopeless and hateful as I was. I wanted them to think God was dead. I wanted them to choke on their fine, churchy talk until they finally spit it out and said, 'If this is what a good God does, I don't want anything to do with Him.'

"But I was wrong. God isn't dead at all. I was the dead one," said Walter, reaching inside his shirt pocket and pulling out a long, shiny chain. Larry's heart jumped at the sight of the dog tags. Indeed, the entire courtroom had an electrical air about it, not unlike the atmosphere of a presidential inauguration just before the president arrives.

"But when a dead man puts his children in the ground, and then those children write him somehow, that dead man can't stay dead for long, can he? It has a way of perking his ears up . . . making him come alive . . . making him believe again. Well, I believe again," said Walter. "Or maybe I believe for the first time, I don't know. Anyhow, I'm not trying to mock Mr. Combs. But the letters in that boot box—and everything else on that table—*are* from heaven and hell, no matter what he says. If you doubt it, then take a look at these tags, and tell me different."

Walter held the tags up high.

"Impermissible evidence. Let me see those," shouted Combs, leaping toward the stand. In a flash, Combs was holding the dog tags in his hands and Judge Pickens was rapping on his bench.

"BENTLEY ALLEN CONNISTON," read Combs aloud, unaware of the bedlam the tag's inscription was about to unleash.

"Bent Conniston?" said one man, standing in the middle of the room. "Why, those are Bent Conniston's tags."

"That's impossible," exclaimed another. "I saw him buried with those tags. They were in his casket as plain as day."

"Order," shouted Judge Pickens. "Order. Orrrder. Mr. Combs, there'll be a major fine for this, I hope you know. Hand me those tags this instant."

Coincidentally, that was the same instant Ripskin chose to make his last appearance in this world. With a wet wheezing sound, he heaved himself out from under the table Ace had been watching throughout the trial, and crawled toward the witness stand.

"Pax," shouted Homer, as he watched his long-lost friend hoist himself with the aid of the railing.

The opportunity to do one final wrong upon this earth was foremost in Ripskin's mind. He had already achieved his vengeance upon Satan by delivering the tags from hell, thereby calling the world's attention once again to hell's existence. Now, the thought of Walter renewing his faith in the One who'd kicked him out of heaven pricked him sorely.

"I'll get you, little mailman," croaked Ripskin. "You won't believe in God again if I can help it. You certainly won't tell others about Him. Without the all-important, incriminating tags, you're history."

"Pax, no!" yelled Homer.

Ripskin lunged at Combs, clawing wildly for the tags.

"Never!" shouted Combs, in answer to Judge Pickens's demands for him to hand over the evidence. His mouth was twisted grossly, as if some force pulled downward on his features. "You can have me disbarred if you like, sir. But believe me, with this kind of religious tripe being spun here—"

Ripskin swiped at the tags again and Combs ran from the courtroom, never suspecting that just three feet behind him hobbled something ugly enough to give him nightmares for a lifetime. Behind the demon and the lawyer ran reporters, police officers, the bailiff, the clerk, half the town of Ellenbach, and three shining angels. When the courtroom was empty, Judge Pickens rubbed his eyes and walked to his chambers.

Outside the courthouse, Combs was making decent time toward his car when suddenly he tripped. The tags went flying from his fingers, twirling end over end, until they came to rest on the crossbar of a gutter grate. The sound of water winding toward the sewer could be heard from below. And for a moment, the dog tags dangled there.

"Don't anybody move," breathed Combs. "I've worked my entire career to find a landmark case that shows what kind of wackos Christians really are. I'm not going to let it all go down the drain, now."

\* \* \*

But without a care for Combs's career, Ripskin shoved past the white-faced attorney and made a final lunge at the dog tags. He hit the grate just as the tags slithered into the darkness.

"Uuuph," groaned Ripskin, as he collided with the metal. And just as the tags had fallen back to hell, his own body began to slip through the crossbars toward his black, eternal home.

In a second, Homer was at his side.

"Pax," he sighed.

"Don't try to change things, Homer. There's nothing to change."

"What about Bent? Will he be punished?"

"We all get punished in the end. Good-bye, Homer," said Ripskin.

And the demon fell without a splash.

When Combs was finally detained, the excitement had died away, and the people were reassembled in the courtroom, they were greeted by an ashen Judge Pickens. He sat in his chair wearing an old cotton suit; his robe was draped across the bench.

"Go on home, Jack," Judge Pickens said to the bewildered attorney. "All of you. Go on back to your families. There's not going to be any more trial today."

"But, Roy," said Emma Sanger.

"No buts about it, Emma. It's a mistrial, plain and simple. The client's Fourth Amendment rights were violated the minute those officers went into his attic and found that box. Unreasonable search and seizure, no question about it. Give the man his job back."

"But that isn't fair."

"What *is* fair, Emma?" said the tired judge.

"Then you're throwing the case out of court, your honor?" asked Jack.

"I am."

"And it's over?"

"It is."

"Yes," shouted Jack, clapping his hand on Walter's shoulder. The room erupted in mirth and madness. Otherwise unemotional farmers lifted their wives into the air and shouted Amen! and Hallelujah! Fights began, broke up, then, broke out again. Some people stood on chairs in tears. Others were shown the door by the bristling bailiff. Jack stooped to hug his father-in-law. Then there was another hug around Walter's neck, a woman's hug, that Walter had longed to feel for years, but chose to push aside.

Walter turned and gazed into his wife's eyes. He reached for Donna's face. Ever so gently, he pulled her toward him with his weathered hands and kissed her, saying softly, "I aim to pay you back for all those years. I promise."

"You can start by buying me a Coke," said Donna.

"Hey," said Larry, "the best drugstore in the county is right across the street. Why don't the two of you go on? Rose and I will take Dallas home. Besides, he has a letter all ready to deliver. The ride to Ellenbach will give me a chance to encourage him. I've got a feeling he'll never do it unless I push him a little. You all go on."

"Is it a date, ma'am?" asked Walter.

"It's a date," said Donna, smiling.

It took a long time for the Johnson County Courthouse to close down that evening on account of several attorneys burning the billable candle at both ends. One by one, the office lights winked off. The tax assessor shuffled out and down the steps. The collector followed him, just minutes behind. Finally, when the last paralegal had filed his day's worth of paper and closed the door behind himself, a solitary light shone dimly above the bench in the courtroom. Below it sat Judge Pickens with Buttercup's letter in his lap.

*   *   *

"It's been a long day, boys," said Ace, in the balcony above.

"All the more reason to wonder why the judge still sits there," said François.

"Give him time, François. There's nothing harder for a man than learning his watertight world has a roof that leaks. He'll be okay. He might turn out for the better. Only Jesus knows."

"You're right, monsieur. I just wish there was something we could do for him."

"I'm afraid that's someone else's assignment."

"I'm starved," said Homer. "Are we going to sit here all night?"

"No. Time to go," said Ace. "I just wanted to think about what we've done for a while, before it all slips away."

"You're not getting sentimental on us are you, Captain?"

"Of course not," said Ace, straightening himself. "It's just that the two of you did a mighty fine job back on that—"

"*Football field*," all three chimed in unison. And they leaped up to go in search of Chaney. But suddenly Ace stopped them.

"Wait a minute," he said. "I just got the strangest feeling that even now we're not through with Walter, yet."

"You're kidding, aren't you?" said Homer, holding his stomach.

"No, I'm not. Come on. Chaney can wait. We're needed in Ellenbach."

## ~ 25 ~

*Across the gateway of my heart*
*I wrote "No Thoroughfare."*
*But love came laughing by, and cried:*
*"I enter everywhere."*

—Herbert Shipman, *No Thoroughfare*

WALTER half-expected the flashing lights again when he and Donna arrived home that night to find Deputy Turner Tubbs sitting in front of their house. For a dozen years of cynicism that could not be released with a single letting ran in Walter's blood.

"Evening Turner," said Walter.

"Walt, Donna," said Tubbs, tipping his hat.

"What's the matter, Deputy? Are there still some things I have to sign or something?"

"No, nothing like that."

"What is it then?" asked Donna worriedly. "Is something wrong?"

"Folks, I think you'd best come with me. There's been an accident."

All the way back to Laird General Hospital, Ace and company rode in the backseat of the squad car. François patted Donna's shoulder while Homer and Ace prayed for Jesus' peace to do its work. Surprisingly, Walter was calm.

"It's going to be okay, Boats," he said as he held Donna's hand. "I don't know what we'll find when we get there, but it's going to be okay."

At the hospital, a sea of people were in the parking lot, more even than had been at the trial that afternoon. Apparently the news had reached Ellenbach before Walter and Donna. And when the townsfolk found out about the crash, they came rushing back to Laird like an evening tide.

In the emergency room's waiting area, the crowd had thinned some. But the low-ceilinged hallway with all the gurneys, oxygen tanks, wheelchairs, and IV poles seemed to magnify the sound of mourning.

"I'm so sorry, Donna. You, too, Walt," said Emma when the Connistons passed the chair where she was sitting. "If there's anything I can do . . ."

"That goes for me, as well," said Scottie Lundy. "Oh, Donna, it's just awful," she sobbed.

"Are you the boy's parents?" came a voice from the end of the hallway.

Walter nodded at the green-scrubbed figure coming toward him. Behind him, the door of an operating room swung loosely on its hinges. At the sight of blood on the man's shirt, Donna looked away.

"Why don't we step in here to talk," the doctor suggested, motioning toward a side room. His words flew around the waiting room, and people crowded about the door to hear the prognosis.

"Folks, please! Give the family some breathing room," said the doctor.

"It's okay, sir," said Walter. "They're close enough to be kin. I'm Walt Conniston. Go on with what you were saying."

"Your friends, the Ravelles, got banged up pretty badly. But they're in stable condition. The pickup hit them on the passenger side. Your son—"

"Dallas," said Donna, leaning heavily against her husband.

"Easy, Boats, I've got you," said Walter.

From the rooftop of Laird General, a voice called to Ace the moment Tubbs's squad car arrived in the parking lot.

"Evermore," cried Citizen Pogromme.

"Does he ever quit, monsieur?"

"No, he doesn't, François," said Ace. "But neither do I. You and Homer go inside with the Connistons. I'll take care of this."

"There's no use fighting alone, monsieur."

"I won't be," replied Ace, firmly. "Do as I say, François. The family needs you."

As François and Homer followed orders, Ace streaked toward the top of Laird General, spraying tar and gravel as he landed on the roof in front of Citizen Pogromme.

"You stupid brute of an angel," said Pogromme. His lips curled back against great, stained teeth, and Ace could see them gleaming under the August moon. "Did you think your Jesus could dispose of me so easily? Why, you're stupider than I thought!"

"It's over, Pogromme," said Ace. "Walter's taken everything your boss can dish out. Today in court all the pain came to an end."

"Did it now? Let me fill you in on what happened this afternoon."

The doctor talked over the sound of Donna's muffled sobs. "Your boy has suffered a shattered innominate bone and a cranial contusion. There's a significant amount of internal bleeding. By far, however, my greatest concern for him is his kidney. Preliminary scans reveal he only has one. How long has . . . ?"

"Since birth," said Walter.

"I see. The one that's left was damaged in the impact. It's shut down, I'm afraid."

\* \* \*

"That is so like you, Pogromme," said Ace. The two spirits had begun to circle one another, each looking for an opening. "You've always enjoyed picking on those who are smaller than you, haven't you? Are you happy now? Did you enjoy hurting the boy?"

"Captain, you have me all wrong," said Pogromme. "I was merely helping a cow across the road. How was I to know that pickup was coming? Am I to blame because the driver swerved?"

"You're to blame for all the pain in the world, Pogromme. You and that black-hearted boss of yours."

"That's a bit simplistic, don't you think, Evermore?" said Pogromme, drawing his sword.

"He's going to need a new one. There's no way around it," said the doctor.

"Can we get one?" asked Donna.

"Not with availability being what it is, ma'am. There's the cost to think of, too. Laird General simply doesn't have the funds. And even if it did, it could take some time. We'll do what we can. The demand for kidneys is great," said the doctor, wishing more and more he was making this speech in private.

"And my wallet is fat," came a voice from the hallway.

The crowd behind Walter and Donna parted, and the face of Foster Jenson III poked through the mass of bodies.

"We're finally alone, my Captain," sneered Pogromme.

"I'm never alone," said Ace.

"That's right. You call upon Jesus whenever the action gets a bit too heated. Go ahead, Evermore, bellow for Him like a little lost sheep. If you do, you'll never know whether I'm stronger than you. Why, you're wondering about that even now, aren't you?" said Pogromme.

"Come on, devil, fight me," said Ace. With a thrust of his sword, he slashed off a piece of Pogromme's collar.

＊ ＊ ＊

"Let me pass," demanded Foster Jenson, and the crowd obeyed. "Listen, young man," said Foster to the doctor. "I've got more clout in my back pocket than you'll make in a lifetime. More than is good for me, probably. I'm prepared to buy the boy a kidney at any price. You just name the numbers, and I'll write out a check."

"But, sir . . ."

"Time's precious, Doctor," said Foster as he took out his checkbook. "How much do I make this for?"

"Sir, money is not the issue. Like I said, availability—"

"Then I'll give him *my* kidney," said Foster.

"Mr. Jenson!" exclaimed Donna, looking from the banker to her husband, then back again.

"I know I'm old, but I believe all my parts are still working," said Foster above the buzz that had filled the hallway. The doctor cocked his head at the offer.

"I suppose it's possible," said the doctor. "We can run the necessary tests. But as you can guess, there's a one in a million chance it will work."

"Touché, Pogromme," shouted Ace as he systematically humiliated Satan's chief of staff. "There's a zipper off your jacket. I'll have the pockets next." Scattered about the rooftop were scraps of leather and metal and cloth.

"Unfair," shrieked Pogromme. "You've been practicing. That's all you angels do up there, isn't it?"

"On the contrary, Pogromme. We rarely take up the blade. I have been praying more, though."

"Prayer, bah!"

"It works, Pogromme. You really ought to try it."

"I will not be defeated," screamed Pogromme. "There will be no evangelism in Ellenbach."

"We shall see," said Ace. He parried an incoming thrust, following with his own counterattack.

Foster turned to address Walter. "A thousand apologies couldn't begin to say how bad I feel for putting you through everything, Walt. And a thousand thanks couldn't express the joy I feel for the future."

Overwhelmed by Foster's concern for Dallas, Walter grasped the beaming banker by his shoulders. "Are you sure you want to do this?"

"I'm a changed man after what went on in court today. As much as I hate to admit it, that son-in-law of yours was right. I'm *not* going to live in the shadow of my father anymore. In fact, I'm looking forward to being a little more like him from now on, and seeing him someday, too."

The two men hugged each other, and the doctor hurried Foster off for testing. From that day forth, the wine of generosity flowed from Foster Jenson III just as naturally as the gospel once flowed from Walter's lips.

On the roof Ace pressed the point of his sword against Pogromme's chest.

"Let it be known," said Ace, "that from now on, Walter Conniston, U.S. Postal Carrier 1009, is free to spread the news of Jesus' kingdom protected from your foul harassment."

"There'll be an appeal," squealed Pogromme as the point began to prick his skin. "I'll file a complaint. I'll—"

"Go home," said Ace.

At that, Pogromme turned and fled for hell, spouting threats and curses over his shoulder like the tail of a comet.

By the end of the surgery at three-thirty, Foster Jenson III had given a kidney and gained a friend. Miraculously, the bean-shaped organ was compatible with its younger, more active host. Walter and Donna were touched when several others had gathered courage and offered their assistance if ever a future transplant was necessary. All in all, the people of Ellenbach were in shock that the greatest miser among them had turned out to be the greatest giver.

When Dallas finally slept in the recovery room, most of the townsfolk went back to Ellenbach, leaving only the

Connistons, Emma Sanger, and the Lundys. Eddy was there, too, having driven back from enrollment the minute her parents phoned her about the accident. She sat cross-legged on the floor of the waiting room reading Dallas's love letter, which someone had secured from the wreckage before it was towed away.

"I hope Dally's okay," said Eddy. "I prayed for him all the way home from school."

"We've been praying for that boy since the day you were born," said Dolf Lundy, smiling at his daughter.

"I think we've done all we can," said Walter. "There's no use hanging around the rest of the night. The doctor says Dallas'll still be out of it in the morning, says to come at noon to check on him."

"The surgery went okay, then?" asked Emma.

"No problems. Of course he won't be playing much ball this season. Other than that, he'll be fit as ever as long as the kidney lasts. Come on, Boats. Let's go home."

Cistern Street looked different to Walter with the purple light of dawn slipping over the rooftops. He was glad he'd never seen it at that time—glad he'd always been there in the safe hours of the day with that beautiful woman.

"Looks like an envelope taped to the mailbox," said Donna, as they stopped in front of Marla's house on the way home. Both got out of the car to retrieve it. They leaned against the hood while Walter opened the letter and read its words out loud.

Dear Connistons,

Please forgive me for not being at the trial. I could tell someone's been watching me lately, and I thought it best for all involved if I moved as soon as possible. I'm going to Pontiac for a while, but I assure you it's not for the same reason I came to

Ellenbach. I just need time to clear my head before answering to the authorities and returning to my family.

"Family."

I can't believe I'm saying that word. It's true, though. I <u>do</u> have a family. You can't imagine how good it was to hear their voices on the phone last night. Soon I'll be "home," another word that has escaped me for a long time.

For reasons I'll not go into, I've hated church and religion since I was a child. In fact, when I arrived in your town I was an atheist. Nevertheless, the friendship of a mailman has changed a lot of things for me. And I stress the word "friend," Donna. By the way, I never thanked you for stopping by to clarify things. So, thank you.

Anyway, I'm open to the possibility of God's existence again. I don't really know Him personally, yet. But whoever this God is, I'm sure He fishes.

Thanks for Coon Creek, Walter.

Sincerely, Marla Coe

P.S. I'll not come back to Ellenbach.

Walter sighed, folding the note. "She's gone, I guess."

For a long time, he and Donna stood listening to the crickets. Overhead, the moon hung three days short of full. It was bright enough to light the marigolds where Walter first knelt, watching the woman who had reminded him of Muriel and who had vanished just as suddenly.

"We ought to be happy for her," said Donna. "I'm sure Pontiac is heaven compared to Ellenbach."

Walter laughed at that. And the sound of it, regardless of its flat and unpracticed quality, was a tune to Donna's ears.

"I don't know," said Walter. "Pontiac hasn't got the Bulldogs. When is that opener with Laird?"

"Tomorrow night."

"That doesn't give a man time to get his boy's arm back in shape," said Walter half-jokingly, half-disappointed that Dallas would be out for the season.

"You've got all the time in the world," said Donna, laying her head on Walter's shoulder. She ran her hand across his chest until she came to the U.S. Mail emblem on the breast pocket of his shirt. Beneath it, she felt the warm, methodic thumping of a human heart. And it seemed not the least bit strange to her when the idea crossed her mind.

"Let's walk home from here," she said, suddenly. "It'll be like old times."

"I don't want old times," said Walter. But when he saw how easily his rusty humor creased Donna's brow, Walter took her hand. "I want *these* times," he said. "I want now."

"Now is nice," said Donna, smiling again.

"I'm a fast walker, so you have to keep up with me." With a lightness in their steps, they set off in the direction of home.

At the corner of Springdale and Troost, Walter hardly gave a thought to the looming privet where Fern once lay, for all fear had ebbed from his life. Ahead he saw Ellenbach spreading out before him: the inky shape of elms and oaks, the birth of gold on ridgetops, here a bedroom light, there the glow of the doughnut shop, and Cyrus making good things for the day. Walter squeezed Donna's hand.

"What are you thinking about?" she asked.

"Oh, you know, just my job and things," said Walter. "Come next week Foster Jenson will be back to his same old self, complaining about his *Journal* being late. The Widow Spradling will be yakking at me for crossing through her garden."

"That's just their way," said Donna.

"I see that now, Boats. A man can see a lot of things when he finally opens his eyes. Boats?" said Walter.

"Hmm?"

"I love this town."

"This town loves *you*, Walter. And don't you forget it if all the griping starts again. That's just Ellenbach crying out for the mail."

Walter smiled and sniffed the air.

"Would you like an eclair?" he asked.

Donna looked at her watch, knowing that her husband's job should be starting soon. "You sure you have the time?" she replied.

"I have all the time in the world," said Walter. He kissed his wife, and together they walked toward Paradise.

Swing/Exhaaaaaaaaale

Swing

Swing

Swing/Puff Out

Swing/Short Inhale

Swing

Swing

Swing

Swing . . .

# ~ Afterword ~

Many years have passed since that summer. Yet, in the house of God there is still a golden mail slot, through which flows a river of communication. Satan's mail mingles daily in that slot with a host of other correspondence from the underworld. But someday Jesus will silence the fiend. He will wall him off in a kingdom so uncomfortable that Satan will scarcely be able to dictate a memo, let alone assault God's children with his unholy whisperings. His mail will cease to go through. Inevitably, however, questions arise from this story. Most common is the one that asks, "What was it for?"

Walter regained his faith and again exercised his gift of evangelism. Donna was immeasurably happier after the events of that summer. Her love for Walter blossomed, and *Hearts on Fire* became a best-seller.

It should surprise no one that Ace rose to the position of colonel in the heavenly host, and he will fight without fear until all of Adam's children are either damned or delivered. François returned to the Alps to help the mountain people. Muriel rejoiced at her father's healing. Bent, on the other hand, spiraled into the joylessness of hell. But of considerable surprise was Homer's eventual lot. Upon assignment to beach patrol at Lahaina, Maui, he requested a relocation. And when Jesus asked him where he wanted to go, he said, "Anyplace where sin leads people close to the rocks, my Lord. That's where I want to be, that's the place for me." So, for the rest of time Homer S. Windkook will be surfing the edges of mean lives, watching, praying, and every so often snatching one from the edge of the deep beyond.

After being found chained to a washroom basin beneath the bleachers of the Foster Jenson II Memorial Stadium and whisked back to heaven, T. Chaney Goodwin apologized profusely to Jesus for ad-libbing orders, and received forgiveness. Then, he hand-delivered Donna's message to Muriel and watched as the woman read and reread her mother's words.

Dallas Conniston's new kidney took, and he rejoined the team at the end of the season, throwing for three touchdowns to beat Laird in the state championship game. Afterward at the school dance, he told Eddy that he liked her, and she didn't seem to mind at all when he held her hand. Six years later, they were married missionaries in New Guinea.

Emma Sanger remained a chain-smoking pessimist, though the editors at *Reader's Digest* said her article, "Scent of Papa," was the best they'd ever read. Bill Ray quit getting drunk and got his thinking clear enough to hear God. The Pittencheeses became the most hospitable family on Hampton Way. But far and away the crowning result of that strange summer came four months later on a December afternoon as Walter was finishing his route.

He had just rounded the corner of the cul-de-sac and was walking across the street toward his own home when a movement at the old Commons's place caught his eye and he turned to see what it was. There at the end of his drive stood the mole of Mulberry Court himself.

"I've been waiting for you, young man. I've been standing here for hours," said the pale recluse, though it had been no more than twenty minutes at most. As he breathed there was a distinct rattling in his chest, and Walter thought he'd remembered Mr. Commons's eyes being less cloudy. But a long time had gone by since the old man's last venture out into the sun.

"Is something ailing you, Henry?" asked Walter. Walter usually slipped the mail beneath the old man's mat, and then there was only cause for Henry to crack the door, reach out, and snatch the letters back into his dark world. "You know, I always put your things under—"

"It's got nothing to do with today's mail. It's about something you brought me a week ago," said Henry. "A letter said my sister died of cancer in Salt Lake City. From now on, if you haven't got anything nice for me in that bag, then go on about your business."

"I'm sorry to hear that, Henry," said Walter. "I wished I'd have—"

Henry waved Walter off with the back of his blue-veined hand, then hobbled back to his house and disappeared with the *clap* of a screen door. He died the day after Christmas.

At his funeral, Mulberry Court alone turned out to pay respects. They stood in crescent formation around Henry Commons's casket, breaths puffing white into the elms above, while Coach Ravelle did the service. For once, Emma didn't utter her usual hmmph when the amen was spoken. Carol Edgerley wrung her hands together as if to squeeze some invisible rag and produce more tears for her neighbor. Richard Allison was his normal restless self. He rocked back and forth from one foot to the other, trying hard to keep the snow from seeping through the seams of his expensive shoes. Twice he stepped to the edge of the grave and looked into the hole. Then he told Connie he had a meeting in Topeka, kissed her on the cheek, and sloshed off to his car.

One by one, the neighbors turned away toward home until there was only Walter left in the cemetery. Some workers had lowered the casket, covered it with good Kansas dirt, and shaped a decent mound above the site. In a week or two, there'd be a proper marker there.

Walter knelt and smiled at the hump of earth. He thought about the hours he'd spent on Christmas Eve, spooning cocoa to the man, and telling him about Jesus.

"You know, Henry, I wouldn't have done it six months ago," said Walter to the ground. "I would have told you Jesus was a worse mole than you yourself.

"But when you shared how your sister died, well, it was as if some voice told me plain as day, *you* were the reason all those bad things happened to me. You were the one soul in Ellenbach waiting for his mail, and I was the one supposed to bring it to you. Sorry I kept you waiting so long."

Walter squinted across the cemetery at two particular stones that seemed to catch the sun's red glow just right.

"We both feel different about God now, don't we Henry?" said Walter, standing to brush the dirt from his knees. He was no longer speaking to the old man's grave; rather, he was talking to some point between the earth and the painted clouds above. "We know God never means us harm. He'll go with us through any storm. He put a story in us all, and He wants us to tell it no matter what's ailing us. Anyway, I aim to tell it now. Say hello to Him for me when you see Him. Say I'm much obliged to Him for letting the mail come through. Oh, and Henry, give my girl a kiss when you see her. It'll be okay. She'll remember you."

Then Walter turned his back on the cemetery and went about his job. And the finest man to ever tote the mail in Ellenbach became a teller of the Story once again, and there was joy throughout the town.

"I say to you that likewise there will be more joy in heaven over one sinner who repents . . ."

Luke 15:7

"Go therefore and make disciples . . ."

Matt. 28:19

# About the Author

WILL Cunningham is a marriage and family counselor in Oklahoma City, Oklahoma. A devoted husband and father of two young sons, he is the author of *It Happened at the Sunset Grille.*